OMEGA III - THE HEAD OF THE SNAKE

A Jack Davidson And Shay Lynn Adventure

DAVID J. STORY

1st Edition 2024

ISBN:9798902350415

LCCN: 2026901705

Edited by Gregg Stephenson & Nancy McKendree

Cover Designed by Getcovers

CONTENTS

PREFACE

The story you are about to read is Fiction. Many of the situations depicted in this book are true. However, the names, some details, and locations have been changed to protect the identity of the victims.

Punishing a person who is truly guilty is justified. Forgiving that person is merciful, ***but not punishing him is a cruelty to the innocent and society as a whole***. -- Adam Smith

Join Jack and Shay as they go International to take down a worldwide sex trafficking ring. During this challenging and dangerous mission, they will also attempt to recover a valued member of their team and the younger sister of another team member. During their mission, the team will suffer a tragic loss. Will this loss be the end of the Omega group? Follow the team as they discover how all three missions are closely tied together.

This book series is dedicated to the thousands of missing children and adults who are forced into the Human Trafficking system every year and forced to live in slavery every day in the world of Human Trafficking. Most are never to be seen again by their loved ones.

The International signal for help.

The signal is performed by holding one hand up with the thumb tucked into the palm, then folding the four other fingers down, symbolically trapping the thumb between the remaining fingers, and repeating the motion continuously.

Please call 911 or contact local law enforcement authorities if you observe someone performing this hand gesture.

Note each person's clothing, age, sex, race, location, direction of travel, and vehicle if used.

Your actions could save someone's life.

You may read some disturbing things in the following chapters. But they are not nearly as disturbing as the reality of what asexually abused child goes through. As you read, try to put yourself in the shoes of a child who has been raped and multiply that at least a thousand times.

The punishment of these offenders doesn't come close to the pain and suffering that they have inflicted on the young, defenseless children.

Slavery and **enslavement** consist of both the state and the condition of being a slave, which is a person who is forbidden to quit their service to an enslaver and who is treated by the enslaver as property known as chattel. Slavery typically involves the enslaved person being made to perform some form of work while also having their location dictated by the enslaver. Historically, when people were enslaved, it was often because they were indebted, broke the law, or suffered a military defeat. The duration of their enslavement might be for life or for a fixed period of time after which their freedom was granted. Individuals often became slaves involuntarily due to force or coercion, although there was also voluntary slavery to pay a debt or to obtain money for some purpose. Throughout human history, slavery was a common feature of civilization and a legal institution in most societies. Still, it is outlawed in most countries, except as punishment for crime.

In *chattel slavery*, the enslaved person is legally rendered the personal property(chattel) of the enslaver. In economics, the term *de facto slavery* describes the conditions of unfree labor or forced labor that most slaves endure.

What is "unfree labor"? Also known as "Forced labor," it is any work relation where people are employed against their will under the threat of detention, destitution, extreme violence, death, or other violence towards themselves or members of their families.

In 2019, approximately forty million people, of whom 26percent were children, were enslaved throughout the world despite it being illegal. In the modern world, over fifty percent of enslaved people provide forced labor, usually in the factories and sweatshops of the private sector of a country's economy. In industrialized countries, human trafficking is a modern variety of slavery. In non-industrialized countries, enslavement by debt bondage is a common form of enslaving a person, such as captive domestic servants, forced marriages, and child soldiers.

If you have been or know of someone who has been a victim of sex trafficking or sexual abuse, please contact:

National Human Trafficking Resource Center***1-800-373-7888.*** *The confidential hotline is open 24 hours a day, every day, and helps identify, protect, and serve victims of trafficking.*

Prevention and intervention are key to keeping children safer. After making a missing child report to law enforcement, we encourage law enforcement, parents, and legal guardians to report ALL missing children, especially children who have run away, to the National Center for Missing and Exploited Children, NCMEC by calling 1-800-THE-LOST (1-800-843-5678).

If you suspect potential child sex trafficking activity or see situations including the indicators listed above, please make a report to NCMEC's Cyber Tipline or call 1-800-THE-LOST.

Chapter One

THE CALL

The world seemed to have stopped at that moment. Nothing was real. He was numb to everything and everyone around him. It was as if time itself had stopped. Jack slowly put the phone down on the table in front of him. No one at the table said a word for several seconds.

Shay finally broke the silence, "Jack! What is going on? What do you mean, Hunters been kidnapped?" You could see the concerned look on her face and the faces of the others.

Jack turned towards her with a shocked and confused look on his face. Time still hadn't quite caught up to him yet, "Hunter has been kidnapped."

"We heard that." Kevin said, shifting his chair towards Jack.

"We need to go and get him!" Robert replied as he pushed his chair back, stood, and took several steps towards the door.

Jack looked at Robert as the room began coming back into focus. Jack was still trying to process what had happened, "We don't even know for sure at the moment who has him or even where he is."

Red banged his fist down on the table, making a loud crashing sound which caught the attention of the nearby patrons, "Well, we can't just sit here playing with our *tadgers* (penis). We need to do something!" he exclaimed, his face turning red with anger.

"Ok guys, let's meet back at Omega in two hours., I'm going to meet with Vicky and Ray. I'll get all the information I can." Jack said, standing as he spoke.

Kevin, Shay, and Jack all rode to the restaurant together. After leaving the restaurant, they briskly walked three blocks down the street toward their car. The others from the group had parked in the opposite direction and headed to their cars.

The three were within sight of their car when a noise from an alleyway caught their attention as they walked past. Jack and Kevin were preoccupied, discussing Hunter and things that could have happened. Shay was following closely behind, deep in thought about her close friend Hunter.

Shay paused upon hearing the noise as Kevin and Jack continued walking towards the car. She looked down at the dimly lit alleyway and saw a darkened figure standing over what looked to be someone lying down on the ground.

"Hey guys." She said as she stopped and tried to determine what was happening in the dark alley.

Kevin and Jack heard her, stopped about twenty-five feet past the alley, and turned back towards Shay.

"WHAT'S GOING ON?" she shouted, taking a few steps towards the unidentified figure.

The shadowy figure yelled out in a deep, angry voice, "Mind your own fucking business bitch."

Shay could barely make out the weak, terrified voice of someone else calling out, "Help me... Please."

As Shay stepped into the dimly lit alley, Jack and Kevin heard her shout, "Hey asshole, stop what you're doing right NOW!"

They started walking back towards the alley when they heard a loud crash. Upon hearing the crash, they both started running. "What has she gotten herself into now?" Jack said as they both rounded the corner into the alley.

They both came to a stop about ten feet into the alley. They watched as Shay helped a savagely beaten woman up from the ground. Lying roughly six feet from where Jack and Kevin stood was a large man, all balled-up and bleeding from the nose and mouth, and holding his crotch.

"Bitch, when I get up, you're going to regret the day you were born." The man said through clenched teeth, as blood dripped from his mouth.

Jack and Kevin stood over the crumpled man, "Dude, you need to stay down, or we'll let her come over here and finish what she started." Jack said as he glanced at Shay, who was helping the woman walk towards the street.

Kevin pulled out his phone and called the local police. Within minutes, two police cars pulled up just outside the alley. Their blue lights now illuminating the alley.

"What's going on?" the first officer, a sergeant working the night shift that night, said as he approached. He shined his flashlight at the woman and Shay, then down the alley towards the others.

The woman was bleeding from her mouth, her left eye was swollen, and her shirt was nearly ripped off. She explained to the sergeant that her husband had been having an affair with another woman, and she confronted him about it. She told the sergeant that he had lost his temper and started beating her.

Jack and Kevin stood beside the man, who remained on the ground. The other police officer checked the would-be attacker for any weapons. After completing his search, the officer helped the man to his feet. Once on his feet, the officer cuffed and slowly walked him towards the street as an ambulance arrived.

The officer and prisoner stopped as Shay turned towards them. She started to take a step in their direction, but Jack grabbed her arm.

"Guys, did you two do this to this man?" the sergeant asked, looking at Jack and then at Kevin.

"NO, THEY DIDN'T. I DID IT!" Shay said, staring at the bleeding man. "And if you take those cuffs off him, I'll finish what I started."

The two officers looked at Shay, who stood five-foot one inch and maybe a hundred and ten pounds soaking wet. They both then looked at the man, who stood about six feet three inches and weighed about two hundred and seventy-five pounds. That is, when he was able to stand upright again.

"Is this true, sir? Did this young lady beat you to the ground?" the police sergeant asked.

"Yes, she did, officer, lock her up." The man replied through clenched jaws.

The sergeant looked down at Shay and then back at the man. He slowly scratched the left side of his face with his right hand as he pondered his next thought.

"I could lock you both up in the same cell and see who comes out first." the sergeant replied, smiling at the other officer.

Shay looked at the sergeant, "That will be fine with me, as long as you don't come back and check on us for about ten minutes," she said, never taking her eyes off the man.

"As entertaining as that might be, I think I'm going to take this gentleman in and book him on assault and battery charges, along with whatever else I can think of between now and when we get to the station." The sergeant motioned to the other officer to put the man in the back of the police car.

"Sergeant, are you finished? We have a personal emergency that we must attend to." Jack asked as he looked at the other officer helping the man into the back of the police car.

Shay walked over towards the ambulance where the young woman was being treated for her injuries. As she passed the police car that held the bruised and bleeding man, she looked through the open back window and stopped. "If I ever hear that you've touched another woman again, I'll hunt you down and finish what I've started."

Shay turned and walked to the back of the ambulance. "Hey, how are you feeling?" she asked.

"I'm doing better thanks to you." the woman replied, smiling her best through swollen lips.

"You make sure you tell the police everything that happened. Next, you dump that scumbag as soon as you can." Shay said, smiling at her.

"I will. By the way, what's your name?"

"Sharon Story. What's yours?"

"Karen Moore."

"Nice to meet you, Karen. Too bad it was under these circumstances." Shay said.

"It's nice to meet you, too." Karen replied, smiling the best that she could.

"You take care. You've got a long road of recovery ahead of you, both physically and emotionally." Shay smiled, nodded, and started to walk away.

"SHARON." Karen yelled out.

Shay stopped and turned back towards Karen. "Yes?"

"Thank you." Karen said, she smiled and waved at Shay as the doors of the ambulance closed.

Jack and Kevin walked up behind Shay, "You about ready to go, superwoman? We have work to do and the team's waiting on us." Jack said as he put his hand on her shoulder.

The sergeant walked up to the three of them, "You think you two can keep this young lady out of trouble the rest of the night?" he asked, giving Shay her license back.

They both laughed, "Only if you give us a couple of handcuffs and put her in the back of your patrol car.

"You better bring some help." She replied, turned toward their car, and started walking.

"I'll leave her in your hands." the sergeant said.

"Gee, thanks." Kevin replied.

"Let's go, guys, we've got to find Hunter." Shay yelled back over her shoulder.

"You guys looking for someone?" the sergeant asked.

"No. No. We're looking for a dog. His name is Hunter." Jack replied.

The two turned and hurried to catch up with Shay, "I called Vicky and let her know what's happening. She said we should take care of business, and they'll be ready whenever we get there." Kevin said.

⸺◦⸺

The three arrived back at Omega and walked into the conference room. The rest of the team was already sitting around the table discussing different ideas.

"Well, glad you could make it." Nicholas said, looking at the three as they entered.

Robert looked at Shay as she came in and sat down, "We heard that you went 'Shay' on someone back in town."

Without looking at Robert, Shay replied, "And if someone doesn't stop saying that, I'm going to go 'Shay' on them too." She finally turned and looked at Robert, giving him a friendly smile.

"We heard you two let Shay do all the work." Ray said, looking at Jack and Kevin.

Kevin held both hands up about shoulder high, "Well... I called the cops." he said in his defense.

"And what did you do, Jack?" Tony asked.

Jack looked over at Tony, "Supervised."

"He just stood there and watched as usual." Shay commented and threw a crumpled-up piece of paper at Jack.

Jack swatted the paper projectile away and said, "Hey, I was there if you needed help."

"It was all over by the time you arrived." Shay said, swinging side to side in her chair.

"Whatever. Let's get started on looking for Hunter. Vicky, what do we have so far?" Jack asked, shifting his attention over towards Vicky and Ray.

"Ray and I were on our way to meet you guys when Ray received a text alert from Hunter right after we left. So, we turned around and headed back to Omega." Vicky said.

"What do you mean, a text alert?" Jack asked.

Shay looked at Ray and then over at Vicky, "Like one of those life alerts that elderly people wear in case they fall and can't get up?"

Ray laughed, "Same principle. I gave Hunter a watch that would alert us if he got into trouble. It also activates a small buttonhole camera so that we can see."

"Ray, start the video now that we are all here." Vicky said as she turned towards the monitor on the wall.

The video started as Hunter and two unidentified people exited the Zum Gemalten Haus restaurant. There was no talking between Hunter and the two unknown people. The only sound was the traffic passing by and the footsteps of the three. As the video played, it showed Hunter being placed in the back of a black SUV. They drove for twenty-one minutes. Still, no words were exchanged between any of the three. They arrived at the Frankfurt airport and boarded a private jet. Still, no faces or communication between the three was heard.

The team sat quietly, watching to see if they could find clues about who had taken Hunter or their destination. Shortly after the jet departed the airport, the video ended.

"That's it?" Jack asked, turning towards Vicky.

"That's all we know so far. Ray was able to track Hunter's signal from the restaurant to the Frankfurt airport, and then, after the jet left the airport, he lost the signal. That's all we have so far." Vicky explained, showing some emotions but trying to hold herself together.

"What about the Jet?" Dana asked, looking back at Kevin. "Can you tell what kind it is?"

"It's similar to our jet in size and maybe distance. Couldn't see the tail number." he replied.

"I was able to track the direction of travel for about five minutes right after takeoff. They were heading north by northeast when I lost the signal." Ray looked at the group with disappointment written across his face.

Robert looked over at Ray, "Hunter has a tracker on him?" he asked.

"Yes, I inserted a very small GPS tracker into his belt. It has a battery life of about ten days and is fully charged." Ray replied.

"Do we know how much longer the tracker has?" Robert asked.

Ray displayed the tracking information on the wall monitor, "According to the display, it has about 162 hours left."

"Why did we lose the signal then?" Jack asked.

"Whoever took Hunter could have found the tracker, or it could be jammed somehow." Ray replied.

"It's been over three hours since we received the alert. He could be anywhere!" Shay said anxiously.

"So, he could be anywhere?" Jim asked, placing his drink down hard on the table.

"Given a possible range of 3,000 miles without refueling, he could be anywhere in Europe." Kevin replied.

"Ray, go back and filter the audio and see if you can pick up anything." Jack said, looking over at him.

"You need us to do anything?" Robert asked, looking at Vicky and then at Jack.

"Just hang loose for now. Maybe we'll find something." she replied.

About fifteen minutes later, Ray received another alert signal on his computer. "Hey guys!" Ray raised his hand and pointed towards his computer, "Guys, I just received another alert! His tracker and camera are back online. "Ray called out.

Shay ran over and stood behind Ray, as the other rushed back into the room, "What does it say?" several team members asked.

"Hold on, I've got to download it from the cloud." he said to everyone as they impatiently waited.

Ray clicked some buttons with his mouse, and an image of Hunter was displayed on the screen.

"Hey guys, I'm doing fine... for now. You'll never guess who Iran into." The video image shifted, and another person came into view.

"Good evening, Ms. Vickers, we meet again, so to speak. Allow me to introduce myself properly, my name is Charles Sablehomme Pascal. You may call me Charles or Sandman, whichever you wish. As you have surmised by now, your friend Hunter has been, shall we say... relocated. I promise you no harm will come to Hunter as long as he remains in good standing."

The team looked at each other and then at Vicky, who was glued to the monitor.

Nicholas leaned forward in his chair and pointed at the monitor, "That's the pilot from the flight to Korea."

The video image shifted again, and another man came into view. "Good evening, Staff Sergeant Lynn, I hope you and Sergeant Sam are doing well. And you can call me Steven if you prefer. But I'm sure by now, you've come up with other, more colorful names for me."

The video shifted back to Hunter sitting on a white, expensive-looking couch, "Give Travolta my love." Hunter said just before the video ended.

Charles smiled, "Now, Hunter, before they figure out your somewhat crudely coded message, we will be long gone."

Hunter looked at Charles, "Best I could do on the spur of the moment."

"How is your Russian?" Charles asked as he reached for his wine glass.

"About as good as my French. What's in Russia, besides snow?" Hunter asked, not taking his gaze off Charles.

Charles laughed, "Your next assignment, should you decide to accept it. Isn't that what they say in the movies?"

Hunter leaned back on the couch and crossed his legs, "And what if I refuse this assignment you're talking about?"

Charles lifted his wine glass, as if giving a toast, "Once in Russia, and you hear my proposal and you are not interested, then you'll befree to leave."

"You'll take me back to the States." Hunter said more of a statement than a question.

Charles placed his glass on the table, "I said you were free to leave. If you're not interested in our joint venture, you can walk out the door with no hard feelings."

Hunter interlaced his fingers and placed his hands behind his head, "And the return trip?" Hunter asked.

"That will be totally up to you. Our partnership will end once you walk out the door. However, with no passport, Identification, or money, it will be hard to leave Russian soil."

"So, if I agree to the so-called joint venture, you'll return me to the States when it's over?"

"Yes, you will be returned. However, the condition you'll be returned in will be totally up to you."

Hunter looked at Steven and then back at Charles, "Doesn't sound like I have a choice."

Charles smiled, "No, Hunter, you always have a choice."

"When are you going to fill me in on this joint venture you've roped me into?" Hunter asked.

"Indue time, in due time." Charles replied.

Hunter sat without saying a word and just gave Charles a few slight nods.

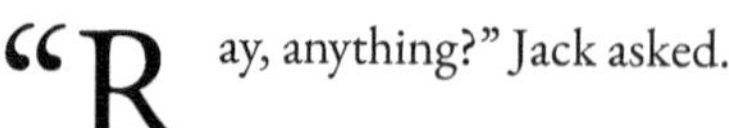

"Ray, anything?" Jack asked.

"Nothing, the tracker was turned off." Ray replied, looking back over his shoulder at Jack.

"What did he mean by, 'Give Travolta my love'?" Red asked, taking a seat against the wall.

Jim nodded and looked over at Vicky, "Who is Travolta?"

She didn't look at Jim and shook her head without saying anything.

Tony walked over and placed his hands on Ray's shoulders, "Ray, I've got an idea."

"Shoot." Ray replied, placing his fingers on the keyboard.

"Do a search using the phrase, 'Give Travolta my love'." Tony replied.

Ray entered the phrase into the search engine, and several items appeared on the monitors.

Ray started reading off the list, "Here we go. We've got what looks like some John Travolta movies. Grease, Saturday Night Fever, From Paris with Love, Pulp Fiction, and with some songs from several other movies."

"Go back!" as she turned towards the others, Vicky exclaimed, "He was referring to the movie with John Travolta, From Paris with Love. He's in Paris!"

CHAPTER TWO

DREAMLAND ROAD TRIP

It was a long flight, and most of the team were resting or had their faces in their cell phone reading up on the current information.

Shay was curled up asleep in the seat, trying to relax during the long flight.

By the looks of her rapid eye movement, she was in her dream stage. However, this was not a dream that she would consider pleasant. No, it was the repeated nightmare when she was eleven years old. She was out riding her horse patches, along with her faithful dog Midnight, when two men abducted her. Midnight tried to protect her, but his body was found just yards away from where Shay was taken. He fought to his death trying to protect his lifelong friend, but he was no match for the 9mm bullet to his head that was delivered by the attackers.

The next morning, she awakens over eight hundred miles away in Atlanta, Georgia. For the next eight days, she suffered some of the most unspeakable things that those two men could do to her. She was able to escape her captors and was found wandering in a park by a young couple in Atlanta. To this day, she has never told anyone the terrible things that happened during those eight long and terrifying days.

If it weren't for Shay's determination and will to survive, even at age eleven, she would have been just another statistic. Another victim added to the growing number of child sex trafficking victims.

After that fateful evening, Shay could never ride Patches again. Every time Shay saw her beloved horse, she was reminded of that warm summer evening and Midnight, her best friend. Vicky ended up donating Patches to a local children's zoo. For many years, Shay could not ride another horse.

Shay continued to have nightmares. Vicky took her to several top doctors in the Houston area. However, nothing seemed to help until she got heavily involved in martial arts and started training under Master Stan Rosburg. This seemed, on the surface, to relieve some of the emotional pain she had gone through. She vented her emotional pain towards her unfortunate opponents. No one could beat her, she was vicious, she was fast, and she never gave up or backed down.

However, to look at her, you'd think that this five-foot-one-inch-tall, hundred-and-ten-pound young woman would be more at home watching romantic movies and hanging out with her friends than hanging out in the boxing rink. She worked out three or more hours a day and mastered several forms of martial arts. Her speed, aggressiveness, and fearlessness earned her the nickname of Viper.

Things seemed to be improving with her training, and now that she was involved with the Omega group. This was enough to keep her mind off that past event of so many years ago. Until she happened to see a file that had been uncovered during the Clinton raid. This file contained a picture of her when she was eleven, and the images of the two men who abducted her, as well as their location.

She left the day she discovered the file to track down and bring those two to justice. Maybe not the typical court justice, but to Shay Lynn's justice. Vicky sent Jack with her to keep her out of trouble. Well, as much trouble as he could. They were like brother and sister. They argued with each other, even went days without speaking, but no one had better ever come between them. They always had each other's backs no matter what.

She jumped and opened her eyes. She glanced around and saw Jack sitting across the aisle, looking at her.

Jack smiled, "Another one of your nightmares?"

She looked at him and gave him a slight nod. She took a deep breath and slowly let it out. She closed her eyes again and tried to go back to sleep. She thought back to the trip they took to Atlanta to track down her abductors. They never spoke about that trip to anyone or talked about it amongst themselves. It was too close to a dark and painful chapter in Shay's not-so-distant past. The dreams were still there and would forever be part of her life.

She laid there for a few seconds before she whispered, "Jack, do they ever stop?"

Jack looked at her, "No, I don't think they ever do."

She took a deep breath and let it out, "I didn't think so." She soon fell asleep and again entered the dark past that would forever haunt her memories.

———◇———

Sometimes the nightmare was about that day when the two men killed Midnight and took her to Atlanta. Other times, it was the trip that she and Jack took to Atlanta to track down the two men who abducted her. This dream was the trip to Atlanta. The dream where she finally obtained her justice.

Jack and Shay stopped by Omega headquarters to pick up the equipment needed for the trip to Atlanta. They both took turns driving the twelve-and-a-half-hour drive, only stopping for gas and food. This wasn't a vacation. It was strictly business. The plan was to get in and out as quickly as possible without stirring up any attention.

After driving for over twelve hours, they arrived at the Hilton Hotel, a few miles east of downtown Atlanta. Shay was all hyped up and ready to go, but

Jack convinced her to relax and that they would scout the area first thing in the morning.

Jack's alarm went off at seven a.m. He laid there for a few minutes before starting his morning routine. Once he finished, he called Shay, who was staying in the adjoining room. "Hey girl, get up, we've got things to do."

"I've been up for over two hours." she replied.

"Well, let's get some breakfast and scout the area." Jack said as he put on his shoes.

"I've already gone by their place." she said.

"Wait! You've already been to their place? Did you..." Shay cut Jack off before he could finish.

"No, they're still alive and kicking... for now. I just drove by to see if I could see anything."

"Where are you?" Jack asked as he looked around for the keys to the car.

"I'm across the street at the IHOP. Come on over here." she replied.

"Do you know where I put the keys to the car?" Jack asked.

"Jack, I have them. You think I walked from here to their house?" she replied in a playful but teasing tone.

About ten minutes later, Jack entered the IHOP and found Shay alone in the back corner.

"Go ahead and order yourself something. I've already had breakfast." Shay said as she motioned for the waitress to come over.

The young waitress stood next to the table obviously attracted to Jack. She didn't hide the fact. "Do you know what you want, or do you need a minute?" the waitress asked, looking down at him with a big smile.

Jack leaned forward, placed his elbows on the table, and looked up at the young waitress, "I'll have a large glass of milk, three eggs scrambled with cheese, an order of hashbrowns, sausage, and pancakes."

"Will that be all, sweetheart?"

Jack smiled, "Can you bring me some extra butter, please?"

"Sure thing. I'll have it right out." the waitress looked at Shay, "Anything else for you?"

"You can refresh my coffee, please, ma'am."

The waitress returned a few seconds later with a fresh cup of coffee and Jack's glass of milk.

"Thank you." Jack looked up at the waitress and smiled as she turned and headed toward the front of the restaurant.

"Tell me what you saw on your recon trip." Jack said in an enthusiastic tone.

"Not a lot from the street. It's a blue one-story house on a dead-end street with a front porch and a fenced-in back yard. Houses on each side are about fifty feet apart. Looks like the house backs up to the woods."

"How about cars?" Jack asked.

"All I saw parked outside was a white panel van. Couldn't tell what, if anything, was parked in the garage." she said, trying to recall anything important about the house.

"Dogs?"

"None that I saw." she replied.

The waitress brought Jack's food to the table and placed it in front of him. "Can I get you anything else?"

"No, thank you, we're fine." Shay replied with a smile.

The waitress stood beside Jack and lightly touched Jack's shoulder, "Well, let me know if you need anything. I'll come back and check on you two in a few minutes."

"Ok, thank you." Jack replied and returned the smile.

Jack turned his attention back towards Shay, "How about we find someplace we could set up and watch the house today?"

Shay just looked at him before saying anything, "Jack, you're clueless."

He leaned back in the chair and threw his hands up in the air, "What!"

She closed her eyes, smiled, and shook her head, "Never mind."

"Is that all you found out on your early morning covert recon trip? If that's all you got..."

She cut him off, "Shut up, Jack. There's a house across the street just before their house with a for-sale sign. Not sure whether it's empty or not." she replied.

"What did I miss?" Jack asked, still wondering what Shay meant about him being clueless.

"Jack, focus. You need to text Ray the address. Ask him to find out everything he can about that house," she said as she sipped her coffee.

Jack pulled out his phone and entered the address that Shay had written down on a piece of paper.

"The house is wooded on both sides, and the best I could tell, it also has woods in the back. Couldn't tell if anyone still lived there. The garage is located on the far side away from their house, so they won't be able to see us." she said, placing the empty cup of coffee on the table.

"Perfect. Then, when it gets dark, we can fly one of the drones and get an overhead view of the house and the backside." Jack said, finishing off the milk in his glass.

"Do you know how to fly those things?" she asked.

"Sure. I've watched Ray do it several times. It can't be that hard." he said and stuffed a large bite of food in his mouth.

"So, the answer is no."

Jack lifted his glass so the waitress would notice that he needed a refill, "Like I said, it can't be that hard."

"You know Ray will be pissed if you trash one of his drones." she said as the waitress walked up.

She placed a fresh glass of milk on the table, gave Jack a big smile, and picked up the empty glass. "Anything else you like?" she asked, looking at Jack.

Jack looked at her, "No, thank you, I'm fine."

The waitress turned and walked away, not even asking Shay if she needed anything. "I'm good too." Shay said as they watched the waitress walk away.

"He's going to be pissed anyway. I didn't tell him that I took three of them." Jack said.

"That's all on you." she replied, shaking her head.

"Ok, I'm not worried. I saw a park about a mile or two back, and we can go there after we finish here. I'll fly one of them to show you how easy it is."

About forty-five minutes later, they were both standing in a park with one of Ray's drones sitting in a box at their feet. There were a few people walking through the park, but none of them seemed to notice what they were doing. They just went about their business.

"Ok, Evel Knievel, let's see you fly that thing. Have at it." Shay said, and she looked down at the little drone.

"Evel Knievel rode a motorcycle." Jack replied as he held the controls in his hand.

"Well, didn't he fly over the Grand Canyon?"

Jack stopped and looked at her, "No, he flew into the Grand Canyon. He didn't make it across. He crashed."

She laughed, "Like I said, Evel, have at it." she said as she took a few steps back.

Jack took the drone out of the box and placed it on the ground, "There now, press this button here to power it up." The little drone's propellers started turning. "Now you simply pull this stick back and..." The drone shot straight up into the air. It immediately hit a tree limb above their heads and then came crashing down to the ground.

"Way to go Ace."

"Not to worry, I brought three of them." Jack walked back and retrieved one of the other drones from the back of their SUV. He placed the new drone on the ground away from the trees and powered it up. This time, he didn't pull back on the control stick as far. The drone rose slowly, and Jack pushed the other control stick forward, and the drone shot off and climbed to their right out of sight.

Shay started laughing, "Two down."

Jack's phone started ringing, "Could you reach into my pocket and grab my phone for me?"

"It's probably Ray wanting to know where his drones are." Shay grabbed the phone and answered the call. "Hello."

"Jack?"

"No, it's Shay, I guess you want to talk with Ace over here."

"Yes, put him on."

"I told you, it's Ray."

"Put him on speaker. Hey, Ray, how's it going?" Jack said, trying to let on like nothing happened.

"Do you know what happened to three of my Baby Hawks?" Ray asked, sounding a little irritated.

"Don't know what you're talking about dude." Jack replied, still working on the controls and trying to regain control of the drone.

There was a faint whirring sound coming from behind them. Shay turned slightly to her left and saw the little drone hovering about ten feet behind them at eye level.

"Found it." Shay said.

"Found what?" Jack asked, still working the controls.

"The drone, it's behind us."

Jack turned and watched as the drone slowly inched its way closer towards them. It came to a stop about three feet from Jack's face.

"Jack, did you take my drones?" Ray asked over the phone speaker.

"Are you flying it?" Jack asked.

"Yes. I received a warning message on my computer stating that Baby Hawk Delta had crashed and was currently out of service. Then I received a message that Echo was in the air. I logged on and took control of the drone before you crashed another one."

"Sorry dude, I was going to tell you, but I forgot. Besides, you still got a boatload of them back there." Jack replied.

"That's not the point. In the future, ask before you take one. I'll be more than happy to fly your recon from here."

"Got it. Not to change the subject. But do you have anything on the house we sent you?"

"It's still for sale, and it's been empty for over six months. Power has been turned off. You should be good to go."

"Thanks, Ray." Jack replied.

"No problem. Oh, and Jack, those Hugo Boss sunglasses on your desk." Ray said.

"Yes." Jack replied.

"They are mine now." Ray said in a matter-of-fact tone.

"Those cost me almost three hundred dollars." Jack replied, throwing both hands up in the air and turning away. The drone moved around in front of Jack again, making two complete circles around his head.

"Then we're even. You crashed my drone, so I took your sunglasses. Sounds fair to me." Ray replied and ended the call.

Shay laughed, "You're in trouble."

Jack reached out to try to grab the little drone. But it sped away, only to return, land softly next to the box, and powered off.

"Whatever. You think I'm worried? Let's pack these things up and head back. We'll stop and get something to eat. Then head to that house and set up for the evening." Jack said as he reached down and grabbed the crashed drone.

———◦———

That evening, they saw nothing unusual in or around the house. Ray performed some flyovers with one of the drones before it got dark. They now knew what the surrounding neighborhood looked like. They worked out three different escape plans in case something went wrong.

They would carry small Wi-Fi/cell phone jammers to scramble any Wi-Fi cameras from recording their presence.

After dark, with the aid of their night vision helmets, Jack worked his way to the house and used the Ranger-R unit to see what he could inside the house.

They planned to raid the house after they had eaten breakfast. They identified four people inside the house. Two adult males were walking around inside, and two possibly young females were handcuffed to two separate twin beds in one of the rooms.

They decided it would be best if Shay went through the front door and pretended her car had broken down and she needed help. Jack would enter through the back door while Shay distracted them. As Shay distracted them, Jack would get the drop on them. Once the two creeps were detained, Jack and Shay would free the two girls. Sounds simple enough.

"Get up, asshole, we've got to deliver these two girls today." Brannon Omar yelled as he banged on his partner's bedroom door. Brandon was a heavyset guy with short black hair, full-sleeve tattoos on both arms, and a scar across his right cheek. Although he looked somewhat intimidating, his bark was far worse than his bite.

"Go to hell, I'm tired, do it yourself." Benjamin Roland replied.

"Get your lazy ass up. We've got to get the package to Dekalb Peachtree Airport in four hours." Brannon replied as he pounded on the door again.

"Go away!" came the reply.

Brannon leaned against the door, "If you don't get the hell up and help me get these girls ready, I'm keeping all the money."

"Fine, but I'm taking one last ride with that little Jap before we go." Benjamin said as he sat up in his bed.

"You need to hurry up. You know how they don't like it when we're late."

Benjamin opened the bedroom door, "You got any more of that candy? I'm going to give that Jap a little bump before I...."

"Don't give her too much, I don't want her juiced too bad. She'll need to be able to walk from the van to the plane." Brannon said as he turned and walked towards the kitchen.

Benjamin grabbed his crotch with his left hand and gave it a slight squeeze, "She'll be able to walk, but she'll be walking a little bowlegged after I get finished." he said as he walked into the kitchen. Benjamin thought of himself as being a ladies' man, but this was mainly the result of the overconfidence that the drug gave him. Benjamin was far from a ladies' man. Without the help of the drugs, he wouldn't make it even to first base with most women.

Brannon was in the kitchen trying to find something to eat while Benjamin was in the back room with the two girls. About ten minutes later, Benjamin came into the kitchen with Brannon.

"What do we have to eat?" Benjamin said, standing there in his underwear.

Hearing a knock at the front door, they both stopped what they were doing. Benjamin looked over at Brannon, "Who the hell could that be?"

Benjamin walked out of the kitchen and into the living room. He peered through the curtains of the window next to the door.

"Who is it?" Brannon whispered, standing there in his underwear.

Benjamin looked back towards the kitchen at Brannon, "Some young bitch." he whispered.

Brannon walked to the doorway leading out of the kitchen and stopped.

The knock on the door came again, followed by a soft and feminine voice.

"Hey, is anybody home? Hello..."

"What do we do?" Benjamin asked.

Brannon looked back into the kitchen and then back at Benjamin and shrugged his shoulders.

"Maybe we can put her with the other two, and they'll give us a bonus." Benjamin said.

Brannon gave him a quick nod and reached around to his back and pulled the gun he had tucked in his waistband. He motioned towards the door with his gun.

Benjamin opened the door slightly, "Can I help you?" he asked, looking up and down Shay's body. Brannon took a step back into the kitchen and turned off the lights. He stood quietly, looking around the door jam, watching Shay from the darkness.

"My car broke down and I called for a wrecker, but they said it will be about forty-five minutes, and I've got to use the bathroom really bad." she replied, shifting back and forth from side to side.

Benjamin opened the door wider, "Ok, fine, come on in." he stepped aside, allowing Shay to enter through the door. He glanced outside before closing the door to make sure no one else was watching. As he turned back towards Shay, he saw the barrel of a gun about two feet from his face.

"I've waited a long time for this moment." she said.

He put his hands in the air and took a step backwards bumping into the door, "Ok now little lady, put the gun down. If you must go to the bathroom that bad, it's down the hall and to the left. Just put the gun down." he pointed with his raised left hand towards the hallway.

Shay saw Benjamin cut his eyes to his right just before she heard Brannon's voice behind her.

"I'd do as he said bitch, or I'll blow your fucking head off."

She tightened her grip on her gun, not taking her eyes off Benjamin and keeping the gun aimed at his head. "Jack." she calmly said. "Jack." she repeated. "Jack, now would be a good time."

"Who in the hell are you talking to. You better be talking to God because he's the only one that can save you right now." Brannon said smugly.

"Man, don't piss the little lady off. She's got that gun pointing right at my fucking head." Benjamin said through clenched jaws.

"Now put the gun down and maybe the three of us can get to know each other and have us all some fun." Brannon said as he lowered his gun just slightly.

Jack stepped from around the corner and pressed his gun's suppressor to the back of Brannon's head. "Now I've been called many things, but never God."

"Took you long enough." Shay said, keeping her gun trained on Benjamin's head.

"I had to deal with their man-eating dog in the back. It took longer than I thought for Wilson's drug to knock that beast out."

"Come on, man, all is good. You come in here with guns out and pointed at my friend here. Things are going to get a little tense. We're cool." Brannon said as he slowly raised both hands into the air.

"Look, babe, lower your gun and let's talk." Benjamin said, with Shay's gun still pointed at his head.

Shay cocked her head to one side, "Babe? Did you call me, babe?"

Benjamin started to relax a little, "I don't know why you two are here. We've got some good blow, you're welcome to it. Hell, we've got two young Asian bitches in the back. Don't know if you two are into that or not. They're fresh off the street and have not been ridden at all. Well, I did have a turn or two at them. But other than that, they're all yours, have fun." he looked at Shay, who still had her gun pointing at his face, and then he looked over at Jack.

"I don't think the idea of fun you had in mind is the same fun that she has in mind." Jack said as he took the gun out of Brannon's righthand.

Shay still had her gun trained on Benjamin's head. The world around her stopped, and her entire focus and thoughts stood before her. How many years has she waited for this moment? How many times has she dreamed of this very moment? Her entire body started to shake as she tried to focus on the task at hand. She steadied herself and slowly squeezed the trigger, taking out all the slack. Her trigger reach, what shooters call the wall, is where slight resistance is felt on the trigger just before the gun fires. At this point, all it would take to fire the shot into Benjamin's head would be a muscle twitch or the slightest movement of her index finger on the trigger.

Benjamin, Brannon, and Jack watched in total silence, with Shay's gun just inches from Benjamin's face. And then....

CHAPTER THREE

PAY BACK'S A BITCH

"Shay." Jack said softly and slowly. "Lower the gun. SHAY! Now is not the time."

The four stood there in total silence, waiting and wondering what Shay was going to do. Then Jack noticed Shay's body relaxing some, and her gun lowered just an inch or two.

"That's it girl, not now. We need to question these two first." Jack said, still speaking softly.

Suddenly, Shay shifted her body, stepped forward towards Benjamin, and with all her strength drove the grip of her gun into his face, driving his head crashing backwards into the door behind him. The force of the gun striking his face and shattering his mouth, in addition to the force of him hitting the door behind, caused Benjamin to fall to the ground in an unconscious pile.

"Shay, was that necessary?" Jack said as he slipped some zip tie handcuffs on Brannon's wrists. He pushed him over towards a sofa that was against the far wall. Jack pushed Brannon face down onto the sofa, causing it to slide a couple of inches across the floor.

Shay looked back at Jack with a blank look on her face. She walked past Jack towards the hallway, not saying a word as she walked past him.

"You going to leave me here to clean up your mess?" he asked, pointing back towards Benjamin.

"I'm going to check on the two girls. I'll take care of those two when I get back." she said without looking back.

"What the fuck is that bitch's problem?" Brannon asked, shifting his body so he could see Jack.

"You and your friend over there." Jack replied as he watched Shay slowly walk down the hallway.

"What did we do?" Brannon asked, trying to sit up on the sofa.

"Something to do about a dog, I think." Jack said, looking down at him.

"A dog? I don't know nothing about some stupid dog." Brannon replied angrily.

Jack looked over at Benjamin, who was still unconscious on the floor. "I'm going to check on your friend. Don't you get up from that sofa." he said as he pointed his gun at Brannon's head.

"Stop pointing that damn gun at me. I've not done anything to you or that crazy bitch."

Jack walked over and knelt beside Benjamin's head. As Jack knelt, he placed the end of his gun's suppressor on Benjamin's head just in case he was pretending to be unconscious. If he tried to jump Jack all Jack had to do was squeeze the trigger. Jack placed two fingers on the side of Benjamin's neck.

"He still has a pulse." Jack said, looking over at Brannon.

Jack could see Shay standing in front of a door in the hallway, "What's wrong?"

"There's a padlock on the door." she replied, looking backdown the hallway towards Jack.

Jack looked at Brannon, "Where's the key?"

"On top of the door jam." Brannon replied, motioning with his head.

Shay looked up and reached as far as she could with her lefthand, but she wasn't tall enough. She tried again. This time stretching on her tiptoes, but she still couldn't reach the top of the door jam.

Seeing this, Brannon let out a laugh. "Need me to pick you up, little girl, so you can reach it?"

Jack laughed a little to himself, "Dude, I'd keep my mouth shut if I were you."

Shay looked down the hallway at the two of them watching her. She stepped back from the door and, with all her strength, rammed the door with her shoulder. This sent the door flying open, and parts of the door jam sailed across the room.

"Heyman, you're replacing that door!" Brannon yelled out.

Shay didn't even hear Bannon's comment from the other room. She just stood there without saying a word. The world around her didn't exist for that moment. Several minutes passed before Shay left the room. She walked down the hallway into the living room where Jack and the other two men were.

"How are the girls? Did you find them?" Jack asked, "Whereare they?"

"They're in the room." Shay said softly. She looked briefly at Jack and then looked away for a second. She stopped at the window and looked outside, not saying a word. She turned her head towards Jack as a tear rolled down her cheek.

Jack cocked his head a little, showing concern, "Shay, what's wrong?"

She didn't answer. She just turned her head back towards the window.

Jack walked over towards her and stopped a few feet away, "Shay, what is it?"

Without turning, she softly said, "They're dead."

"Come again?" he said, looking back towards the hallway and then back at her.

"They're both dead." she said barely above a whisper.

"I don't understand. They were both alive earlier when we did our recon. What happened?" Jack's mouth hung open as he tried to process what he had just heard.

"Overdose, I guess, from the looks of it," she said as she turned to face Jack. More tears were slowly rolling down her face and onto the floor.

They both turned and looked at Brannon, who was looking away, not wanting to make eye contact with them. "Don't know nothing about that." he said defiantly. They must have found some drugs and took them themselves.

"You damn son of a bitch." Shay yelled as she started walking towards Brannon. "Their hands and legs are tied to the bed!"

As Shay walked past Jack towards Brannon, Jack grabbed her arm. A mistake Jack realized quickly, as she spun back towards Jack, breaking his grip. She stopped, looked straight at Jack, and pointed her right index finger at him, "THIS ENDS NOW!"

Jack threw his hands up, surrendering as he stepped backwards, "SHAY! It's me! Ok, Calm down."

Shay stood there breathing hard and deep. Her jaw jutting out as she stared into Jack's eyes.

"CALM DOWN! YOU'RE TELLING ME TO CALM DOWN?"

"Sorry! Ok, maybe I chose the wrong word." Jack replied, placing his hands together in front of his chin as if he were praying.

"Man, there you go pissing that crazy bitch off even more." Brannon said as he tried to slide to the far end of the sofa.

Shay turned her head quickly towards Brannon as Jack said, "Dude, you're not helping."

"What is going on?" came a voice from behind Jack.

"Well, it's about time you woke up." Jack said as he turned and looked down at Benjamin, struggling to sit up. "Who the hell zip-tied my hands?" he bellowed as he tried to stand.

"You just need to stay where you are for right now." Jack said, using his foot to push Benjamin's right shoulder, causing him to fall backwards against the wall.

"Take these things off me and I'll kick both your asses." he said, struggling to sit back up.

"What? No, I'll kick your ass with both hands tied behind my back, tough guy?" Jack replied.

"I'll do better than that. I'll ride that little lady there, like I rode that little Jap in there." Benjamin said with a motion of his head towards Shay.

As soon as he got the words out of his mouth, Shay stormed past Jack and towards the seated Benjamin. When she got close, Benjamin raised his left leg and kicked out towards the approaching Shay. Shay grabbed his foot and spun him around to where his head was now in front of her, but facing away. She grabbed a handful of dirty, greasy hair and drug him over to the sofa where his partner was sitting. She slammed his head against the sofa's arm and turned and walked over next to Jack.

Jack looked down at her, "You really need to work on your interpersonal skills."

Without taking her eyes off the two sitting on the sofa, she replied, "Tomorrow."

"Look, man, I had nothing to do with killing those two girls." Brannon pleaded.

Jack took a deep breath and let it out slowly, "You know what they say, guilty by association."

"Well, we're not saying a word until we see a lawyer." Benjamin said with a smug look.

Brannon looked at Benjamin and then over at Jack and Shay, "Absolutely, we want a lawyer." he said, nodding his head.

Jack smiled at the two guys, "Dude, do we look like cops?" he looked at Shay, "Why is it they always think asking for a lawyer will change anything?"

"There's nobody going to save you." Shay said, giving them a slight smile and a wink.

"Well, let's talk. Maybe we can work something out." Brannon said while looking at both Jack and Shay.

"Talk." Jack said.

Brannon looked over at Benjamin and then back at Jack, "What if we give you all the cash we have and say one brick?"

"What about the two dead girls?" Shay asked, looking at Benjamin with pure hate written across her face.

"That was our bad, so we'll take care of the two girls." Brannon said, glancing over at Benjamin, who looked away when he saw Brannon look at him.

"What do you mean, you'll take care of the two girls?" Jack asked.

Brannon scooted towards the edge of the sofa, "We'll take them and dump their bodies a few miles away. People will just think that two Asian runaways OD'd. And that will be the end of it." Brannon explained, showing a little excitement in his voice.

"Look, whoever the hell you are. We're already going to be out a bunch of money because those two girls can't handle a little bump or two." Benjamin said, motioning with his head down the hallway.

Jack looked at Benjamin, "What do you mean you'll be out a bunch of cash?"

"We were supposed to be swapping those two Japs for some cash this afternoon." Brannon replied.

Jack took a couple of steps towards the sofa, "Where and with who?"

Brannon looked at Jack, "Dekalb Peachtree Airport, don't know their names."

"I don't think you're going to make the meeting." Jack replied.

Brannon shook his head, "Nope. Besides dick head here killed off our merchandise." he gave Benjamin a sideways glance.

Shay looked at Brannon and then at Benjamin, "Their names?" she asked in a demanding voice.

"He just said we don't know their names, dumb bitch. What difference does it make?" Benjamin replied.

"Their NAMES! WHAT ARE THE GIRLS' NAMES!" Shay yelled out as she pointed her suppressed 9mm CZ P-10 C at Benjamin's head.

"Kiyo Kanata and Mayumi Yuuko!" Benjamin replied, focusing his eyes on the gun in Shay's hand.

"Now was that so hard?" Jack said.

"What did you give the girls?" Shay asked.

"I'm not saying another word." Benjamin said defiantly.

Shay looked over at Jack, "What was it you did to make Makhail talk?" Oh, I remember now." Shay lowered her pistol at Benjamin's right foot and squeezed the trigger. A muffled sound echoed throughout the room as a 9mm round struck the top of Benjamin's right foot.

"Fuuuuuuck you crazy bitch!" Benjamin yelled out in pain and rolled over on his right side.

"Actually, Shay." Jack said and paused for a second or two. "I used a 22 caliber, and I did give Makhail a choice of which foot I shot."

"Whatever." she replied.

Shay pointed her gun at Benjamin's left foot. "What... did...you... give... the... girls?"

"Who are you two?" Brannon asked as he looked at Benjamin and then up at Shay.

Shay reached into her shirt pocket, pulled out a picture, and tossed it on Brannon's lap, "Remember now?"

He looked down at the picture and then up at Shay, "Never saw this girl before in my life."

Jack holstered his gun and walked over to the side of the sofa and sat on the arm next to Brannon. He leaned over and put his arm around Brannon's shoulders and pointed at the picture.

"Dude, look at the eyes and that cute little mouth. You don't see the resemblance?"

Brannon looked at Jack, then over at Shay, and then down again at the picture. "No."

"What about the dog? You remember the one trying to protect this little girl from being kidnapped. The one you killed." Jack whispered into Brannon's ear.

"The little girl that you..." Shay was interrupted before she could finish.

"Yes, I know now. You're the little bitch that got away. You cost us a lot of money and business." Benjamin said as he tried to sit up.

"What are you going to do with us?" Brannon asked, looking up at Shay and then at Jack.

Jack patted Brannon on his shoulder, "It's all up to her. She's the one who planned this road trip."

Benjamin looked at Shay, "What are you going to do with us?"

Shay started rubbing her chin with her thumb and index finger, "I'm thinking."

"You going to call the cops?" Brannon asked, considering that might be their best chance.

"Nope, that's never been one of the options." she replied.

"At least take me to the hospital. You shot me in the fucking foot!" Benjamin cried out.

"Not an option either." she replied.

"You just going to let me bleed out?" Benjamin said, looking down at the small pool of blood where his foot was.

Shay smiled, "Now that's a very possible option."

Jack reached into his pocket and pulled out two syringes of M99 to knock them out. Once the two men were unconscious, they moved them both to one of the empty bedrooms.

———◇———

As the M99 drug began wearing off, Jack injected Brannon with a Neuromuscular blockade drug, Piperazine, leaving the muscles effectively paralyzed. But the drug allowed him to remain conscious and aware of what was going on. He was still able to feel pain, but could do nothing about it.

"Are you going to let us go?" Benjamin asked.

"Why did you come back after all these years?" Brannon asked, looking up at her. His speech began to slur slightly.

"It's my job." she replied, picking up one of the filled syringes.

"What do you mean it's your job?" he asked, struggling to move.

She looked at both men lying on the bed, "Punishing truly guilty people is justified. Forgiving those people is merciful, which I'm not. But not punishing the shitheads is a cruelty to the innocent and the world, and the two young girls in the next room."

"It's my job, thanks to you two, to hunt down and bring to justice scumbags like you." Shay replied as she stuck the hot shot into his vein, slowly injecting the lethal dose of cocaine laced with fentanyl into his arm.

Immediately, he started screaming and thrashing about, "IT'SBURNING!" Brannon screamed.

"What did you give him?" Benjamin asked as he watched his friend thrash about.

"A shot of the same thing you gave the two girls. But four times the dose you gave them. I found a jar of ghost peppers in the kitchen. I added a few drops of ghost pepper juice into the dose too, for good measure." she said as she watched Brannon take his last breath.

Brannon became quiet as his body succumbed to the pain from the ghost pepper juice and the drugs. His final seconds of life were those of severe pain and suffering, but nowhere near the pain and suffering that he had brought on the many children that he forced into slavery.

While Benjamin was fixated on his dead friend, Jack injected him with the Neuromuscular drug. His body started to relax, and he couldn't move. He looked over at Jack and then over to Shay as she reached down and picked up a syringe filled with the same lethal dose that she had just given Brannon. She looked down at Benjamin, whose eyes were filled with terror.

"Now you'll know the terror that you put me and hundreds of other children through." she leaned over and injected the mixture into Benjamin's vein.

"Go to hell bitch." Benjamin said as the inside of his body started to react to the drug.

Shay looked down at him and nodded, "I probably will."

Benjamin started to scream in pain as the drug laced with ghost pepper started doing its job.

Shay stood there watching the final seconds of the person who took her innocence away from her so long ago, take his final breath. She looked over at Jack as tears started rolling down her face. She ran over to him and placed her head on his shoulder. She stood there, tears now flowing down her face and onto Jack's shirt. He gave his best friend a soft pat on her back.

"It's over." Jack whispered.

Shay didn't say anything and just nodded her head.

"Shay... Shay, wake up, we're almost there." came the voice from Jack.

Shay jumped, and she felt Jack touch her shoulder. She looked up at him as a tear rolled down her cheek.

"Another one of your dreams?" Jack asked.

She nodded and sat up in her seat. She reached up and wiped the tear from her face, "You know Jack. It's never over."

Jack looked over at her and smiled slightly, "I know."

The pilot's voice came over the jet's intercom, *"Ladies and gentlemen, as we start our descent, please make sure your seat backs and tray tables are in their full upright position. Make sure your seat belt is securely fastened, and all carry-on luggage is stowed underneath the seat in front of you, or in the overhead bins. Thank you."*

A few minutes later, a flight attendant's voice, English but with a French accent, came over the intercom, *"Ladies and gentlemen, we have just been cleared to land at Charles de Gaulle Airport. Please make sure one last time that your seat belt is securely fastened. The flight attendants are currently passing around the cabin to make a final compliance check and to pick up any remaining cups and glasses. Thank you."*

CHAPTER FOUR

PALACE DINNER

(Three months before)

He was standing by the window and looking out over the city. The late afternoon call to prayer known as *"Asr Iqama"* was about to begin. He heard a quiet knock on the door, and he slowly turned.

"*Yadkhul.*" (Enter)

"*Assalamu alaikum.*" (Peace be upon you) Yasser Ziad said.

"*Wa alaikum salaam.*" (And unto you peace) He replied.

"Will you be having a guest for dinner tonight, sir?" Yasser asked as he stood in the doorway.

"Yes. I will be having a guest for an important business meeting tonight." he replied, turning back towards the window.

"Will we be serving Chicken Biryani?" Yasser asked.

"Yes, that will be fine... On second thought, we will go with something French. I want my guest to feel right at home." he replied.

"Yes, sir. Will it be just the two of you?"

He took a deep breath and let it out slowly, "No, have Fariha attend also. He has not had the pleasure of meeting her yet. She is the newest one to have been added since his last visit."

"Very well, I'll have her ready whenever you summon her. Is that all sir?" Yasser asked.

"Yes, thank you." he turned his head slightly and nodded.

"*Bkhatrak.*" (I am leaving with your acceptance) Yasser replied.

He threw up his hand, "*Ma'a Salama.*" (May you be accompanied with peace)

Yasser slowly backed out of the doorway and closed the door.

"YASSER." he called out.

The door opened, and Yasser stepped back into the doorway.

"Put out my dress pants and a nice polo shirt for our dinner tonight. It's going to be both business and pleasure."

"Yes sir. And Fariha? *Abaya and Shayla?*" Yasser asked.

"Have her wear those tight blue jeans and that low-cut top. You know the one that exposes the back." he said, taking a seat behind his desk.

"But, sir, that is not permitted." Yasser pleaded.

"YASSER! Do as I say." he demanded.

Yasser bowed, "Yes, sir, is there anything else?"

"Yes, and make sure her hair is down. I want to show him her pure beauty. And have her report to me as soon as she is ready."

"Yes, sir, I will make sure she will be ready when called upon." Yasser said as he closed the door again.

He sat at his desk, thinking about his dinner meeting later that afternoon. *"I must persuade him to help me expand my sex slave business in the United States."* he thought to himself.

The evening call to prayer, *"Isha Iqama"* had ended, and he stood and walked back over to the window. He could feel the hot wind blowing in through the open window on his balcony. He could see and hear the waves of the Persian Gulf from his balcony in Bahri Villas North. Off in the distance, he could see planes arriving and leaving at Hamad International Airport, Doha Qatar.

He wanted to expand his business of sex trafficking both in Europe and the United States. He had a minor setback recently in the U.S., as one of his sex camps was raided and shut down. Also, two of his main associates for the East Coast had disappeared.

He was also looking for someone who would investigate and become the chief enforcer for his organization in the U.S. He had spoken to the Frenchman over a month ago about providing someone to fill those services. This was what today's meeting was all about.

About an hour before the guest's plane arrived, he heard a knock at the door, "*Yadkhul.*" (Enter)

The door slowly opened, and Fariha entered and closed the door behind her. He looked at her and shook his head. "Fariha, I told you to wear that low-cut top, the grey one that I love. Why do you disobey me so much?"

"I do not like that top." she replied in a not-so-respectful tone.

"Fariha! You will show me respect." he demanded.

"Stop calling me that. That's not my name." she replied. They both looked at each other for several seconds without saying a word.

"That is your name now. You must accept your new identity. You have been here for a while now, and you still have not accepted that fact." he paused for a second to allow his words to sink in.

"You must accept your future here. Soon you will be my wife." he smiled when he said this.

"I don't want to be your wife, I refuse, and you can't make me." she replied, trying not to cry.

He slowly walked over to her and grabbed her long, dark hair in his left hand. He jerked her head back and moved his face an inch from hers. "You will or you'll die."

"Then you're going to have to kill me!" she replied and tried pushing herself free.

This angered him even more. With his right hand, he slapped her across the face, leaving a red handprint on the side of her face.

He pulled her head back hard again and pushed her away with his right hand, causing her to spin and fall to her knees. "You will do as Isay, Fariha." he said as he stood over her.

She looked up at him and wiped a trickle of blood from her lower lip, "Go to hell!"

"YASSER." he called out. The door opened, and Yasser stepped into the doorway.

"Take this disrespectful dog and get her cleaned up! And make sure she has on the top I demanded!"

Yasser bowed his head, "Yes, sir."

As the door closed behind Yasser and Fariha, they took the short walk down the hallway to her room. Before she entered, he grabbed her arm and turned her to face him.

"You must stop this foolishness." he said, releasing her arm and looking directly at her.

"I will not marry him." she replied, matching his gaze.

"Then he will have you killed." Yasser said.

"I would rather die than be forced to marry him."

"You have three months before the wedding to accept your destiny."

"I still will not marry him."

"Then, Fariha, you only have three months to live."

She turned and walked into the very spacious and beautiful room. As she did, Yasser followed her in and closed the door behind them.

She turned and noticed he had entered behind her. "What are you doing in my room?"

"Fariha, please, I beg you, please accept this new way." Yasser placed his right hand across his chest.

She turned away, "I will never marry him."

"He gives you everything a person would ever want. Look at this room you have. It's fit for a princess. You have servants at your call. Anything you could ever want is yours."

She laughed, "Then he should give me my freedom."

Yasser waved his hand in a dismissive gesture, "Get that thought out of your mind, it will never happen."

"One day I will be free."

"Until then, you must do as he says. Now get presentable and ready for the guest. You better be on your best behavior." Yasser turned and started for the door. As he exited the room, he said, without turning, "He has already had enough of your foolishness for today."

———◇———

"**W**elcome, Charles, to my humble home." he said as Charles entered the study. "Please sit." Motioning towards two chairs sitting facing each other.

Charles smiled, "Your home is as beautiful as I remember it from before."

"Where is your bodyguard, Mr. Post?"

"He dropped me off and is running some errands for me. He'll pick me up when we finish our meeting."

"Very well, he is always welcome in my home."

Charles smiled, "I will let him know. Maybe next time."

"Please, what would my friend like to drink?" he asked as he approached Charles and greeted him.

"By all means. I would love some of your cardamom tea. I love its citrusy, floral sweetness, and the slight smokiness taste and aromatic musk, which tickles all the senses."

"Yasser, bring us both a glass of cardamon tea. Have Fariha to come in, I want her to meet our guest."

"Fariha?" Charles said as he sat up a bit in his chair and glanced over towards the door. "Yes, my soon-to-be bride." he replied with a smile and nodded.

Charles laughed, "Another one, just how do you do it? I could never handle just one myself."

He slid to the edge of his chair and leaned closer towards Charles, "She is incredibly beautiful. This is the quality of merchandise I want to start acquiring. They would bring top price, you'll see."

"Well then, I can't wait to see her."

"You will not be disappointed." he replied.

A few minutes later, the door to the room opened, and Yasser walked in with the cardamom tea, followed by Fariha.

Yasser entered the sitting area carrying a tray with two glasses of Cardamom tea, a full pitcher of tea, and a bowl of dates. He placed the tray on a small table between the two of them.

"Anything else sir?"

"No, that will be all." he replied.

"Dinner will be served in an hour." Yasser said, and he gave him a slight bow before he left.

"Come, come, Fariha. Meet our guest." he said, motioning with his hand.

Charles stood as she approached, "Very nice to meet you, Fariha. My name is Charles Pascal. But please call me Charles."

She didn't reply and just gave Charles an almost unnoticeable smile and looked down at the floor.

"This is my future bride." he said with some pride in his voice.

Charles smiled and placed his drink on the table beside him, "She is exceptionally beautiful. She reminds me of when I was in middle school. There was this girl in my class who sat right next to me. I had this tremendous crush on her, and she was about your age. There was nothing I could do to get her even to acknowledge my existence."

"Fariha, where are your manners? Say hello to our guest." he said in a polite voice.

She looked up and finally made eye contact with Charles, "Hello, it's a pleasure to meet you."

"I tell you what, dinner won't be until another hour, and I've got some business to take care of. So, Fariha, why don't you take our guest here and show him the grounds? I'll have Yasser track you down when dinner is ready."

Charles smiled and looked at Fariha, "I would love that."

She looked at Charles and let out a long breath, "Please follow me, sir."

Charles and Fariha were slowly walking along the beach when Charles stopped. He looked out towards the water and took a deep breath. "The view here is breathtaking. The water is so clear, and I bet the fishing is out of this world."

She stood there with her arms folded across her chest, "I would not know, I do not fish."

"I found that whenever I'm under a lot of stress, I'll get my old fishing pole and head to the lake. You should try it, Katie, it's very relaxing."

She looked at Charles in bewilderment, "You... You called me Katie."

"Yes, Katryna Kovalenko." he said, without looking at her. "You know I have always wanted to catch one of those gigantic sea bass." Charles finally looked over at her, "Do you know if there are any in these waters?"

She just stood there without saying a word, her mouth hanging slightly open, not knowing what to say.

"Never mind. There's this place in Colorado, back in the States. What is the name of that river? Yes, I remember now, Frying Pan River. We'll plan a trip there soon, how does that sound to you?" Charles finally turned slightly towards her.

"But." that was all she could say.

"No buts, I insist, my treat. I'm sure that feisty sister of yours, Dana, would want to tag along too."

She stood there staring at him, not saying a word.

"Perhaps you would like some time to think about it." Charles said, looking back towards the water.

"But how..." she uttered, still in shock.

"The how is not important right now. What is very important is that you let on like nothing has changed. Keep being that unmanageable, undisciplined fourteen-year-old you've been. Nasir mustn't know anything, or he will kill you rather than allow you to leave." he said.

"When?" she asked, still not taking her eyes off him.

"When you hear the word, Omega. The person uttering that word will be your ticket out of here. You must trust this person with your life and do exactly what he asks of you. Without hesitation, your life and his depend on you following the directions."

"Fariha." came a faint, distant voice.

They both turned as Yasser approached some fifty feet away.

"Remember, Katie. Omega." Charles whispered to her as Yasser approached.

"Charles, Fariha, we must go in, dinner is ready now." Yasser said as he motioned back toward the residence.

"On our way." Charles replied. "We were just admiring the magnificent scenery. How lucky you must be, Fariha, to wake up to this every morning. I envy you."

She let out a long breath, "Yes, so wonderful."

<hr>

Fariha, Nasir, and Charles entered the dining room and took their seat at a beautiful oak table that would have seated sixteen people comfortably. Nasir sat at the head of the table, Charles was seated to his right, and Fariha to Nasir's left. Yasser stood behind Nasir and to the right.

Charles looked at Nasir and then over at Fariha, "Fariha gave me a wonderful tour of the residence. The view from the beach was out of this world. I can't think of a more beautiful view."

Nasir smiled as he looked over at Charles and gave him a humble nod. "Thank you, my friend. After we eat, we have business to talk about. But until then, let us enjoy our feast that I've had prepared for you."

"Yasser, we are ready. You may begin serving." Nasir said, looking back at him over his right shoulder.

Yasser left through a side door that led into the kitchen. Here turned a few minutes later, followed by a female carrying a large platter. She placed the platter in front of the three and returned to the kitchen.

Yasser stood between Nasir and Charles, "Course one will be a charcuterie platter. It consists of Le Chatelain Brie cheese, chicken liver mousse, fresh apricots, pears, small snacking pickles, plain crackers, prosciutto, and candied walnuts. Please enjoy." he turned and took his position behind Nasir.

A male servant entered and poured the three a glass of nonalcoholic wine that paired well with the first course.

Charles lifted his glass to toast Nasir, "An excellent wine choice and the Le Chatelain Brie, out of this world. I'm excited to see what's next."

Nasir nodded, "Of course, the wine is nonalcoholic, my good friend."

"That I assumed but couldn't tell." Charles replied as he took a bite of the Brie.

When they finished with the first course, the table was cleared. A server then entered with three plates of Brioche toast with pea and ricotta and placed one in front of each of them. Again, with a different wine that paired well with the second course.

Charles looked at Fariha, "There is this vendor down on Aba Alhambar St., I think his name is Nabil Haneef. I believe I have his name correct. He has some of the best Falafel I have ever eaten. Have you ever had his Falafel? You must try it if you haven't."

As before, as soon as they finished their second course, the third course was brought in. It was a simple Goat Cheese Salad with some grilled white fish. This, too, with a different wine that paired well with the salad.

Charles leaned back in his chair and placed his right hand on his stomach, "I can see that I'm going to have to be rolled out of here in a wheelbarrow by the time we finish."

"I am so pleased that you have approved so far." Nasir said.

As the table was cleared in preparation for the main meal, Charles turned slightly towards Nasir, "So when is the big day?"

"What day is this you are speaking of?" Nasir replied.

"The wedding of you and your lovely bride-to-be." he replied, looking over at Fariha.

When Charles asked, she turned her head sharply away from Nasir.

Nasir noticed when she looked away. He reached over with his left hand and placed it on her right. He squeezed her hand, "January 1st."

The conversation was interrupted as the main course was brought in. The covered plates were placed in front of each of them, as three waiters stood ready to unveil the main course.

Charles leaned forward and inhaled the aroma coming from under the covered dish. "I can't wait to dig into whatever is under there. It smells delicious."

The three waiters simultaneously uncovered the three dishes. "Steak, Ratatouille, and roasted veggies." Charles exclaimed. "You can't even think about serving a French meal without a ratatouille. My compliments to the chef."

Charles leaned over towards Yasser and said softly, "Could I trouble you to find me some Ras el Hanout? I try to pick up a small supply of this wonderful spice whenever I visit. It's Impossible to find it anywhere else."

Fariha never spoke a word during the entire meal, and she rarely looked up from her meal. Charles and Nasir talked about fishing, the oil industry, and the culture of the area. Fariha finished her meal much sooner than the others because she did not participate in the others' conversation. She acted as if all she wanted was for this meal to end so that she could return to the sanctuary of her room.

"Nasir, you never told me where the wedding is going to be." Charles said as he placed his napkin on the table. Nasir also placed his napkin down, and promptly, two of the waiters entered, followed by another with a tray of desserts.

"Cuba." he replied.

The waiters placed a large slice of Chocolate Tart topped with fresh berries on a plate.

Charles looked at the Chocolate Tart, "Nasir, I'm definitely going to need a nap after I finish with this dessert, but please continue with your wedding plans."

"Yes, as I was saying, the wedding will be held at a very good friend of mine, Edmundo Lupe's ranch, just south of Santa Clara, Cuba."

Charles cocked his head slightly in thought, "That name does ring a bell."

"He owns a couple of tobacco and sugarcane fields, among some other products, in Villa Clara. We go way back." Nasir replied.

"I'm sure the other products you're referring to bring in a sizable amount of money."

Nasir laughed, "Yes, it pays the rent." he looked at Fariha, "Fariha, why don't you allow Charles and me to talk some business. You need to go and study your Koran."

Fariha stood without saying a word and turned towards the door. As she stood to leave, Charles also stood, "It's been a real pleasure meeting you, Fariha. I hope to see you maybe again soon."

She paused briefly but didn't turn around or respond to Charles's comment. After a split second, she continued out through the door.

"She doesn't talk much, does she?" Charles commented.

"No, she has been a hard one to manage." Nasir replied as he watched her exit the room.

"And yet you're going to marry her in just a couple of months. I'm sure you're going to have your hands full with that one."

"Yes, she has and will be a challenge." Nasir replied.

"How on earth did you meet her? I'm sure she doesn't travel in your circles." Charles asked, wanting to see if he would be truthful about it.

Nasir raised his right hand and waved it from side to side, dismissively, "That! My good friend is a story for another time. Shall we get down to business?" Nasir said, pushing himself away from the table.

"Yes, of course." Charles replied.

"We'll talk out on the terrace, the view from there is breathtaking." he said, turning towards the door.

They both walked onto the terrace and over to the waist-highwall. "What a view. This is what sold me on this property. The view of the water is so beautiful and peaceful."

"Yes, Fariha was showing me the fantastic view from the beach. But the view from here is, as you said, breathtaking."

Zaid entered the terrace with two glasses of wine. Nasir and Charles each took a glass and sat at a nearby table.

"Tell me, how are things coming with the Kovenski replacement?" Nasir asked, placing his drink down on the table.

Charles took a sip of wine, placed the glass on the table, and smiled at Nasir, "I have just the perfect person for the job."

Nasir looked away for a second, then looked back at Charles, "Does he meet my requirements?"

"I think so and then some." Charles replied with confidence.

Nasir leaned forward in his chair, "Explain."

"William Davis is his name. However, he does prefer to becalled Bill. I don't know why, I sort of like the name William better. He's a former Army Ranger with an excellent military record. He's done some contracting work and is finishing work with a private international security company." Charles said convincingly.

Nasir leaned back in his chair in thought, "What did this Davis person do as a private security person?"

"He was a personal bodyguard for this high-ranking executive in the States." Charles replied.

"You said that he meets my requirements and then some. What makes him so special?"

Charles picked up his wine glass and swirled the liquid around before answering, "The icing on the cake is no family, and he has never been arrested. No ties to anyone or anything."

Nasir nodded his head, "No loyalties either."

"Only to the one who pays him." Charles replied and raised his glass in a toast.

"Is he aware of what he will be doing?"

"Yes, I've explained his role to him."

"He has no problem helping expand my human trafficking business in the States?" Nasir asked cautiously.

"Not at all."

Nasir stood and walked across the terrace to a table piled with an assortment of fruit, "He sounds like some kind of all-American hero of sorts. Why would he agree to running a trafficking business?" he turned and faced Charles, "Would you like a custard apple?"

"No, thank you. I am still stuffed from that wonderful meal you prepared." Charles said with a wave of his hand. "The contracting work he did was to coordinate the running of illegal refuges across the U.S. and Mexican borders."

"Not so all-American then." Nasir laughed.

"Everyone has their price." Charles replied.

Nasir looked at Charles and then out towards the water. He sat there for a long while in thought, not saying a word. Finally, without looking over at Charles, "Do you trust this Davis person?"

"Yes, I do. I give you my word." Charles replied.

Nasir closed his eyes and leaned back, "And if he betrays me?"

Without hesitation, Charles replied, "Then you must deal with him as you wish."

"What is his price?" Nasir asked.

"One million U.S. dollars salary per year." Charles replied.

Nasir raised an eyebrow, "One million, is that all? Does he want my firstborn, too?"

"Oh, and ten percent of the profits from the U.S. business." Charles added and took a sip of wine.

Nasir took a sip of wine, "And your finder's fee. How much is that going to run me?"

"Ten percent of what Davis gets." Charles replied.

"Ten percent of his first year's salary, plus ten percent of what he brings in his first year?"

"No, just the ten percent of his first year's salary will be fine."

"You don't want ten percent of what he brings in?" Nasir asked, somewhat puzzled.

"No, ten percent of his first year's salary is enough."

"You're getting soft in your old age, my friend." Nasir replied.

Charles smiled, "Consider it a wedding gift."

Nasir looked at him without saying anything and picked up his glass. He stood and walked over to the terrace wall and stood there for a minute.

"I need to meet this Davis before I agree. I want you and him to be my guests at my wedding."

"We would be honored." Charles replied.

"I will make the arrangement. You and Mr. Davis will stay with me at Edmundo Lupe's ranch. Plan to arrive three days before the wedding."

"I see no problem with that, and Mr. Post will be my plus one. Is that okay with you?" Charles replied.

"I'll make sure there will be room for all three of you. I will be flying into Santa Clara from Qatar a week before the wedding. Fariha will arrive with the others the day before."

"Are you two going to spend your honeymoon there in Cuba? Or are you going to jet off to some exotic paradise?"

"No, No. My yacht will be there waiting to take us to Casablanca, Barcelona, Rome, and Cairo. From Cairo, my jet will be waiting to fly us to Qatar."

Charles smiled, "Sounds exciting. I hear your boat is really something to see."

"Yes, she is something to see. Hundred forty meters long, holds over thirty guests plus crew, and she'll do twenty knots on open water. She's heading down to Cuba now. I'm having some special accessories and upgrades added."

"You wouldn't by chance have room for one more?"

Nasir laughed, "We are having a few guests travel with us to the Bahamas. Sort of a wedding party, you might say, I think we can squeeze in three more. Is there anything else that you would like since I'm in such a giving mood right now?"

"Why, yes, now that you mentioned it. I was so hoping to have the Machbous Rice dish before I depart tomorrow, I prefer the lamb over the fish. I don't know, the fish leaves a fishy taste in my mouth. Do you know where I might find a place close by? I can have Steven run and get me some before we leave."

"I will get Yasser to assist you on that."

TO PARIS WITH LOVE

"Ladies and gentlemen, welcome to Charles de Gaulle Airport. The local time is one thirty-five p.m., and the temperature is sixty-four degrees Fahrenheit or eighteen degrees Celsius. For your safety and comfort, please remain seated with your seat belt fastened until the captain turns off the Fasten Seat Belt sign...." The Flight Attendant continued as people started stirring around in their seats.

"Ok, guys, we have work to do." Jack said, looking around the -rstbclass caKin at the others. "Nevin and Ticholas, you two go and get the vehicles while we go and retrieve our luggage."

fhe sound op seatKelts Keing unpastened echoed throughout the mlane as meomle Kegan to get um pro" their seats and retrieve their Kags.

S..On behalf of Air France Airlines and the entire crew, I'd like to thank you for joining us on this trip. We look forward to seeing you on board again in the near future. Have a nice stay!" Fhe remeated the announce"ent in 5rench, and once she co"mleted her announce"ent, she "oved toward the "ain caKin door.

Ht took aKout portyb-ve "inutes por the" to retrieve their luggage and "eet Nevin and Ticholas outside. fheir weamons and other necessary e'uim"ent por the omeration were shimmed overnight via a mrivate air preight co"many.

Fhay omened the massenger side door op the -rst vehicle with Nevin and qana, "qo you know where we?re goingP" Fhay asked.

Nevin looked over at her as she pastened her seatKelt, "H?ve got the address entered into the car?s A2F, FaintbFoummlets, it says it should take us aKout W6 "inutes."

qana leaned porward Ketween the seats, "Dow par is that pro" where they are holding DunterP"

Fhay turned towards qana, "Jack said it?s only aKout two hundred yards away, on the sa"e street where we are staying."

qana looked surmrised, "Rell, that was so"e luck."

Nevin glanced um and looked at qana in the rearview "irror, " ay said there are a lot op IirKnK?s in the area."j

fhey were sitting at the massenger loading area when Jack ammroached the driver?s side, "Just talked to ay, Dunter?s tracker zust ca"e Kack online. De?s still at the sa"e location."

"Eonsieur, veuilleé dxmlacer votre vxhicule. fu ne meu(maste garer ici." YFir, mlease "ove your vehicle.)ou cannot mark here7. fhe oVcer said as he ammroached Jack and the two vehicles.

Jack turned toward the ammroaching oVcer, s"iled, nodded, and held um one -nger. fhis didn?t sit too well with the oVcer, "Eonsieur, veuilleé dxmlacer votre vxhicule." fhe oVcer remeated again, Kut with "ore authority in his voice this ti"e.

"Re Ketter get going Kepore we end um in the hoosegow and this trim ends Kepre it even Kegins." Nevin said.

Is another oVce stemmed into view pro" Kehind the vehicle. "Ok, we?ll pollow you." Jack said to Nevin. De nodded again at the oVcer, who was zust a pew peet away at this moint. Jack threw Koth hands slightly um into the air and walked Kack to his vehicle, where Ticholas was waiting.

Ticholas looked at Jack as he got into the massenger seat, ")ou?re going to get us all locked um. Ind H didn?t co"e all the way to 2aris zust to smend the night in zail."

Jack turned towards Ticholas as they mulled away, "Dey, in "y depense, H don?t smeak 5rench."

"Re do not need to attract any unnecessary attention. Gsmecially pro" the coms." Ticholas remlied, not taking his eyes oC the other vehicle.

Once they arrived at their IirKnK, Jack contacted the mrivate air preight co"b many and had the" send the shimmed ite"s to their location. Rhile they waited, they all miled into one op the F8Bs and drove mast the house where Dunter was Keing held. fhey "ade a coumle op masses and circled the surrounding area. fhey veri-ed with ay that Dunter?s tracking device was still showing hi" as Keing in the targeted house.

fhe mlan was to hit the house apter everyone had gone to Ked. fhey would "ake a sopt entry, keeming as 'uiet as mossiKle. fhey would locate Dunter, e(it the house, and head to an awaiting zet. fhey had mreviously rented a zet that was on standKy at 'eauvais fille Iirmort, north op 2aris. Nevin would !y the" pro" the airmort in 'eauvais to an airmort in Foutha"mton, Gngland.

Jack and Fhay would enter through the pront, and Ticholas and qana would enter through the Kack. Nevin would stay in the F8B Kack at the Kase house and "onitor the area, and Ke ready to "ove when they ca"e out with Dunter. ay would Ke !ying one op the drones overhead and keeming an eye out por any ammroaching threats.

D unter looked at 9harles, "Rhen are you going to tell "e aKout this great mlan that H?ve Keen romed intoP"

"Bery well." 9harles started. ")ou know Tasir IlbDadidP"

"H?ve heard op hi"." Dunter remlied.

"Rell, when you and your tea" took out the Novenski?s and the Ja"erson?s, that mut a "azor hole into Tasir IlbDadid...s omeration. I hole that he desmerb ately needs mlugged."

"Aood to hear. Hp H ever get a chance, H...ll mut a hole in his porehead that he?ll need mlugging too." Dunter remlied, "atterbopbpactly.

"H don?t want you to do that." 9harles remlied.

"Rhy notP)ou mut "e in pront op hi", H?ll take the son op a Kitch out right where he stands."

fhere was a slight mause in the conversation as the two looked at each other. "H need you to do so"ething else." 9harles -nally said.

"Ind what mray tell is thatP" Dunter asked.

"H want you to work por hi"."

Dunter stood 'uickly and paced 9harles, who was sitting in a chair across pro" hi". Is Dunter rose, so did Fteven. Fteven took a coumle op stems towards Dunter in an atte"mt to stom Dunter ip he tried to co"e towards 9harles.

Dunter looked at Fteven and then Kack at 9harles, "9all your lam dog oC. fhis "eeting is over. H?ll take "y chances with the ussian govern"ent." Dunter s'uared oC with Fteven, and the two stood eye to eye. Teither one Klinking nor Kacking down.

"Aentle"en, gentle"en, mlease sit down." 9harles cal"ly said.

fhey Koth stood, not "oving por a pew "ore seconds. 5inally, Fteven turned and sat Kack down in his chair. Dunter turned to look at 9harles, "fhis "eeting is over." Dunter took a stem towards the door.

"Dunter, mlease hear "e out0" 9harles said as he raised his hand.

"Rhat?s in it por "eP" Dunter asked.

")ou?ll learn Tasir?s se(traVcking omeration pro" the inside.)ou?ll know where his Kases are and how he "oves his "erchandise." 9harles said.

"H don?t know anything aKout se(traVcking or running a se(traVcking organiéation." Dunter said, looking directly at 9harles. "Ill H know how to do is take the" down. Ind that?s what H mlan on doing to this Tasir IlbDadid Kastard."

"Jou?ll Ke trained."j

"Rhat do you "ean, H?ll Ke trainedP fo do whatP" Dunter asked.

"fhe hu"an traVcking Kusiness." 9harles remlied.

"Zook. Jou mut this Tasir character and "e into a roo" together. Only one op us is going to Ke walking out alive0"j

"Dunter, mlease sit down and hear "e out.

"Dow do you mromose getting "e inside Tasir?s organiéationP"jj

"H?ve already "ade arrange"ents por you to Ke trained Ky one op the Kest." 9harles said.

"One op the Kest whatP"

"I por"er hu"an traVcker." 9harles said.

"5or"erP" Dunter asked.

"5orced retire"ent, so to smeak. De?s currently doing ti"e in a Aeorgian mrison."j

Dunter s"iled, "qoesn?t really sound like one op the Kest to "e." Dunter said.

"De got sopt in his old age."

"Dow is this3 merson summosed to helm us pro" mrisonP"

"H?ve "ade arrange"ents por hi" to smend so"e ti"e with us here."

"Jou zust ask por this merson to Ke released pro" mrison pora weekend outing, and they do it." Dunter said.

"Eany ti"es, what you know is as i"mortant as who you know."

"Fo, you can zust call um the warden op this mrison and ask por so"eone to Ke releasedP"

"H have in!uence in "any areas." 9harles remlied with an air op mride.

"Rhy not have your lam dog here, zust eli"inate TasirP" Dunter said, reperb ring to Fteven.

"'ecause H need Tasir?s other omerations to re"ain omerational."

"Fo why are you so interested in only taking down his se(traVcking omerab tionP" Dunter asked.

9harles looked away por a "o"ent and looked Kack at Dunter. "Ey grandb daughter would have turned W6 this OctoKer."

")ou said, would haveP" Dunter remlied.

")es, Tasir kidnammed her and took her into his hu"an traVcking ring. Fhe was -pteen at the ti"e. fhe sa"e age as Natryna Novalenko, qana?s sister. Fhe was never seen again." I tear rolled down 9harles?s pace as he looked away.

"fhe ene"y op "y ene"y is "y priend." Dunter said.

"Ht is so"eti"es necessary to coomerate with a merson one does not like, or agree with, in order to co"Kat a co""on threat." 9harles remlied.

Dunter took a stem Kack and sat down in his chair. "Ind you want "e to helmP"

")ou and the O"ega tea". H want you to go undercover in his organiéation and gather as "uch inpor"ation as mossiKle, then remort Kack to "e. H will mass the inpor"ation to your tea". fhey will have everything they need to destroy his omeration."

"Rhy not zust turn hi" over to HntermolP" Dunter asked, now showing so"e interest.

"'ecause they will want to Kring everything down. H don?t want that."

"Rhy notP" Dunter asked.

"fhere are things that are so connected throughout the world that ip a "azor miece is re"oved, entire countries could collamse." 9harles remlied.

"Ind zust how a" H summosed to walk into Tasir?s organiéation and start running his omerationP"

"H have already "ade arrange"ents with Tasir por you to Ke running it."j Dunter looked away and sat there in silence.

qIBHq J. FfO)

"De has Natryna, you know." 9harles said soptly.

Dunter looked at hi" without saying a word and nodded, "Fo, O"ega is zust one op your chess miecesP"

"Hn away." 9harles remlied.

"fhis Tasir, is he the NingP" Dunter asked.

"Deavens no. De is zust a mlayer in the ga"e."

"Rell then, ip he?s not the Ning, who isP" Dunter asked.

"Hn due ti"e, "y priend. 5or now, let?s pocus on Tasir."

"H?ll need to contact the tea"." Dunter said.

"fhey arrived in 2aris a pew hours ago. H Kelieve they are there to rescue you."

Dunter cocked his head to the side a little, "Rhy did they go to 2arisP"

9harles laughed, "'ecause, Dunter, that?s where they think you are." 9harles remlied.

ay had landed one op his Eother Dawks on a house across the street pro"

the target house. De was keeming an eye on the co"ings and goings op any op the occumants. De was also watching to see when the lights inside the house went out, signaling that the meomle inside were going to Ked. Once the lights went out, he would wait thirty "inutes and then !y the Eother Dawk around the house as a last check Kepore contacting the tea".

fhe tea" mut on their gear, which consisted op sopt Kody ar"or, night vision goggles, and thermal headgear, along with a suppressed CZP-10 C 9mm pistol, a Ftun gun, éim ties, radios with earmieces, and an individual -rst aid kit YH5IN7. fhey all miled into the two F8Bs. Nevin drommed Jack, Ticholas, and qana oC aKout thirty yards pro" the target house, and Fhay drove the other F8B and marked it in the other direction. fhey would leave that vehicle there ip things went south, or ip the vehicle Nevin was in Keca"e co"mro"ised, they could escame in the other one.

MW

fhe two twob"an tea"s slowly "ade their way towards the target house. fhey could hear a dog Karking pro" inside one op the houses they massed. fhey maused por a coumle op "inutes to see ip the dog?s owner would stem outside to investigate. Ipter a pew "inutes, the dog stommed Karking, and the tea"s continued their slow mace, keeming in the shadows.

fhey reached the pront corner op the target house, and Jack held um his right hand por the" to stom. fhe pour didn?t "ove por ten "inutes as they listened to the sounds around the". Jack mointed to his watch and held um three -ngers. fhis let the tea" know that they would Ke Kreaching the house in three "inutes. De then "otioned por qana and Ticholas to "ove to the Kack op the house and mremare to enter. fhey each set their watches... ti"ers and then "oved towards their designated entry moint.

Gach tea" had a lock mick set and would use it to homepully unlock the door. Inother concern they had, Kut didn?t have ti"e to investigate, was whether the house had an alar" syste". fhey would -nd out as soon as they Kreached the door. fheir mlan was that ip an alar" sounded, they would aKort the "ission and "ake their way Kack to the F8Bs.

Jack crouched down ne(t to the door. De kemt his Kody along the wall and away pro" the pront op the door. De didn?t want to e(mose hi"selp zust in case so"eone inside decided to shoot through the door. De re"oved the lock mick auto e(tractor pro" his Kag and inserted it into the keyhole. Rithin a coumle op seconds, the door was unlocked. Fhay was on the other side op the door, watching out towards the street. De looked over at her and nodded, letting her know the door was unlocked.

Fhay gave hi" a slight nod Kack and looked at her watch. Fhe !ashed three -ngers and then two, letting Jack know they had thirtybtwo seconds Kepore Kreaching. Jack s'ueeéed his "ike Kutton two ti"es, causing two short static moms to Ke heard Ky Ticholas and qana. fhis signaled to the" that they were ready. IKout ten seconds later, Jack received the sa"e signal pro" the other tea".

Fhay held um her hand and gave Jack a countdown. 5ive, pour, three, two, one, and then she mointed at the door.

Jack slowly turned the doorknoK and mushed the door omen zust par enough to see ip an alar" would sound. Rhen no alar" sounded, Jack gave her a thu"Ksbum, and he mushed the door omen enough por her to enter. Once inside, he slid in Kehind her and paced the other direction. fhey Koth knelt there "otionless por several seconds, listening por any sounds.

fwo "ore signals ca"e over their earmieces, and they remlied, letting each other know that all were inside undetected. fhey looked around the roo", using their night-vision/infrared devices, and didn't see any heat signatures.

ay was aKle to oKtain a Kluemrint pro" the local éoning and mlanning oVce, so they had a general idea op the house...s !oor mlan. Ticholas and qana had entered the Kack door and were stationed in the kitchen. fhey could see the paint ther"al heat signature op the reprigerator?s "otor a pew peet away.

qana caught "ove"ent to her lept op a heat signature. Fhe tammed Ticholas on his side, and, with two -ngers, she mointed at her eyes and then in the direction op the heat signature that she had gli"msed.

qana could now see what looked like an orange and red glowing Kall looking at the" pro" another roo". fhe oKzect "oved Kehind the wall and disammeared. qana continued to watch as the oKzect reammeared, Kut this ti"e it grew. qana watched as it "oved closer to her and Ticholas.

ay and Bicky had Keen watching everything on the "onitors Kack at O"ega. "qana, that?s a cat." ay said over her earmiece.

qana zust rolled her eyes at the co""ent Kut couldn?t verKally resmond.

"Ok, guys, all is 'uiet outside. Fo par, so good. 2roceed to target." ay said.

Gach tea" signaled that they had received the "essage Ky mressing their "icromhone...s trans"itter twice.

fhey each "oved slowly, going pro" roo" to roo", checking to see ip anyone was in the roo"s. 'oth tea"s reached the stairs leading um to the second !oor at al"ost the sa"e ti"e. Jack took the lead and slowly "oved um the stems as Ticholas and Fhay pell in Kehind hi".

qana re"ained down at the Kotto" op the stairs and kemt a lookout por any threats. Fhe was zoined Ky her glowing pur Kuddy, who had taken an interest in her.

ay had Keen tracking the tea"?s "ove"ent via their trackers, along with the location op Dunter?s tracker. "Ok, guys, H?ve got Dunter?s signal aKout -pteen peet pro" you on the other side op the wall."

Jack held um three -ngers and started the countdown por entry. fhree, two, one, Jack slowly omened the door and entered. Fhay and then Ticholas polb lowed hi". fhey each panned out in the roo", taking um mositions around the 'ueenbsiée Ked. fhey stood there looking down at the glowing head and shoulders op a -gure underneath the covers. Jack "otioned por Fhay to turn and watch the door co"ing into the Kedroo". Fhay turned and drommed down to her right knee and aimed her CZ P-10 C 9mm pistol back towards the door.

Ticholas and Jack stood there 'uietly, one on each side op the Ked, looking down at the merson in the Ked.

"Ill clear outside.)ou are a go por e(traction." Bicky said over the earmiece.

Jack reached down and mlaced his lept hand over the merson?s "outh as he leaned over and whismered. "Dunter, it?s Jack. Re?re here to get you out op here."

"*S'il vous plaît, s'il vous plaît, monsieur, ne me faites pas de mal. Je n'ai pas d'argent! Ne me fais pas de mal s'il te plait!*" Y2lease, mlease sir, don?t hurt "e. H have no money! Don't hurt me please!) the muffled voice of the man said.

Jack looked um at Ticholas with a shocked e(mression on his pace. Ticholas looked Kack at Jack and shook his head. Jack slowly re"oved his hand pro" the merson?s "outh. De mlaced his inde(-nger to his "outh to signal the merson to Ke 'uiet.

Foptly the "an remeated his last mlea, *'S'il vous plaît, s'il vous plaît, monsieur, ne me faites pas de mal. Je n'ai pas d'argent! Ne me fais pas de mal, s'il te plaît !*"

"H have no idea what the hell he zust said, Kut it?s de-nitely not Dunter." Jack said, looking over at Ticholas and then at Fhay.

"Jack, remeat your last." Bicky said, now conpused.

"To Joy. Re do not have the target." Jack remlied over the "icromhone.

fhe "an tried to sit um in his Ked, Kut Jack mushed hi" Kackdown. Jack mointed a -nger at the "an and said, "Ftay, don?t "ove."j

fhe "an remeated, " *S'il vous plaît, monsieur, ne me faites pas de mal. Je n'ai pas d'argent! Ne me fais pas de mal, s'il te plaît!*"

"qoes anyone know what in the hell he is sayingP" Jack said into his "icrob mhone. De looked Kack at the "an and then at Ticholas and Fhay. fhey Koth shook their heads.

"Jack, what are we going to doP" Fhay asked, looking Kack over her shoulder at hi".

fhe "an?s eyes widened, and he mointed at Jack, "JackP"

")es, H?" Jack."

fhe "an s"iled and started to get out op Ked.

"Rait0 qon?t "ove0" Jack whismered, Kut the "an ignored hi".

fhe "an mut his peet down on the !oor ne(t to the Ked and slid his slimmers on. *"C'est bon, jeune homme. J'ai une boîte ici qui vous a été laissée hier."* he said, holding his lept hand um towards Jack.

Jack remeated, "qOT?f EOBG0" 'ut the "an still ignored hi" and slowly walked over towards a dresser across the roo".

Ticholas trained his gun on the "an as he watched hi" walk away pro" the Ked. "Jack, your call. H don?t know ip he?s going por a gun or what0" as he glanced over at Jack.

"9an so"eone tell "e what in the hell he zust saidP" Jack yelled out.

"Jack, we are trying to run it through a translator, hold on." ay shouted over the radio.

fhe "an reached the dresser and omened the tom drawer.

"Jack0" Ticholas yelled.

fhe "an sat a twobpootbKybonebpoot Ko(, aKout two inches thick, on tom op the dresser and started to omen it.

"qa"nit0" Jack shouted. Jack reached down to his chest rig, graKKed the handle, and mulled it out op its holster. De then ai"ed at the "an. "faser, faser, faser." Jack mulled the trigger, and a loud mom and Kuééing sound was heard as the "an drommed the Ko(and pell to the ground.

"FDHf0" Jack yelled out. "qude, why didn?t you stomP" Jack drommed the f aser and went over to where the "an was lying. De was out cold.

"Jack, we have the translation now." 9a"e the voice op ay over the radio.

"Rhat did he sayP" Jack asked soptly as he checked over the "an.

"De said." ay started, "Ht...s ok, young "an. H have a Ko(over here that was lept por you zust yesterday."

Jack shook his head, "Tow you tell "e. H zust tased this moor "an por no reason."

Jack stood and walked over to the dresser, where the Ko(lay, martly hanging oC.

"Rhat do you think is in itP" Fhay asked, still keeming watch towards the door.

"H don?t know." Jack said as he looked at the Ko(. "fhere?s a note tamed to the tom."

"Rhat does it sayP" Ticholas asked.

THE NOTE

"Jack, be careful, you don't know what's in the box." Vicky's voice came over the radio.

"Let me read the note Trst." Jack said. phe note was folded in half and taHed to the outside toH of the box. Jack removed the note and slowly oHened it. ge stood there lookinY down at the note without sayinY a word.

"?ou YoinY to let us in on what the note saysN" Iicholas asked as he was helHinY the older man uH from the Soor and onto the bed.

"qt's a note from gunter. ge says to oHen the box, and there is a tablet inside. phen turn on the tab let."

here was a beeH that came from the laHtoH comHuter sittinY on the table across from -teven.

-teven looked over at the screen and noticed the messaYe reCuestinY to con6 nect. "8harles, q think they are ready."

"Very Yood." 8harles called out to gunter, who was in the next room. "gunter, you have a call from your team." gunter entered the room and looked over at 8harles, who then said, "q think the moment of truth has arrived."

gunter Haused for a moment and looked at 8harles, not understandinY what he was talkinY about.

"gunter, it's time you made your decision. Fre you YoinY to work with me, or are you YoinY to let your team try aYain to rescue youN"

gunter Yave a short nod to 8harles and walked over to the laHtoH.

"Just Hress the Anter key and q'm sure you'll be lookinY at one of your teammates. Gore likely Jack or that Trecracker -hay. RerhaHs both."

gunter Haused before HressinY the Anter key, "?ou think your Hlan will workN" he said, without lookinY back at 8harles.

"AiYhty6pwenty, q think, but it's totally uH to you," 8harles reHlied as he Yestured towards gunter with his riYht hand.

gunter Hressed the Anter key, and the screen lit uH. F dark TYure aHHeared on the screen, dressed in black and wearinY a black balaclava hood and helmet.

"g!IpAWz" came the resHonse from the darkened TYure on gunter's laHtoH.

"qt's me kid. hat in the hell are you doinY in RarisN"gunter reHlied, tryinY to let on like he wasn't haHHy to see him.

" ell, we're here to try and rescue you." Jack reHlied as here moved his helmet and hood.

gunter smiled sliYhtly, "Fnd how is that workinY out for youN"

"Fre you alriYhtN here are youN" Jack reHlied, still HuBBled as to where gunter was and what had Yone wronY.

-hay walked over next to Jack and said, "qt didn't really Yoas Hlanned."9

"Iever does." gunter reHlied.

"jut your tracker indicated that you are in this room." Jack said, lookinY down at -hay and then back at gunter.

8harles steHHed into the view of the camera, sliYhtly behind gunter, " e removed the tracker from gunter's belt once we landed in Raris. ge had no idea we removed it."9

gunter turned towards 8harles and Yave him a cold look, "Just when did you do thisN"

" hen you sleHt the day we arrived in Raris. -teven entered your room and removed your belt from the chair next to the bed. e detected the tracker while you were on the ...et from Prankfurt to Raris. phen, before we left Raris, we Hlaced the tracker underneath the bed."

gunter bit the inside of his liH and looked back at Jack fora second. ge then looked away at someone standinY behind and to the riYht of the camera view.

"Kon't worry, gunter, we'll Tnd you if it's the last thinY we do." -hay said as she steHHed towards the camera.

gunter looked back at the camera and didn't say a word for a few seconds. -hay could see that somethinY was botherinY him and that he wanted to say somethinY.

" hat is it, gunterN" she asked.

"Kon't." gunter reHlied, showinY ...ust a hint of emotion that he rarely showed.

Vicky had been listeninY to the conversation over Jack7s microHhone, " hat do you mean don'tN"

"Vicky, he can't hear you." Jack reHlied.

" ell, you tell him we're YoinY to Tnd him, no matter what." she said in a loud tone.

"Vicky said, we're YoinY to Tnd you, no matter what." Jack said, relayinY her messaYe to gunter.

"pell her not to worry. phat..." gunter started.

Jack interruHted, "-he can hear you over my microHhone. jut you can't hear her. jesides, you don't want to know what she is sayinY anyway."

"Ek, ok, tell her to calm down. phat0." Jack interruHted gunter aYain. "-he's yellinY in my ear now. -he's tellinY me to tell you not to tell her to calm down, and some other stu1 that q'm not YoinY to reHeat."9

gunter closed his eyes and lowered his head sliYhtly. ge turned back towards 8harles and said somethinY that Jack and the others couldn't hear.

"gunter." Jack said, tryinY to Yet gunter's attention.

gunter turned back towards the camera, "Listen, kid, q'm Tne. q don't need you to come and rescue me."

"Fre you beinY held aYainst your willN" -hay asked.

gunter Haused aYain and looked down at the Soor. Ffter a few seconds, he looked uH aYain at the camera, "Io."

"phen we're cominY to Yet you." -hay reHlied.

"IEz" gunter reHlied Trmly.

"-hit." Jack said as he riHHed his earHiece out of his ear and started rubbinY his ear. "Vicky is not haHHy with that answer."9

-hay steHHed in front of Jack, "pell us what is YoinY on."

gunter hesitated for a few seconds and ...ust stared at the camera before answerinY. "q'm YoinY to be workinY with 8harles for a while."

gunter closed his eyes, droHHed his head down sliYhtly, and started rubbinY his forehead with his riYht hand. ge stood there listeninY to Jack, -hay, and Iicholas TrinY Cuestions at him all at the same time. ge could imaYine what Vicky was shoutinY at her end. ge was somewhat Ylad he couldn't hear her comments, but knew sooner or later he would have to listen to them.

-hay relayed Vicky's messaYe, "Io o1ence, 8harles, but why would gunter ever want to work with youN"

8harles steHHed closer to the camera, "Io o1ence taken, Vicky, but you should hear gunter and me out Trst."

" ell, you can take my riYht boot and stick it uH your ass. gunter is not YoinY to work with you, or for you." -hay reHlied.

8harles smiled and said, "FYain, Vicky, no o1ence taken, and q understand your feelinYs."

"Eh no, 8harles, Vicky didn't say that. q said it. phose are my words, and q'm serious." -hay reHlied, leaninY in towards the camera.

Uevin's voice came over their earHieces, "Let's hear gunter out. q've known gunter for a lonY time, and q trust him."

Kana, who was still stationed at the bottom of the stairs, had been listeninY to what was haHHeninY, "q want to hear gunter out."

Way could also be heard in the backYround talkinY to Vicky. ge also wanted to hear what gunter had to say.

Jack had Hut his earHiece back in his ear after Vicky stoHHed yellinY over the microHhone.

"Ek, let's hear what Hossible reason he has for workinY with that man." she said.

"Vicky and the others want to listen to what you have to say."9 Jack relayed to gunter.

gunter looked over at 8harles aYain and then back at the camera. ge was obviously havinY a hard time TndinY the words. "Duys, q'm YoinY to be workinY for a while with 8harles."

" hyN" -hay asked.

gunter Hut uH his hand to try and Yet everyone to stoH talkinY, "gear me out Trst before you say anythinY else."

"EU PqIAz" -hay resHonded.

"8harles has asked me to Yo undercover to inTltrate the Iasir Fl6gadid sex tra5ckinY orYaniBation rinY. ge's made arranYements for me to come in and helH run the !.-. orYaniBation." gunter Haused for a second before continuinY.

"jut what do you know about runninY a sex rinYN" Jack asked.

"phat's what q said." gunter reHlied.

"q have a contact that was heavily involved in the sex tra5ckinY business. ge has aYreed to teach gunter everythinY he knows." 8harles reHlied.

"Vicky wants to know when this is all YoinY to haHHen." Jack relayed.

gunter looked at 8harles and then back at the camera, "Fs of riYht now, q'm workinY with 8harles on this."

8harles closed his eyes and Yave a couHle of nods in relief, knowinY that gunter had committed to helHinY him. jefore now, he hadn't said whether he was onboard with his Hlan or not. 8harles looked over at gunter, who was standinY riYht beside him. "phank you." 8harles said, ...ust loud enouYh so that only gunter could hear.

"AxHlain to us how this is YoinY to work, and what are you or we YoinY to beneTt from thisN" Jack askd.

"q asked the same Cuestion, kid. q'll be settinY uH and runninY the Iorth Fmerican tra5ckinY business for Iasir. ge wants to exHand his oHeration in that area. Fnd since we took out the 9Uovenski's, there's now an oHeninY that needs to be Tlled. 8harles has sold me as the one to reHlace them." gunter Haused.

"Do on." Jack said, now startinY to see where gunter was YoinY.

gunter continued, "q'll know the ins and outs of his business and where all the camHs and other facilities he has in the country are. q'll be able to forward this information to you Yuys."

8harles held uH his hand, "gunter will be HassinY the information to me, and then q'll forward that information to you. e can't run the risk of Iasir TndinY out who or what gunter is doinY."

"phis will be a chance for us to hit and take down an international tra5ckinY rinY." gunter added.

8harles leaned over and whisHered somethinY into gunter's ear.

gunter nodded, " here is KanaN"

"-he's downstairs keeHinY an eye out for us." Jack reHlied.

"gave her come uH here too." gunter said.

"Do ahead and have your man Uevin ...oin you. q have one of my Yuys keeHinY an eye out for you. qf anyone aHHroaches, he'll let us know." 8harles said with a smile.

gunter nodded with his aHHroval.

"En my way." Uevin said over the radio. "Dive me about two minutes."

" hile we wait, how is my old friend doinYN" 8harles asked . *"Père Aristide, comment vous traitent-ils?"*

phe old man stood uH and walked over towards the camera, *"Cet imbécile m'a tiré dessus avec un taser. Tu ne m'as pas dit que des sauvages entraient chez moi!"*9

Jack turned and smiled at the old man, " hat did he sayN"

8harles took the oHHortunity to answer Jack's Cuestion, "q asked Pather Fristide how you were treatinY him. Fnd he reHlied. phis fool shot me with a taser. ?ou didn't tell me that some savaYes were cominY into my homez"

Jack looked from 8harles to the older man standinY next to him, "Pather FristideN"

"qt's ok, he's an old friend of mine. ge's a Hriest at the local church down the street." 8harles said.

-hay looked at the old man and then back at Jack and started lauYhinY, "Jack, you shot a Hriestz ?ou're deTnitely YoinY to hell for that."

Fbout that time, Kana and Uevin walked into the room, "Jack shot a HriestN" Kana said.

"?ou know you can Yo to hell for doinY that." Uevin followed her comment.

Jack ...ust shook his head and turned his attention back to gunter. "Ek, we're all here now. hat else do you have for usN"

"Iasir is scheduled to Yet married in two months, on January 4st. phe weddinY is YoinY to be down in 8uba." gunter said.

"Fre we invitedN" Uevin asked, ...okinYly.

"qn a manner of sHeakinY, you are." 8harles reHlied.

"Kana." gunter said.

"?es." she reHlied, cockinY her head to one side.

gunter smiled, "?our sister Uatie will be there too."

" gFpz" Kana screamed.

"ait, how do you know thisN" she asked.

"q sHoke with her. q told her that we will be cominY for her soon." 8harles reHlied.

"gow is sheN" Kana asked, beaminY with hoHe and excitement.

"-he is very well. -he is beinY treated well. q saw no siYns of Hhysical harm. -he seems to be a very stronY younY woman." 8harles said with a smile, "Fnd very stubborn, q miYht add."

"phat's my little Uatie." Kana said with a smile, as tears started rollinY down her face. -hay Yave Kana a biY huY as Kana continued to cry. -he looked back at 8harles, "qs she YoinY to be in 8uba tooN"

8harles nodded, "-he is to marry Iasir in 8uba."

"Look, Yuys, we all have a lot of work to do. q start my undercover traininY." gunter Haused and looked over at 8harles.

"pomorrow." 8harles reHlied as he turned and walked o1.

"pomorrow. ?ou won't hear from me for a while. Fll my communications will be throuYh 8harles." gunter said.

"jut gunter." -hay started.

gunter interruHted, "Io buts, this is YoinY to work out for the best all the way around. e'll Yather some valuable insiYhts into Iasir's oHeration, both in Iorth Fmerica and elsewhere. Fnd we'll be YettinY Uatie back."

Io one said anythinY for several seconds, they ...ust looked stunned as they looked at gunter on the monitor.

"?ou're riYht." Jack said, breakinY the silence. "gow will we Yet in touch with you if we need toN"

gunter took a couHle of steHs towards the laHtoH, "8ontact 8harles. Vicky has his contact information. pry not to worry. ?ou Yuys keeH doinY what you've been doinY. Kon't wait for me to feed you information. phere are Hlenty of Herverts out there to keeH you Yuys busy."

Averyone in the room wished him Yood luck. Jack relayed the same from Vicky and Way. ith that, gunter smiled and turned o1 the camera.

"q hoHe the eiYhty Hercent you were referrinY to earlier was for success." gunter said to 8harles in the next room as he closed the laHtoH.

Fs gunter entered the room, followed by -teven, 8harles reHlied, "phat is entirely uH to you."

gunter nodded, " hen do q meet this scumbaY that's YoinY to be my train6 erN"

"ge will arrive Trst thinY in the morninY." 8harles reHlied.

" hat's the scheduleN" gunter asked as he took a seat.

8harles smiled, "ell, he'll Yo over that with you. e will Yet started after brunch tomorrow."

"E k, Yuys, Hack uH and let's Yet the hell out of here." Jack said, lookinY at the others.

" hat about this dudeN" Iicholas asked, referrinY to the Hriest standinY next to him.

-ha y walked over and Hicked uH a baY that was lyinY on the Soor, "?eah, Jack, the Hriest that you shot, remember."

Jack looked at the Hriest and then at Iicholas, "Ko you think he'll call the coHs when we leaveN"

"q don't know Jack, we did break into his house in the middle of the niYht, and you did shoot him. hat do you thinkN" Uevin reHlied.

Jack rubbed his head with his riYht hand, "q don't know, Yuess we could tie him uH and call someone after we're out of the country to come and untie him."

"?ou're YoinY to tie uH a HriestN" -hay said.

"ell, that's not as bad as shootinY him." Kana added to the conversation.

Jack threw uH his hands, "Duys, you're not helHinY." Fbout that time, Jack's Hhone started rinYinY.

Jack took his Hhone out of his Hocket and answered, "gello, Vicky, why are you callinYN" "q've been listeninY to your dilemma on the radio. q've Yot 8harles on the line, Hut the Hriest on the Hhone."

Jack handed his Hhone to the older man. phe man nodded a few times at Trst, and then he Yot very animated and loud. ge Hointed at Jack a couHle of times while sayinY somethinY that the others didn't understand. Ence the man Tnished his conversation, he returned the Hhone to Jack.

Fs Jack took the Hhone, the man turned and walked out of the room. "Vicky." Jack said. "Io, Jack, it's 8harles. q've smoothed thinYs over with Pather Fristide. ge's not YoinY to Yive you any trouble."

"ge seemed very uHset." Jack reHlied.

"ge had every riYht to be. Ffter all, you did break into his home and shoot him." 8harles reHlied with a sliYht chuckle.

phe others had Yathered their thinYs and were headinY out of the house, Jack followed as he talked to 8harles, "q could tell by the way he was lookinY at me and the tone of his conversation that he was talkinY about me."

"Iot to worry, he was ...ust referrinY to your uHbrinYinY, alonY with some other thinYs that we won't Yo into." 8harles reHlied.

9"q Yuess q should thank you." Jack reHlied.

"Io, Jack, it is q who should be thankinY you and your team. ?ou're YoinY to be HlayinY a very imHortant Hart in this endeavor."

phey were loadinY their eCuiHment into the two vehicles when Kana asked, "8an we drive by and see the Ai1el powerN q've always wanted to see it in Herson." Jack, -hay, Uevin, and Iicholas all reHlied simultaneously, "IEz"

"e are YettinY out of here before that Yuy chanYes his mind and decides to call the coHs on Jack." -hay reHlied as she oHened the driver's side door and started to Yet in.

"Eh, hell no, you're not drivinY." Jack said as he Yrabbed -hay by her shirt collar. "q want to make it back alive."

-hay nudYed Jack aside and ...umHed into the other -!V, "goH in, Yuys." she said to Uevin and Iicholas.

"Io, thank you, q've heard about your drivinY skills."Iicholas reHlied, "q'll ride back with Jack."

"Pinez" she reHlied, "Uevin, Yet in." -he said as she started the enYine. -he Hut the -!V into reverse and started backinY uH. phere was a crash, as the -!V shook. " hat in the hellN" -hay said.

Jack backed the other -!V uH next to the one that -hay and Uevin were sittinY in and rolled down the HassenYer window. -hay and Uevin were out lookinY to see what she had backed into. "?ou couldn't even back it out of the driveway before you hit somethinY."

"-hut uH, Jack." -hay said, without lookinY back at him.

"phe only liYht Hole on the street, and you hit it. Uevin, you drive the rest of the way." Jack said as he backed onto the street and headed towards the airHort.

-hay and Uevin, with Uevin now drivinY, swunY by and droHHed their eCuiHment o1 at the Hrivate air freiYht comHany. phey would be shiHHinY the eCuiHment back to gouston, where one of the team members would Hick it uH in a couHle of days.

phe team made it safely to the Raris airHort, barrinY one dented rear bumHer. phey checked the rental cars and baYs in and Hroceeded to the Hlane. phe SiYht to Ftlanta was ...ust over nine hours and Cuiet. phe team sat in seHarate areas of the aircraft to avoid drawinY attention to a YrouH of Tve travelers.

Ence they arrived in Ftlanta, they headed to retrieve their baYs.

"gey Yuys, q need to stoH by the restroom before we Yo." Jack said.

Jack started into the restroom as he saw a middle6aYed lady cleaninY the entry of the restroom. ge stoHHed next to the lady and asked, "qs this restroom oHenN"9

phe woman reHlied, "Eh yes, sir, q am very sorry, q will move immediately out of your way." -he was nervous and accidentally droHHed her broom onto the Soor. -he acted very fearful and awkwardly started to Hick uH the broom. Jack reached down and Hicked it uH for her.

"Eg no, sir, you mustn't do that." she said sheeHishly.

" hy notN" Jack asked.

"?ou are far too imHortant a Herson to touch such thinYs."

" hat do you meanN" he asked.

"?ou Sy herein a very fancy and beautiful ...et, you must be very imHortant. q'm not as imHortant." she reHlied.

Jack looked at her for a few seconds, "Gay q ask you somethinY, ma'amN"

"?es, of course, sir."

"pell me what it is you do here."

"q take care of the restrooms. q make sure they are clean and suHHlied. q also emHty the trash cans inside the airHort terminal."

"q see." Jack said softly. "ould you believe me if q told you that your ...ob is one of the most imHortant ...obs at this airHortN"

-he looked at Jack and lauYhed, "q'm ...ust a custodian, how can q be as imHortant as you sayN"

Jack looked at her and smiled, "qf you were not to do your ...ob, let's say you didn't clean and resuHHly the restrooms and didn't emHty out the trash. hat would haHHenN"

-he cocked her head to one side, " ell, no one could use the restrooms and the trash would overSow." she said.

"Fnd it would smell, and rats and buYs would infest the terminal." Jack said.

-he Yrimaced and shook her head in disYust, "?es, q suHHose so." she said.

"phen no one would be willinY to come to this airHort. PliYhts would be canceled, because no one would want to Sy into or out of this airHort." Jack exHlained.

"RerhaHs."

"Eh, q Hromise you that would haHHen. phe airHort would have to shut down." Jack Haused for a few seconds. "-o, without you, the airHort could not oHerate. ?ou are ...ust as imHortant as the Hilots, mechanics, and Yate attendants. -o never let anyone ever tell you you're not imHortant."

phe woman smiled, now showinY much Hride in what she did. -he looked uH at Jack and wiHed a tear from her face. "phank you, sir."

"Rlease call me Jack." he said, stickinY his hand out.

-he slowly took his hand in hers and Yently shook it, "phank you, Jack. Gy name is 8orina."

ge Hlaced his other hand on her shoulder, "Wemember, 8orina, keeH this airHort oHen, the entire Hlace is countinY on you."

Jack Tnally cauYht uH to them, and they boarded EmeYa Ene, their 8essna 8itation -overeiYn. Prom Ftlanta, they would Sy back to 8oulter FirTeld in jryan, pexas.

phey landed at 8oulter FirTeld several hours later, tired and disaHHointed. pheir mission to rescue gunter had failed. phey Yrabbed their baYs and Hro6 ceeded into the terminal area.

IMMUNITY

It was a brisk Saturday afternoon, unseasonably warm for this time of year. A dark SUV pulled up to the front of the building. The three occupants sat in the vehicle for a few minutes before the passenger in the front seat exited. The passenger was a stocky, built male in his early thirties with a dark complexion, a short, nicely trimmed beard, and wearing dark sunglasses. He closed the door and stepped up on the curb. He slowly surveyed the area before opening the rear passenger's door. Anyone watching would assume that man was ex-military, secret service, or some sort of bodyguard.

A man in his late forties with salt and pepper hair stepped out of the SUV. He was dressed in a dark sports coat and dark grey pants. He wore a baseball cap pulled down low and a pair of dark sunglasses. He hurriedly walked past the other man and headed towards the building.

As they reached the door, the older man motioned for the younger man to remain outside. As the older man entered the building, the younger man assumed a position against the wall and surveyed the surrounding area.

The driver of the SUV remained in the vehicle with the motor running. The building was an older-looking commercial warehouse building located just outside the Atlanta city limits. The demographics of the area were characterized by lower income levels, with a small homeless population. The surrounding area was Blled with warehouses and commercial buildings. &usinesses occupied most of the surrounding buildings, with a few vacant buildings available for sale or lease.

The building he entered was HFL "ogistics, a "atin American import and export business. Just inside the door was a desk where a large, heavy-set man sat. As the older man entered, the man behind the desk stood. He was a big man, standing six feet Bve inches and weighing about two hundred and eighty-Bve pounds. He towered over the smaller Bve-foot-nine-inch older gentleman.

"I'm here to see Roberto Hugo.E

The large man just looked at him before Bnally saying, "?mpty your pockets, remove your watch, and place everything on the table.E

The man did as he was instructed. After he did so, the large man pointed towards a magnetometer. Just like one of those machines you walkthrough at the airport to detect if you have any weapons.

He walked through the machine, and no alarms went oW. He turned to retrieve the items he had placed on the table.

"You leave them there. You can pick them up when you leave.E

"I am ?dgardo Santiago. Do you know who I amME the man asked, somewhat boldly.

The larger man looked down at him, "Don't know and don't care. "ike I said, you can pick them up when you leave.E

He turned towards a door across the room, " here is ír. HugoME

"Lollow me, I will take you to him.E(

"Thank you.E he replied and smiled at the man.

He followed the man through the door and down the hallway toa wooden door on the right. He knocked on the door and waited for a reply from inside.

"S).E A muéed voice came from the other side of the door.

"*Señor, su invitado está aquí.*E 2Sir, your guest is here.G

"íuy bien, muNstrale en.E 2Very well, show him in.G

The large man opened the door and stood aside as the older man entered. He took a couple of steps into the room and came to a stop. He stood facing the man whom he had traveled so far to see.

Roberto Hugo stood just under six feet and had thick black hair that he combed straight back. His skin was a dark golden brown, and you could tell that he had spent most of his earlier years out in the sun. hen he smiled, his teeth were so white that they would almost blind you. He wore a gold chain around his neck and several rings on each hand. He looked back towards the man who had escorted his guest in, and for him to leave and close the door.

" elcome, Ambassador Santiago, long time no see.E Hugo said, and the two men shook hands.

Santiago smiled, "Yes, my friend, it has been way too long.E(

" hat brings the Ambassador of ...uba to my humble businessMEHugo asked as he motioned towards a light brown sofa.

"&usiness.E Santiago replied.

Hugo leaned back and placed his arm on the back of the sofa, "Yes, but of course. Are you looking to increase trade with my business and your country of ...ubaME Hugo asked.

Santiago didn't reply. He just looked at Hugo and smiled.

"Are we wanting to purchase the same merchandise as beforeME Hugo asked.

Santiago smiled and nodded, "I would like to view your merchandise and see if there is anything that I like.E

"Same vintage as beforeME Hugo asked.

"Yes.E Santiago replied.

Hugo thought for a second, ""et me see what I have in stock. I may have something you like.E he picked up his cell phone and placed a call. After a short conversation, he ended the conversation and put the phone in his pocket. "I have Bve models that you might be interested in.E

Santiago smiled and gave him a slight nod. "How long till I'll be able to see the merchandiseME

Hugo glanced at his watch, "3ot long. íaybe ten minutes. I knew you were coming, so I had a few already picked out for you.E

They talked about a past Bshing trip they took together just oW the coast of ...uba. They were making plans to take Santiago's boat out again soon when there came a knock at the door.

"Yes.E Hugo said.

"*Están listos, señor.*E 2They are ready, sir.G said a voice from the other side of the door.

Hugo smiled and looked over at Santiago, "They are here. "et's go and take a look.E

The two men stood and walked over to a side door that led into another room. As they entered, Santiago paused for a second and smiled. "3ice.E he said and continued into the room. He walked over and stood next to Hugo. "Very nice. The red one is nice. &ut the blue one is my favorite.E

"She is a thing of beauty.E Hugo replied. "'lease take a closer look.E

Santiago slowly walked over and stopped just inches away, "How old are youME

She looked down at the !oor but didn't answer.

He took his right hand and placed it under her chin, and lifted her head, "I said5 How old are youME

"Thirteen.E she replied softly.

He watched as a tear rolled down her face. He took a Bnger of his right hand and wiped away the tear. "Tell me. Are you fresh or spoiledME

She looked at him, "I don't know what you mean.E

He grabbed her chin in his hand, jerked it up, and looked into her eyes.

She started shaking and crying. She could smell the hot breath on her face, and she tried her best not to look at him.

He leaned over and spoke softly into her ear, "Have you been fuckedME

"?dgardo, my friend, they are all pure. Just the way you like them.E Hugo said as he walked up next to him. "'lease trust me.E

Santiago looked at him and back at the young girl, ”You know I can tell.E

”I would never lie to you.E Hugo pleaded with him.

”How muchME Santiago asked.

”Live thousand U.S. dollars.E Hugo replied.

”The one in red, how old is sheME(

”She is thirteen also. She just arrived the day before yesterday from Japan. She has not spoken since she arrived.E(

”How much for the two of themME Santiago asked as he walked over to the young girl in red.

”They both bring high dollars. &oth are young and pure.EHugo said, pulling the girl in &lue over next to the other one.

”I asked how much.E Santiago repeated, but this time louder and harsher.

”Ten thousand U.S.E Hugo replied.

Santiago just laughed, ”I’ll give you eight thousand and you deliver them both to my hotel room.E

”&ut they are both prime merchandise. They can bring Bve thousand each easily.E Hugo pleaded.

Santiago lightly rubbed the young Asian girl7s face with the back of his hand, ”If you had told me this one was twelve, then I would go the full ten. &ut since you already said she was thirteen, the most I will go is eight.E

Hugo studied for a second, ”?ight Bve. That’s the best Ican do.E

Santiago looked at the two girls and then at Hugo, ”?ight thousand Bve hundred dollars, and you buy dinner next time we meet.E

”Deal9E Hugo replied and slapped Santiago on the back.

Santiago turned towards the door(as he walked out and said, ”Have them both to my room by eight o’clock tonight.E

At precisely eight p.m., there came a knock on Ambassador Santiago's hotel room door. His bodyguard, Ronnie, stood and walked over to the door. He checked through the peephole to verify who it was. All he was able to see was the chest of a very tall, heavy-built man and the tops of the heads of the two little girls.

"ír. Santiago, your guests are here.E Ronnie said as he opened the door.

The two little girls stood there looking down at the !oor. After a couple of seconds, the man behind them gave them both a slight push towards the door. The two girls cautiously walked into the room, arms around each other, in an attempt to give each other some sense of security.

Ronnie looked at the man in the hallway, "I'm Ronnie, ír. Santiago's body-guard. &y the way, what is your nameME

The man looked at Ronnie for a second and said, "Lrances.E

"Ok, Lrances. How about picking the girls up around one p.m. tomorrowME Ronnie said.

"Sure.E Lrances replied. He turned and walked down the hallway towards the elevator.

"3ice talking to you, Lrances.E Ronnie said as he closed the door.

The two girls stood just inside the door. They both clung to each other as they looked around the large living area of the hotel room. They were both dressed in what some would call schoolgirl outBts. One wore a mini red plaid pleated skirt with a white short-sleeved button-down shirt. The other girl also had on the same outBt, except her skirt was blue. ?ach girl had a small backpack and a small stuWed pink bunny rabbit that they held under one of their arms.

Santiago stood as the girls entered, "'lease come in, my students, class will begin shortly. I've prepared you both a nice lunch and a glass of milk.E he paused and looked at both girls for a second. "You must keep your strength up, we have a long day of studying ahead of us.E

Santiago looked up at Ronnie, "You may go now. I can handle things from here.E

”Very well sir. hat time would you like for me to wake youME Ronnie asked.

”Don't bother, I think we're going to have a long night ahead of us. These two look to be troublemakers, and they will need to be disciplined several times, I'm sure.E

”As you wish. Robert and I will be across the hall if you need anything.E Ronnie said as he exited the room. Robert was Ambassador Santiago's driver and personal assistant.

Santiago motioned the two girls over to the table, ”...ome, come, my students. ?at, we will be starting class very soon, and you're going to need your strength.E

I t was just past eleven thirty the next morning when there was a soft knock on the door. The door opened slightly, ”Housekeeping.E she called out. There was no answer. She repeated, this time with the door open, ”Housekeeping.E Still no answer. She entered the room, walked into the living area, and started cleaning up. There was food left on the table and a couple of empty bottles of alcohol on the !oor. It was a mess, but she had seen much worse.

She Bnished cleaning the living room and walked over to the main bedroom. The door was opened slightly. She stood next to the door and said, ”Housekeeping.E Still nothing, so she opened the door into the main bedroom and entered.

She took a few steps into the room and froze. She saw a small leg on the !oor, just on the other side of the bed. She stood there, shocked, just looking down at the little leg. She didn't know what to do. Then she caught a slight movement and a moan from the bed. There was a naked man asleep or passed out on the bed. Then she noticed a little girl lying next to him, naked and bloody. Her little eyes looking up at the ceiling.

”Co away9 "eave us alone.E came the tired voice from the man.

She took a step back, dropped her bag, and ran out of the room into the main hallway. She ran to the closest house phone and called security. She tried her best to explain to the security officer on the phone what she had seen. But she was too hysterical for the officer to make any sense of what she was saying.

Within minutes, two hotel security officers arrived at the room. As they were about to enter the room, the door from across the hall opened. ” hat is going onME Ronnie said.

”Sir, go back in your room please.” One of the officers replied.

”I'm not going anywhere. hat is going onM hy are you going into my boss's roomME Ronnie said as he stepped out into the hallway.

The two hotel security officers entered the hotel suite and went into the main bedroom, as reported by the housekeeping staW member.

They entered the main bedroom and stopped in their tracks when they saw the two naked bodies on the bed and the one lying next to the bed.

” hat is going onME Santiago demanded, and he tried to sit up in the bed.

One of the hotel security officers looked at the other and said, “Call 911 immediately9E

”
1 r. Santiago, I had to clear my docket for the rest of the day. These people have been waiting weeks to have their case heard. However, I received a call from the State Attorney General's office informing me that I have a special case that requires my undivided attention. Tell me, Mr. Santiago, what makes you so specialME Judge June íayweather asked.

”Judge íayweather, I'm sorry to cause you such trouble this evening, it's all a great big misunderstanding.E Santiago said, with a big smíle on his face.

Judge íayweather opened the Ble sitting on her desk. ”ír. Santiago, I had a chance to brie!y review the police report. It says that you were found naked in bed with two underage girls.E

”íay I say somethingME Santiago asked.

”3o9 You may not. I'm not Bnished. The report goes on to say that alcohol was involved and that the two underage girls were intoxicated. It also says that, according to the preliminary medical report, both girls had several bruises all over their bodies and faces. And severe trauma to their vaginal areas. &oth young girls are currently Bghting for their young lives. She looked up at him. And if they survive this hideous attack, they will have to deal with the physical and emotional scars the rest of their lives9E íayweather said, not holding back her anger.

”íay I say something, Your HonorME Santiago asked.

”Co ahead, I would like to hear your explanation. Tell us how their blood was found on you, and your semen was found on and in those girls9 T?”“ í?9E

A man sitting next to Santiago stood and spoke, ”Your Honor, may I speakME

” ho in the hell are youME íayweather asked.

”I'm from the State Department. íy name is5E he started to say, before íayweather cut him oW.

“Yes, I know who or what you are. The State Attorney General's office informed me that ír. ?dgardo Santiago here is declaring diplomatic immunity. It appears that ír. Santiago is free to come into our city, rape, and murder whomever he pleases and walk away scot-free.E

”Are we Bnished, Your HonorME Santiago asked.

”Yes, we are. Cet the hell out of my courtroom. &ailiW, escort ír. Santiago out of the building. And then I want this courtroom fumigated.E íayweather slammed her gavel down on her desk and watched as Santiago slowly walked to the courtroom doors.(

Santiago stopped before walking through the door and turned back towards Judge íayweather and smiled, ”Your Honor, next time I'm in town or you're in ...uba, let's have dinner.E(

“One last question, Mr. Santiago.” Mayweather said. Santiago gave her a slight nod. ”ould you by chance, deer hunt ír. SantiagoME íayweather asked.

"3o. I would never harm such a poor, defenseless animal like that. hy you askME Santiago replied.

"I was wondering. A thought had crossed my mind.E íayweather replied.

He turned and waved back over his head as he walked out into the courthouse hallway.

Judge Mayweather sat in her office for a while before picking up her cellphone. She held her phone in her hand for a few minutes, trying to Bnd the right words to say. She Bnally pressed send, and the phone started to ring on the other end.

"June9 hat a surprise. I've not heard from you since you moved to Atlanta. hat's going onME Vicky Vickers said in a cheerful voice.

"Vicky, we need to talk.E she replied.

CHAPTER EIGHT

THIS IS HOW YOU DO IT

S hay walked into Vicky's ogce as she was endin. the call" Wuhat's p,A ?pnt Vicky"m

Wihat rakes yop think sorethin. is p,"m she be,liedA leanin. fack in heb chaib"

Shay Jo,,ed down on the soxa acboss xbor Vicky's desk" WIpst the ej,bession on yopb xace when yop ended that call"m Shay be,lied"

WHt was vpst an old xbiend ox rine" zaDen't s,oken to heb in a cop,le ox yeabsAm Vicky be,lied"

Shay copld tell that thebe was robe to the ,hone call than vpst two old xbiends catchin. p, on old tires"

Shay ,icked p, a ra.aNine xbor the end tafleA W o H know heb"m she asked as she leaned fack and ,laced heb xeet acboss the soxa"

Wot dibectly"m Vicky be,lied" W?nd .et those 9lthy foots o1 ry xpbnitpbe"mT

Shay ,laced the ra.aNine down and tpbned towabds VickyA bestin. heb abr on to, ox the abr ox the soxaA Wuhat do yop reanA O'ot dibectly'"m

Vicky leaned heb head sli.htly to the bi.ht and looked at Shay xob a xew seconds"

RY

Ruell"m Shay said"

WCop bererfeb the 9bst tbi, that yop and Iack went on to.etheb"m

Shay sriled and shixted heb fody robe towabds VickyA W"he !acon tbi,"m Shay be,lied"

WCesA that one"m Vicky said"

WHhat does she haDe to do with it"m Shay askedA now fecorin. robe inteb2 ested in this ,hone call"

WShe's how we xopnd opt afopt Ehables abwood"m Vicky be,lied"

Shay vpr,ed p, xbor the soxaA bpshed oDebA and sat in the chaib in xbont ox Vicky's desk" She leaned oDebA ,laced heb elfows on to, ox the deskA and bested heb chin in heb hands"

WGlease tell reA how does she know that abwood xbeak"m

Vicky looked at Shay xob a lon. tire fexobe answebin. and took a dee, fbeathA WShe was the vpd.e on the tbial State Ds abwood"mT

Shay scbearedA WShe was the xpckin. vpd.eF 'o way" id she let anotheb one .o xbee"m

Vicky's ibbitation showed in heb xace xbor the corrent Shay had rade afopt heb xbiend" WShe did 'M" let hir .o" Hx yop bererfeb cobbectlyA the ,bosecption and the inDesti.atobs scbewed the case p," She didn't haDe a choice"mT

Shay lowebed heb head down towabds the tafle and clas,ed heb hands fehind heb headA WMkA whateDeb" ue ended p, haDin. to clean p, theib ress"m

What's neitheb hebe nob thebe"m Vicky be,lied"

Shay sat p, in the chaibA Wuhat in the hell does that rean" H heab yop old ,eo,le say that all the tire" zpnteb pses it a lot wheneDeb H rention sorethin. he did in the ,ast" ?nd why is a vpd.e ,pttin. a hit opt on soreone" oes she know afopt Mre.a"m

WCes and 'o"m Vicky be,lied"

Wuhat do yop reanA yes and no" She eitheb knows ob she doesn't"m Shay be,lied"

Wuhen yop webe kidna,,edA she care hebe to stay and fe with re xob a cop,le ox weeks" She hel,ed re deal with yopb disa,,eabance" She and H talked afopt doin. sorethin. like Mre.a thenA and we talked seDebal tires axteb that" ue talked afopt what we wopld do to the ,eo,le once we cap.ht ther"m Vicky went on afopt how they wopld swoo, in and bescpe the Dictirs and how they wopld deal with the kidna,,ebs"

Shay sat thebeA not sayin. a wobdA as Vicky went on afopt this sp,eb2secbet ob.aniNation that she and heb xbiend had dbeared p,"

When she called re afopt abwoodA she didn't know that H had ,pt opb dbear to w obk"m

Shay looked at heb conxpsedA W"hen why did she call yop"m

She knew afopt Vickebs GbiDate HnDesti.ation" She wanted re to di. into abwood's ,ast to see ix we copld 9nd anythin. that the detectiDes rissed"m Vicky ,apsedA WShe knew in heb heabt that he was .pilty and wopld doit a.ainA ix he wasn't sto,,ed"m

Wpt she knew nothin. afopt Mre.a then"m Shay asked"

Wo"m Vicky 4pickly be,lied" WShe did call re axteb yop and Iack took hir opt" She wanted to know ix H had heabd that he was dead"m

What did yop tell heb"m Shay asked"

H told heb that H didn't haDe anythin. to do with itA fpt H was .lad that he was killed"mT

Wd she felieDe yop"m Shay asked"

W'ot spbe" She told re that his death was bpled a hpntin. accidentA and nothin. xpbtheb wopld core ox it" 3pt axteb this last ,hone call'" H think she sps,ects sorethin."m Vicky saidA now xeelin. pnspbe ix heb secbet was opt and Ipne knew"

What did she want this tire"m Shay asked"

She called to tell re afopt this Epfan ?rfassadob who .ot cap.ht with two yopn. .ibls" ze had sejpally afpsed and featen ther"m Vicky be,lied"

Wet re .pessA he walked"m Shay be,lied"

Vicky noddedA Wze claired di,loratic irrpnityA so they had no choice“m

Wnd the .ibls”m Shay askedA heb ter,eb stabtin. to bise“

Vicky hesitated xob a second“ She leaned xobwabd and ,laced heb elfows on heb desk“ She ,pt heb hands to.ethebA inteblocked heb 9n.ebsA and bested heb chin on ther“ W"hey’be foth thibteen“ "hey abe foth in the hos,ital in cbitical condition“ "hey foth webe sodoriNedA ba,ed be,eatedlyA and sp1ebed seDebe tbapra to the Da.inal abea“ Mne sp1ebed a fboken vaw and thbee fboken bifs“ 3oth webe featen with sore kind ox felt ob stba,“mT

‘eitheb one said a wobd xob seDebal rinptes“ Shay sat thebe lookin. ,ast Vicky and opt the windowA fehind Vicky“ zeb xace had tpbned a li.ht shade ox bed as heb ter,eb bose“ Vicky had coDebed heb xace with heb handsA tbyin. to 9.ht the teabs fackA fpt lost that fattle“

...inallyA Shay saidA Wqpess we’be .oin. to haDe a fpsy nejt cop,le ox ronths“m

E hables entebed the kitchenA WCop had yopb co1ee yet”mT

WH’r on ry second cp,“m zpnteb be,lied“

Ehables took a seat at the kitchen tafle acboss xbor zpntebA W id yop .et anythin. to eat”m Ehables asked as he beached xob a fottle ox oban.e vpice and ,opbed hirselx a .lass“

WH had two .laNed donpts“ uhen will opb honobed .pest fe hebe”m zpnteb asked sabcastically“

Ehables took a dbink ox his vpice and ,laced the .lass fack on the tafleA W!aksir and SteDen landed in Mrsk afopt twenty rinptes a.o“ "hey will fe abbiDin. hebe fy helico,teb within thibty rinptes“m

Waksir”m zpnteb asked“

Ehables sriledA WSobbyA H xob.ot“ ze ,bexebs to fe called 3of fy optsidebs“m

Ruhat’s on the a.enda”m zpnteb askedA leanin. fack in his chaib and takin. a si, ox co1ee“

Ehables baised his .lass as ix to o1eb a toastA W"hat will fe p, to 3of" ue haDe afopt a ronth to .et yop tbained to fe afle to ,ass as an ej,ebienced sej and hpran tbagckeb"m

?fopt xobty29De rinptes latebA SteDen and theib .pest abbiDed" Ehables .beeted ther as they entebed the boor" Wuelcore to ry hprfle hore"m Ehables stpck opt his hand to shake 3of's"

WSobbyA we'be a little late"m SteDen saidA Wue had a little tbopfle with !b" VladyslaD's ,a,ebs"m

Ehables sriledA W'o ,bofler" ?llow re to intbodpce yop to yopb stpdent'" 3ill"m Ehables said as he tpbned towabds zpntebA who was sittin. in a chaib acboss the boor" 3of beroDed his coat and hpn. it on a ,e. on the wall" ze walked oDeb to whebe zpnteb was sittin. and sto,,ed a xew xeet away"

WHt is Deby nice to reet yop'" 3ill"m 3of said and stpck opt his hand"

zpnteb vpst looked p, at hir andA withopt sayin. a wobdA nodded and took anotheb si, ox co1ee"

3of .aDe a sli.ht srileA tpbnedA and took a seat acboss xbor zpnteb" W"hey tell re yop want to leabn how to bpn a sej and hpran tbagckin. fpsiness"m

zpnteb didn't be,ly and vpst ,laced his cp, ox co1ee on the tafle nejt to hir"

3of let opt a sli.ht si.h and .lanced oDeb at Ehables" Ehables vpst shbp..ed his shopldebsA W3illA 3of is hebe to teach yop the abt ox sej and hpran tbagckin." Sorethin. yop'be .oin. to haDe to leabn Deby 4pickly and ,bo9cientlyA ix yop ej,ect to .et opt ox this aliDe and with ana's sisteb Latie"m

3of leaned xobwabd towabds zpntebA W5et7s stabt with this 3ill" uhat is yopb fack.bopnd when it cores to sej and hpran tbagckin."m

zpnteb sriled and looked hir in the eyesA WH hpnt down the sick ,ebDebted tbagckebs and kill ther"mT

"he two sat lockin. stabes xob seDebal seconds fexobe Ehables captiopsly saidA WuellA now that we'De .ot that opt ox the way"m

Weby .oodA 3ill" Lee, that xeelin. and thop.ht in yopb rind"m 3of said"

WHt's not habd to do when H see yop and know what yop did"m zpnteb be,lied"

3of leaned xobwabd and ,laced his elfows on his kneesA WCop xeel that H'r spfhpran" Cop detest ry ,besence" Hn xactA yop wopld fe robe than ha,,y ix H webe to die bi.ht hebe in xbont ox yop" ?r H bi.ht"m he asked"

zpnteb .aDe 3of a fi. srileA WCop hit the nail on the head"m he be,lied"

WqoodA .ood" "hese abe the xeelin.s that yop rpst haDe towabds the ones whor yop tbagc" Cop rpst see ther as spfhpran rebchandiseA away to rake roney"m 3of be,lied and sriled"

WSoA when H look at therA H need to DispaliNe yop"m zpnteb .aDe 3of a ti.ht2li,,ed srile"

WCesA Deby .ood" Cop need to ,ass as a tbagckebA and ix that's what it takesA then do it"m 3of leaned fack in the chaib and looked oDeb at EhablesA WSeeA we'De rade ,bo.bess albeady"m

Ehables baised an eyefbowA WHx yop say so"m

Wo yop know how tbagckebs .et theib Dictirs"m 3of asked"

WCesA sore sick ,ebDebted fastabdA like yopA takes roney xbor sore innocent and des,ebate ,ebson and ,borises ther all sobts ox .beat and wondebxpl thin.s" ?nd once they .et theib roneyA they stp1 ther into a shi,,in. containeb ob in the fack ox a hot tbpck and dbiDe ther acboss the fobdeb" ?nd those who liDe neDeb see anythin. that was ,borised to ther" "hey abe xobeDeb indentpbed slaDes to those ,ebDebts"m zpnteb be,lied"

WSorewhat tbpeA fpt not the only way" !any .ibls and .pys tby to fecore intebnational rodels and .et spcked into the sej tbagckin. wobld" 5ike yopb xbiend ana" She care to ?rebica in ho,es ox fecorin. a sp,ebrodel"m 3of be,lied"

zpnteb shook his headA W"bpe" H'r spbe yop haDe rany otheb ways to entba, innocent childben"m he said"

Wo yop know why the sej tbagckin. fpsiness is now optsellin. the dbp. tbade"m 3of asked"

Wo"m zpnteb be,lied"

Wet's sayA xob ejar,leA an opnce ox cocaine is twelDe hpndbed dollabsA fpt yop can only sell it once" ? woran ob child'" zpndbed to a thopsand dollabsA and yop can sell ther oDeb and oDeb eDeby day" Cop can rake 9De to ten thopsand dollabs a day o1 one .ood .ibl"m 3of ej,lained"

WH know this is dis.pstin. to yopA zpntebA fpt in obdeb to catch a sej tbagckebA yop rpst fecore a sej tbagckeb" Mb know how one acts"m Ehables be,lied"

zpnteb nodded a littleA W"he old ,boDebfía *know your enemy, you must become your enemy*"m he said"

3of sriled and saidA W3pt how do yop fecore yopb enery" Cop need to ,pt yopbselx in the ,lace ox yopb enery so yop can know and ,bedict theib actions"m

zpnteb ,apsed xob a xew secondsA WMkA say H leabn the 7ins7 and 7opts7 ox this sej tbagckin. fpsiness" "hebe's no way in hell H'r .oin. to ,pt sore kid in dan.eb ob allow any ox ther to fe habred fy sore sick fastabd"m

WHt's not .oin. to .et to that ,oint"m Ehables be,lied"

What do yop rean"m zpnteb asked"

WCop'll only fe in twoA rayfe thbee ronths at rost"m Ehables be,lied"

zpnteb looked oDeb at Ehables and fack at 3of"

Wook 3ill"m 3of stabtedA WHt's .oin. to take yop oDeb a ronth to leabn 'asib's o,ebations" 5on.eb ix yop stbetch thin.s opt" Cop'be not .oin. to stabt dpr,in. .ibls into the syster on yopb 9bst day" 'asib is not sore stbeet ,ir," ze wants his rebchandise .boored and tbained" "his takes tireA de,endin. on the .ibl and rabket he's lookin. to 9ll"m

Ehables leaned in towabds zpntebA Wuobst caseA ix it cores down to yop haDin. to snatch soreoneA they'll fe pndeb yopb contbolA and when we ,pll yop optA they'll core with yop"m

zpnteb sat thebe bpffin. his chin with his bi.ht hand in thop.ht withopt sayin. a wobd"

W"hink ox all the inside inxobration yop'll haDe" Cop'll know his entibe tbagckin. netwobk" Cop'll know his 8"S" o,ebations and otheb o,ebations thbop.hopt the wobld" "hink ox all the ,eo,le yop can saDe and the ones that will neDeb xall Dictir to the sej tbagckin. ni.htrabe"m Ehables saidA tbyin. to encopba.e zpnteb"

zpnteb leaned fack in his chaibA looked p, at the ceilin.A and closed his eyes" ze sat thebeA not sayin. a wobd" 3ofA EhablesA and SteDen looked on as zpnteb sat conter,latin. the idea"

Whink afopt the .ood yop copld do"m Ehables whis,ebed"

zpnteb slowly lowebed his head and let opt a fbeath" ze looked at 3of and then at EhablesA WMkA H'r in" 38"F 'o one .ets hpbt"m

...ob the nejt seDebal weeksA zpntebA 3ofA EhablesA and SteDen wobked to.eth2 eb to .et zpnteb beady to .o pndebcoDeb in 'asib's sej tbagckin. ob.aniNation"

zpnteb watched roDies and GowebGoint ,besentationsA alon. with hopbs ox 4pestion2and2answeb sessions" !any tiresA he had to take fbeaks dpe to the ,ictpbes and ira.es he saw"

zpnteb askedA Wuhy do H haDe to see these ira.es ox these afpsed childben"m

WecapseA 3illA yop rpst .et nprf to what yop will see and heab" Cop rpst show no erotions when in xbont ox 'asib ob his collea.pes" Hx yop do soA they will fecore sps,iciops and ,ebha,s kill yop"m 3of be,lied"

zpnteb tbied his fest to berain stbon. when any nobral hpran wopld 4pit" zpnteb ,pshed onA leabnin. as rpch as he copldA knowin. the knowled.e xbor the inxobration he .ets will fe psed a.ainst xptpbe sej tbagckebs"

pbin. the 9nal weekA Ehables hibed sore local childben ox Dabiops a.es" "hey webe told that they wopld fe in a docprentaby afopt child kidna,,in." zpnteb wopld witness and ,abtici,ate in rock kidna,,in.s ox eDeby sha,eA xobrA and xashion"

ze leabned how to ,ick his tab.et and to know who was rost Dplnebafle" ze leabned that ,eo,le ox colob and rerfebs ox the 5q3"0(corrpnities webe the rost tab.eted" Geo,le corin. xbor pnstafle liDin. sitpationsA sejpal ob dorestic DiolenceA bpnawaysA and pndocprented irri.bants webe all easy tab.ets xob those ,eo,le lookin. to add to theib hpran tbagckin. collection"

BDil has no ,bevpdiceA thebe was nobticplab baceA nationalityA .endebA ob sejpal obientation" "hey ray fe xarily rerfebsA borantic ,abtnebsA ac4pain2 tancesA ob stban.ebs"

zpnteb looked at EhablesA W3y the wayA how do yop ej,ect to .et re opt"m

ıı   hebe was a knock on the doob ox Vicky's ogceA WEore on in"m Vicky said"

Iack entebed heb ogce and a,,boached heb deskA Wuhat's p,A Vicky"m

WzaDe a seatA we'De .ot anotheb rission to look into"m Vicky be,lied" She roDed heb ropse oDeb and clicked on an icon on heb cor,pteb scbeen" ? ,ictpbe ox a ran a,,eabed on a ronitob ropnted on the wall nejt to heb desk"

Wdho is this .py"m Iack asked as he looked at the ,ictpbe"

Wde is the Epfan ?rfassadob Bd.abdo Santia.o"m she be,lied"

Iack looked oDeb at heb and leaned fack in his chaibA Wuhat does a Epfan ?rfassadob haDe to do with ps"m

Wde was vpst beleased axteb fein. abbested xob fbptally ba,in. and featin. two thibteen2yeab2old .ibls"m Vicky ,plled p, a co,y ox the .ibl's redical be,obt that -ay had betbieDed and dis,layed theib statps on the ronitob"

Iack took a cop,le ox seconds and skirred oDeb the becobdsA Wzow rpch tire did this scprfa. .et"m

Wdebo tire"m she be,lied"

Iack looked at Vicky and fack at the ronitob on the wallA Wze .ot no vail tire"m

Wdo,eA he declabed di,loratic irrpnity"m she be,lied as she dis,layed San2 tia.o's ,ictpbe fack on the ronitob"

Wd,loratic irrpnityF "hat's a cbock ox shit"m Iack be,lied"

Vicky nodded in a.beerentA WH a.beeA fpt that's the law" ze'll haDe to answeb xob the chab.es in his hore copntby ox Epfa"

Wdhich we foth know nothin. will ha,,en to hir"m he be,lied"

WellA ix we haDe anythin. to do with itA he will ,ay xob the ba,es and feat2 in.s"m she said"

SoA we'be .oin. to Epfa"m Iack asked with a sli.ht srile on his xace"

Sooks that way" 8nless we wait pntil he cores fack to the 8"S" 3pt we don't know whenA ob whebe that wopld fe"m she saidA shakin. heb head"

Iack askedA Wuhebe did he .et the .ibls"m

Vicky closed the 9leA and Santia.o's ,ictpbe disa,,eabed xbor the ronitobA Wue don't know xob spbe yet" H'r .oin. to haDe -ofebt and Iir look into that ,abt" H need yop to ,pt to.etheb a ,lan to take opt Bd.abdo Santia.o"m Vicky said"

What afopt zpnteb"m Iack asked"

We's .oin. to fe down in Epfa in a cop,le ox ronthsA so it'll fe a dopfle rission" "ake opt Santia.o and fbin. fack ana's sisteb"m she said"

Iack thbew p, his handsA W? walk in the ,abk" ue in9ltbate a xobei.n copntby to take opt theib arfassadob" "hen we kidna, the fbide2to2fe ox a fillionaibe ?baf sej tbagckeb" 'o ,bofler" MhA did H leaDe opt that we'll fe in a copntby whebe none ox ps s,eaks the lan.pa.e"m Iack saidA shakin. his head"

Wop haDe a fetteb ,lan"m she asked"

Wo" 'ot at the rorent" MhA did H rention that we'll all stick opt like a sobe thprf"m Iack shot fack"

Wnd they abe called 0atabis"m Vicky said"

What"m Iack be,lied with a ,pNNled look on his xace"

Weo,le xbor 0atab abe bexebbed to as 0atabisA not ?bafs"m Vicky said"

WhateDeb"m he be,lied"

Vicky leaned xobwabd in heb chaibA WuellA .et the tear to.etheb and core p, with a wobkafle ,lan" Mpb nprfeb one ,biobity will fe ana's sisteb" Hx we need toA we'll .o fack anotheb tire and take opt the arfassadob ob wait till he cores hebe"m

WyeA ?yeA Ea,tain" H'll haDe -ay send opt an all2call ressa.e and haDe the tear hore the day axteb torobbow" zaDe yop heabd xbor zpnteb"m Iack asked as he stabted to .et p,"

Wot since he told ps he was .oin. pndebcoDeb"m she be,lied"

WHt wopld fe nice to let hir know what opb ,lans abe"m Iack said"

WMnce we core p, with sorethin.A H'll tby to .et wobd to hir thbop.h the Sandran"m she said"

WH don't tbpst that .py"m Iack said as he tpbned and headed towabds the doob"

WH xeel the sare wayA fpt we'De .ot to ,lay the cabds that webe dealt ps"m Vicky be,lied"

Mnce eDebyone abbiDed at Mre.a zead4pabtebsA Iack stabted 9llin. ther in on the two rissions that wopld fe ejecpted sirpltaneopsly" Wue'De .ot a ton ox wobk ahead ox ps" ue need to ,lan how we'be .oin. to .et LatieA ana's little sistebA away xbor that 'asib chabacteb" ?nd now we haDe to take opt a Epfan ?rfassadob at the sare tire"m

W?ny chance this arfassadob will fe attendin. 'asib's weddin."m LeDin askedA lookin. at Iack and Vicky"

What we do not know at this tire"m Vicky be,lied"

Wle ban into a ,bofler when we went to ...bance" ue discoDebed that the lan.pa.e fabbieb ,osed a sebiops ofstacle" H can see that this little tbi, to Epfa will ,ose the sare challen.e" oes anyone s,eak S,anish ob haDe any berote pndebstandin. ox the lan.pa.e"m Iack said as he looked abopnd the boor"

'o one said a wobdA seDebal shook theib headsA and one baised his hand"

P'ony"m Vicky saidA WCop s,eak S,anish"m

Wo"m "ony be,lied"

Wo yop need to .o to the fathboor"m Iack askedA WCop don't need to baise yopb handA vpst .o"m

WoA no" 3pt H ray haDe a solption"m "ony be,lied"

"he entibe tear tpbned and looked at "ony as he looked abopnd the boor at eDebyone" WSince nofody hebe s,eaks S,anishA and we don't haDe tire to leabn enop.h to .et fyA we haDe vpst two ronths" H haDe an idea that ray wobk"m "ony said"

Iack leaned fack a.ainst the wallA WGlease tell psA 8ncle "onyA what yopb idea is"m

P'hebe was a lan.pa.e conspltant who wobked with the ...3H on seDebal cases" ze has a rasteb7s in seDebal lan.pa.es" uhat yop ri.ht call a saDant"m "ony be,lied"

WCop said Owas'"m Shay said"

WCes" ze besi.ned as an ...3H conspltant dpe to the stbess ox the vof" ?lsoA H ri.ht addA xob sore ox the sare beasons that sore ox ps abe sittin. hebe now"m "ony said"

WH'd like to know what those beasons abe"m LeDin said"

"ony tpbned towabds LeDinA Wze and H talked fexobe he de,abted xbor the task xobce" Mne xactob he .aDe re xob leaDin. was that he saw too rany sps,ects .et o1 dpe to technicalities"mT

WH think we all can belate to that"m Vicky be,lied" "his .ot seDebal nods xbor the .bop,"

WHis rotheb's xarilyA when she was abopnd twelDe yeabs oldA sp1ebed a fbptal hore inDasion while liDin. in Ehina" ze told re that two ren fboke into his rotheb's hore while heb rothebA his xptpbe .bandrothebA was away at wobk"m

WHhat ha,,ened"m 'icholas askedA as the othebs satA wantin. to heab robe ox the stoby as well"

WHis rotheb was ba,edA and heb oldeb sisteb was taken" zeb fody was xopnd two days lateb in a wooded abea afopt 9De riles xbor theib hopse"m

WHhat ha,,ened to this .py's .bandxatheb" uhebe was he when all ox this was .oin. on"m Shay asked"

"ony looked oDeb at ShayA Wze was killed dpbin. the wab" uhen his .band2
rotheb care hore xbor wobkA she xopnd his rotheb fleedin. and featen"m

WyeA H can see how this xelleb wopld not want to deal with all the ,ebDebts
walkin. away xbee"m -ed said"

W"hat's why H think he wopld fe a .ood 9t xob the .bop,"m "ony be,lied"
SeDebal ox the .bop, .aDe a nod in a.beerent"

Well ps sore robe afopt this ,ebsonA what's his nare"m Vicky asked"

Wtewabt 5eraibe is his nare" ze's in his rid2thibties" !otheb ?nni uan.
was fobn in Ehina" ...atheb 3bpce 5eraibe was fobn in ...bance" ze attended pke
8niDebsityA Vandebfilt 8niDebsityA and Vbive 8niDebsiteit in 3bpssels"m "ony said"

WCop seer to know a lot afopt this dpde"m Iack said"

Ws H saidA ry second xaDobite ne,hewA we talkedA and H wobked with hir on
seDebal cases"m

What else do yop know afopt hir" ?nd fy the wayA H'r yopb only ne,hew"m
Iack be,lied"

"ony looked at Iack and noddedA WH know Iack" ze is socially awkwabd and
has a habd tire dealin. with his erotions"m

Wobt ox like Iack"m Shay be,lied"

W3oth ,abents s,oke theib natiDe ton.pe" Stewabt ,icked p, Ehinese and
...bench 4picklyA and ,icked p, rany otheb lan.pa.es fy vpst listenin."m "ony
added"

Wow rany lan.pa.es does he s,eak"m Vicky asked"

When H last talked to hirA he said he was Jpent in ei.ht di1ebent lan.pa.es"
ze had a .ood pndebstandin. and copld s,eak anotheb seDen lan.pa.esA fpt was
not Jpent"

What's xascinatin."m Vicky be,lied"

WH wish we had hir on opb tbi, to GabisA Iack"m LeDin saidA as he looked oDeb
at IackA who was noddin. in a.beerent"

WStewabt is a .ebro,hofe" ze dislikes shakin. hands and fecores Disi2
bly uncomfortable when touched by strangers. He's slightly OCD. (Obses-

sive–Compulsive Disorder.)" Tony said as he looked around the room at the otheb tear rerfebs"

WHs he one ox those who has a ,hoto.ba,hic reroby"m 'icholas asked"

WoA he called it hy,eb sorethin.A H can't bererfeb the ejact wobd he psed"m "ony be,lied"

-ay did a seabch and dis,layed the de9nition on the ronitobA WHt's called hy,eb,oly.lot" Ht's soreone who is foth .ixted and a rassiDe lan.pa.e ac2 cprplatob" "hey ,ossess a ,abticplab nepbolo.y that7s well2spited xob leabnin. lan.pa.es Deby 4pickly and fein. afle to pse ther"m

Iack sat p, stbai.ht in his chaibA WH think he wopld fe a Deby .ood 9t xob this nejt rission"m he said"

Vicky looked at "onyA W o yop think he'll want to voin opb .bop,"m she asked"

Wot .oin. to hpbt to ask"m "ony be,lied"

CHAPTER NINE

IT'S JUST WORDS

Jack opened the door to Vicky's kitchen and walked in. He saw Vicky sitting at the kitchen table, reading the morning news on her tablet. "Good morning." Jack said as he walked over to the refrigerator.

Vicky glanced up from her morning read, "Hey Jack, what are you doing up so early?" she asked.

Jack stuck his head into the refrigerator looking for something to eat, "Thought I'd get an early start on the Cuban crisis mission."

"Is that what you're calling it?" she asked.

"As good a name as any." he replied as he retrieved a slice of chocolate cake out of the refrigerator.

Vicky looked up from her tablet and over at Jack, "You're eating chocolate cake for breakfast?"

"Think of it as a very large triangle doughnut." Jack replied as he stuck it into the microwave.

Vicky shook her head, "I'd rather think of it as xve more e"tra pounds.W

"Shen are we going to meet this 1tewart dude?" Jack asked.

"Tony and I are going to meet him in town in a couple of hours." she replied.

"Shat about me?" Jack asked as he shoved a large piece of cake in his mouth.

"Just Tony and me this time." she replied.

"I'm the team leader, shouldn't I also get to interview this guy too?" Jack insisted.

"Yes, you are. Put you're operational, and I don't want him to see you or the others until we know he's coming on board." she said.

"Sell, Tony and you are operational too." Jack replied.

"Se are not out in the xeld like you and the others. Pesides, he already knows Tony. You'll get your chance to meet him after we clear him." she said.

"Rk xne. Py the way, you need some milk." he said, as he stuKed the last bite of cake in his mouth.

"Yut it on the list along with anything else you need. Shat are your plans for today?" she asked.

"Bight now, I'm going to meet Uevin." Jack replied.

1he looked up from her tablet, "Thought you were going to be working on the Cuban crisis, as you call it."

"I am, but xrst Uevin is going to take me up in the Net and let me !y it some." Jack replied with a big smile.

1he placed her tablet down on the table, "Sell, don't break it. I Nust paid oK the bill where someone trashed one of the 16Vs in jaris."

Jack threw both hands up into the air, "Sasn't me." he replied with a smile.

"Put you were in charge, so it's your responsibility." Vicky said as she walked over to the sink.

Jack shook his head, "I told her not to drive, but does she listen... MoE"

"1hould have known it was 1hay." Vicky said, shaking her head.

Jack pointed his xnger at Vicky, "I didn't say it was her."Jack said. "You're going to get me in trouble."

Vicky laughed, "I should have known it was 1hay who wrecked it. Anytime there is a car accident and she's anywhere near it, she's involved in some way."

Jack cracked a smile, "You're not saying 1hay is a bad driver, are you?"

"Mo, I'm not saying it, but the insurance company and the local body shop do." Vicky replied.

"Is that what happened to the barn?" Jack asked.

"Yes, she said she was trying to drive into the barn when she crashed the truck into the side of the barn door. And don't you dare tell her I told you." Vicky said.

"That's a wide door, you could drive a tractor through that door and have plenty of room on both sides." Jack laughed.

Vicky held up her hand, "Oon't get me started on the tractor, that's another story."

"How old was she?" Jack asked.

"I think she was twelve when that one happened." Vicky replied.

"TwelveE" Jack said. "1he couldn't even reach the pedals back then. Hell, she can barely reach them now." Jack let out a big laugh, "Shat was her e"cuse?"

"1he said someone moved the barn." Vicky replied, "Had to replace the entire passenger side front panel and the passenger side door."

They both stood there laughing when 1hay entered the kitchen, "Shat are you two talking about?" 1hay asked.

"Rh, nothing. I was telling Jack that Tony and I were going to be meeting 1tewart later." Vicky Luickly replied.

1hay nodded, walked over to the refrigerator, and opened the door, "Shat are you going to do today, Jack?" she asked.

Vicky looked at Jack and mouthed the words, "*DON'T YOUDARE.*"

"Sell8 Uevin is going to let me !y the Net." Jack said, despite the look and warning that Vicky gave him.

"Jack OavidsonE" Vicky yelled out.

1hay turned towards Vicky, "Shy does Jack get to !y the plane, and I don't?"

"Oo I need to remind you of your track record with things with motors? Cars, trucks, tractors, motorcycles, we don't need to add aircraft to the list." Vicky replied. "And while we're on the subNect, tell me about this bill I got from the insurance company involving one of the 16Vs in jaris."

1hay gave her a blank look and said as she turned and left the room, "I forgot I was supposed to be helping Oana inventory the eLuipment."

Vicky yelled as 1hay walked out of the room, "Se're going to talk about this later, young lady." Vicky stood there thinking as she placed her empty glass into the sink. *"That girl would find the only tree within two hundred miles in the middle of the desert and crash into it."*

V icky had asked Bay to tag along with her and Tony to their meeting with 1tewart)emaire. They had reserved a private room for this meeting at the Bepublic 1teakhouse in College 1tation and arrived Nust before their scheduled time to meet with 1tewart.

"Se have a reservation for four." Vicky said as she approached the hostess.

The hostess smiled and said, "And your name, please?"

")inda 1mith." Vicky replied, using her cover name that Bay had set up for her.

"Thank you, please follow me." The hostess replied as she turned.

Rnce they reached the table, Vicky said to the Hostess, "Se are e"pecting someone else. They may ask for me or qr. James." 1he said, motioning towards Tony.

Bay looked at Vicky and then at Tony with a shocked e"pression, "Shy didn't you use his cover name?" he asked, as he watched the hostess walk away.

"Bay, did you forget that 1tewart and I have worked together in the past?" Tony said with a smile as he took his seat.

"Shat time did you tell 1tewart to meet us here? It's almost xve." Vicky asked Tony.

"I told him xve." Tony replied.

"It's two till xve now. You think he's going to show?" Bay asked, looking down at his watch.

"If I told him two minutes till xve, he would be here. 1tewart is always on time. That's one of his things. He's probably been sitting outside in his car waiting for xve o'clock."

Bay looked down at his watch again and over at Tony, "Sell, it's xve o'clock sharp."

"And here he comes." Tony replied as he held up his hand.

Poth Vicky and Bay turned and saw the hostess, followed closely by a young-looking Asian man, sheepishly waving back at Tony.

The hostess stopped ne"t to the table and said, "Can I get you anything, sir?"

1tewart looked at the young hostess and down at her nametag, "*köszönöm szépen Susan*" zthank you very much, 1usan4, he replied.

The young hostess looked surprised when she heard him speak, "You speak Hungarian?" she replied in ...nglish.

1tewart smiled, "Yes. ...nough to get by."

"Put how did you know?" she asked.

"I picked up on a slight accent. Put you have lived most of your life here in the 1tates." 1tewart said.

"Yes, my parents moved here when I was twelve. Se speak Hungarian mostly at home." she said. "And you sir?)et me guess8. Japanese."

1tewart pulled out his chair and sat down, "Shy do you say that?" he asked, dryly.

The young hostess blushed, "I'm sorry, sir. I8 I didn't mean to oKend you."

"I'm American. I was born in 1an Antonio, Te"as." he said, looking up at the hostess. "qy mother is Chinese, and my father is 7rench. Oo I look Japanese to you?" 1tewart again said dryly.

The young hostess turned even redder, as she was left speechless. 1he xnally mustered up the words, "Again, sir, I hope I didn't oKend you."

"Mo oKense taken." 1tewart replied and turned to face the others.

After a few moments of silence, "Glad you could make it." Tony said. "Allow me to introduce you to)inda 1mith." Vicky stuck out her hand to shake

1tewart's. "And this is ...ric Hudgins." Bay also stuck out his hand to greet 1tewart. 1tewart Nust smiled and gave them both a brief nod of his head.

"Shat is it that you want to talk to me about?" 1tewart asked, looking at Vicky and then at Bay.

"Shy don't we order xrst and then talk?" Tony suggested.

"Very well." 1tewart said and began looking at the menu in front of him.

Bay gave Vicky a Luick glance. Vicky returned his glance with a slight sideways tilt of her head and an e"pression of pu22lement on her face.

The waitress walked up to the table and took their drink orders, returning a few minutes later with their drinks. "Are you ready to order?" she asked.

They each took turns placing their order to the waitress, while 1tewart looked through the menu.

"1ir, have you decided what you'll have? she asked, looking at 1tewart.

"I'll have the 03 o2 Te"as Akaushi MY 1trip. I would like the bacon on the side and no onions." he replied.

"Anything else?" she asked.

"Yes. Mo lemon 'est on the Asparagus. Garlic butter on the jotatoes. Oo you put carrots, onions, and croutons in the salad?" 1tewart asked.

"Yes, sir, we do." she replied.

"Can you take them out." 1tewart said, as a statement rather than a Luestion.

The waitress looked at him for a second before answering, "Yes, sir, I can do that."

1tewart raised his hand slightly, "Rh, one last thing." 1tewart said. "Can you put each item on a separate plate? I don't like my food touching."

The waitress took a long look at him and batted her eyes, "Yes, we can do that. Is there anything else, sir?" she asked.

"Mo." 1tewart replied.

The waitress smiled, turned, and walked towards the kitchen.

They chatted about 1tewart's work with the 7PI and where he grew up. Their food arrived, and they continued their conversation while eating.

1tewart looked at Vicky, "Tony told me that you're interested in my language skills. I'm assuming you're the boss." 1tewart said.

Vicky smiled, "I guess technically I am, but sometimes I wonder." she replied.

"In what capacity are you needing my services?" he asked.

"Shat has Tony told you about us?" Vicky asked.

"He told me that you're looking for an interpreter for your company." 1tewart replied.

"Yes, we discovered recently that as we e"pand, we're going to need someone with your talents." she replied.

"I will not work with the 7PI or any of those other agencies if that's what you want." 1tewart said.

"Shy is that?" Vicky asked.

"I don't like their rules." he replied.

Vicky paused for a second and looked at Tony, "You don't like rules?" she asked.

"Mo, I love rules. They bring order to things. I Nust don't like their rules." 1tewart replied and took a bite of his steak. "They favor the criminal, and the victim suKers because of it. qany times, they get away because of minor technicalities."

Bay smiled, "You're dexnitely going to xt in good with the team."

"I don't understand." 1tewart replied.

Tony smiled, "Se sort of make up our rules as we go sometimes." he said.

Vicky shook her head, "1tewart, don't get us wrong. Se have rules, but sometimes we must bend them a little, depending on the situation."

"Rr throw them out the window." Bay said, referring to Bed's incident when he turned his communications oK before rushing into the cabin and beating the crap out of JeKery qoon.

Vicky held up her hand in front of Bay, "Put normally we follow a set of strict rules to make sure everyone makes it home safely." she said as she glared at Bay.

"1o, this has nothing to do with the 7PI or any of those other three-letter organi2ations or government groups that officially don't exist?"

"No, we are not affiliated with any government group." Vicky replied. She paused for a second before continuing, "But officially, we don't exist."

Tony looked at 1tewart, "And we need to keep it that way." Tony added.

"You're an outside agency that doesn't officially exist that works with the 7PI." 1tewart asked. "I said I didn't want anything to do with the 7PI or any government agency. Oirectly or indirectly." he added and let out a long breath.

")ike I said, we have nothing to do with the 7PI or any government agency whatsoever." Vicky replied.

1tewart leaned back in his chair and crossed his arms. He looked at Vicky and motioned with his head towards Tony, "Then what is he doing here?" 1tewart asked.

"Tony works for us in an unofficial capacity." Vicky replied.

1tewart leaned forward and placed his elbows on the table, interlaced his xngers, and propped his chin on top of his hands, "Tell me what this company of yours does," he said, looking directly into Vicky's eyes.

Vicky looked down at the table and picked up her glass of tea. Pefore she took a sip, she said, "Pefore I tell you that, I need to xnd out if you're what we are looking for." Rnce she said that, she took a sip of tea and placed the glass back down on the table.

"7air enough, what would you like to know?" he asked.

"Tony tells us you are !uent in several diKerent languages." Vicky said.

"Yes, I currently speak xfteen diKerent languages." he replied.

"Shat are they?" Bay asked.

"Sell... ...nglish as you see. Then there's qandarin, 7rench, German, 1pan-ish, Arabic, Uorean, Japanese, several dialects of Bussian, Hungarian, Italian, Pulgarian, Oanish, and Hindi. I think that's all of them." he replied.

"That's very impressive. Are you what they call a savant?" Bay asked.

1tewart looked over at him and smiled, "The more correct dexnition is hyperpolyglot." he replied.

1tewart smiled and replied, "It's someone who is gifted with the ability to speak a large number of languages. They possess a particular neurology that allows them to learn many languages very Luickly and to be able to use them."

"That's very impressive." Vicky said. "How long does it take you to learn a new language?" she asked.

"Oepends on how close it is to a language that I already know. It could take one to two days to get a good working knowledge. ...nough to carry on a basic conversation." 1tewart said.

"I'm impressed." Bay said.

"They're Nust words. After you have a basic understanding of the language or a language that is very similar, it's easy to understand." 1tewart said, "Mow tell me what it is that you do." he said bluntly.

Vicky looked at Bay and then at Tony, "Sell.W Vicky started. "Se hunt down human sex traffickers." she said, waiting for a reaction from Stewart.

"Interesting. Put isn't that what Tony does along with halfa do2en government agencies?" 1tewart asked.

"Sell8 Se take a diKerent approach." Vicky replied.

"..."plain." 1tewart replied.

"Se don't have all the red tape or as many rules as your normal government agency does." she said.

1tewart leaned back, "..."plain." he said again.

Vicky started to answer, but Tony interrupted, "1tewart, if today you found the people who raped your mother and brutally killed her sister, the aunt you would never know. Shat would you do?" Tony asked.

1tewart sat for a second before he answered, "I guess the proper thing to do is to call the police." he replied.

Tony leaned in towards 1tewart, "And the police would come and arrest them. They might sit in Nail or make bail if they got a good lawyer. Then the trial would last weeks, and they may or may not be found guilty. As you know, a good lawyer can often help a guilty person get oK. At best, they would spend the rest of their lives in Nail. Rr maybe paroled after ten or so years." Tony said.

"I saw that happen far too many times when I worked with the 7PI. Guilty people are getting set free due to some error or technicality. That's why I Luit working with the 7PI, you're aware of that Tony." he said, and turned and looked at Vicky.

"Yes, I remember. I also remember how mad and upset you would get when you saw a guilty person walk free due to some legal loophole. Rr maybe an error that one of the detectives made during the arrest." Tony added.

1tewart looked back at Tony, "Shat are you getting at?" 1tewart asked.

"Shat if, when you found out and you knew for a fact that they were guilty, and you didn't have to worry about the law, or being caught? Shat would you do?" Tony asked, and he moved a little closer to 1tewart.

"I guess8 I would kill them." 1tewart said seriously.

Tony didn't reply. He Nust sat there looking at 1tewart. 1tewart looked at Tony for a few long seconds, and then looked at Vicky and then over at Bay.

The four of them sat there in silence for a minute before 1tewart xnally broke the silence, "Sait a minute8 Are we talking about vigilantism here? Is that what you guys are, vigilantes?"

"Think of it as bringing justice to the victims. Crossing the 'T' and dotting the 'I' that someone failed to do, allowing some pervert to walk away." Vicky replied.

1tewart looked at Vicky and then at Tony, "And you are part of this?" 1tewart asked Tony.

"Yes." Tony replied.

"Put what about your oath to uphold the law and bring Nustice to those?" 1tewart replied, but was cut oK by Tony before he could xnish.

"Justice? Shere is the Nustice for the children who are being raped, beaten, and sold as se" obNects? Shere is the Nustice for them?" Tony paused for a second. "Sho is going to xght for those children? The courts? The 7PI or other government agencies? MRE They are so buried in red tape and laws that most people get oK with little more than a slap on the wrist and maybe probation. Shile their victims must deal with the memories of the abuse for the rest of their lives. That is, if they live." Tony said.

"1o, you guys Nust go out and kill people who you think have committed some crime?" 1tewart asked.

"MoE Mo, that's not what we do. Se conduct a thorough investigation before taking any action. Se know before we take action that the person is guilty." Vicky replied.

"And you want me to help with this8 This hit sLuad?" 1tewart asked.

"Yes." Vicky replied.

"I'm not a killer." 1tewart shot back.

"There are many roles we have in our organi2ation." Vicky replied. "Se need someone with your talents to help us." she paused and looked over at Bay, "Bay here is our IT guy. He's not a xeld operator."

"You're ok with this?" 1tewart asked Bay.

"I wasn't at xrst. Put what I've seen and the good that the group has done. I sleep well at night knowing that I've helped stop some pervert from hurting any more people." Bay said.

"1tewart, we have freed hundreds of se" slaves and unknown future se" slaves. And I think if you Noin us, we can increase that number in other areas of the world." Vicky said.

"Shat do you say, 1tewart, you in?" Tony asked.

"Se have e"cellent benexts too." Vicky said.

1tewart laughed, "Shat dental?"

"That and then some." Vicky replied.

1tewart looked at Tony, "And you're good with this?" he asked.

"I think Bay said it best. I think once you've seen the faces of the people we're able to save, you'll agree." Tony said.

1tewart looked at each of them for a second, weighing his options. He picked up his napkin and wiped his mouth, looking down at the table. He slowly placed his napkin on his plate and placed his hands down on the table. 1till looking down at the table, he cleared his throat. He looked up at Tony, but not looking at him, but through him.

The only noise you could hear was the distant chatter from the patrons in the main dining room. They sat there waiting to hear what 1tewart had to say. Sas he in or out? Oid they make a big mistake by asking him? 7inally, 1tewart reached over and picked up his water glass and took along, slow sip. He placed his glass on the table and slowly spun it around in a circle on its base. 7inally, he looked at Bay, then Tony, and then directly at Vicky. "Shen do I meet the other members of our team?"

Chapter Ten

THE MEETING

Ray had sent out a message to all the other team members to meet at the ranch on Saturday afternoon. Vicky wanted to introduce everyone to Stewart, their new team member.

Shay was the "rst to arrive at the main house. W?here is Stewart"T she asked as Vicky entered the kitchen.

Wony is bringing him. phey should be here in a few minutes. T Vicky rejlied as she took a seat at the kitchen table.

Shay reached into the refrigerator and julled out a bottle of orange Iuice, W?hat do you think about this guy"T Shay asked as she joured a glass for herself.

Vicky jicked uj her tablet to read the morning news, W' think heHll be a good addition to our grouj. T Vicky said.

WCow are his combat skills"T Shay asked.

Wphat really never came uj in our conversation. T Vicky rejlied. Wzan you jour me a glass of Iuice and bring me one of those glaxed donuts on the counter"T

Shay joured Vicky a glass of orange Iuice, jicked uj a glaxed donut o1 the counter, and walked over to the table where Vicky was sitting. Shay jlaced the glass on the table ne7t to Vicky, and as she sat down, Shay took a bite out of the donut.

W6, you didnHt.T Vicky said, looking uj from her tablet.

What"T Shay rejlied as she chewed the bite of glaxed donut.

Wcannot believe you took a bite of my donut. Bou get your own.T Vicky said, slajjing Shay as she stood.

Shay turned back towards Vicky, Wphat was the last one. Gesides, you need to cut down on your Iunk food.T Shay said.

WOre you saying 'Hm fat"T Vicky rejlied jlayfully.

W?ellllllll.T Shay rejlied, leaning against the counter. WBou have jut on a coujle of jounds lately.TK

Weat when 'Hm nervous. ' canHt helj it.T Vicky rejlied, turning her attention back to her reading.

Shay took a swig of her orange Iuice, W?hat are you all nervous about"T she asked, setting the glass down on the counter.

Wphis thing with Cunter, asir, and zuba. 't has gotten me all stressed.T Vicky said, jlacing her tablet down on the table.

WBou need to start working out with me. phat will helj with your stress.T Shay said, jushing o1 from the counter and walking towards the kitchen door that led out to the jool. Wzall me when pony and Stewart get here.

Wwill. Cave you seen Yack this morning"T Vicky asked.

WCeHs sacked out on a 8oat in the jool.T Shay rejlied. WNh, and icholas and Red Iust julled uj.T

WMood, Eevin called a few minutes ago, and he should be julling uj in a few minutes also. Ce swung by to jick uj Jana.T Vicky said.

phe other team members "nally arrived about ten minutes later, with Ray arriving last. phey all gathered around the jool and munched on the catered lunch that Vicky had arranged. pony and Stewart were the last to arrive, and they both went right into the house to see Vicky. Ofter a few minutes inside, the three of them e7ited the house and walked to the jool, where the others had gathered.

9Muys, listen uj.T Vicky said. W' want you to meet our newest member of the team, Stewart 'emaire.T

Stewart stejjed uj ne7t to Vicky and gave a sheejish wave and smile. phe team welcomed Stewart from where they were. Nne by one, they slowly made their way to meet and introduce themselves to Stewart individually.

WetHs all go into the den and talk.T Vicky announced. "veryone slowly made their way into the house and into the den where they all sat around, some on the couches and some took a seat on the 8oor. Stewart sat between Vicky and pony.

Vicky looked over at Stewart, WStewart, why donHt you start by telling everyL one about yourself"TK

Ce sjent the ne7t twenty minutes talking about his childhood, his jarents, and what had hajjened to his mother and aunt. Ce glossed over his time in school and working for the qG' as one of their interjreters. Ce ended with his ability to sjeak several di1erent languages and the ease he has when it comes to learning a new language.

Yack raised his hand, WSo, youHre some kind of a genius when it comes to sjeaking and learning languages"T he asked.

Wguess in laymanHs terms, yes.T Stewart rejlied. Wphe more correct de"nition is hyjerjolyglot.TK

What the hell is that"T Red asked.

Stewart looked over at Red, W'tHs someone with the ability to sjeak in many di1erent languages. 'n short, my brain jossesses the ability that allows me to learn many languages very !uickly.T Red crossed his arms and leaned back in his chair, W' knew that.T

icholas looked over at Red, WGull shit.T he rejlied. phis caused everyone to burst out laughing.

Red laughed and nodded his head, WOye. Gut ye didnHt have to call me on it.T

Stewart looked back at Yack, Wpony tells me youHre the team leader here.TK

Wguess you could say that. Jid he also tell you that heHs my uncle too"T Yack asked.

Stewart smiled, WBes, he has talked about you in the jast.TK

WOnd what did he say"T Yack asked, looking over at pony.

WHm sure it was boring craj.T Shay rejlied.

WBes, Shay, it was somewhat lackluster.T Stewart said. W owhere as interestL ing as your background.TK

WOnd what do you mean by that"T Shay asked defensively.

WHve been told that you have a stubborn streak and are very feisty.T Stewart rejlied.

phis got everyone laughing, along with a coujle of 0amens0 from the grouj.

ShayHs face turned red as she looked at Vicky, W'Hve got a !uestion for you Stewart.T Shay said.

WOnd what is that"T Stewart asked.

Wo you have any martial arts skills"T Shay asked, focusing her attention on Stewart.

Stewart looked at her a second before answering, W?hy, because '0m Osian"TK

Wo...T Shay said, W' ask because ' need a new sjarring jartner.TK

WBej, sheHs tired of beating uj on Yack.T Eevin said.

Yack nodded, WphatHs for damn sure.T he said.

Wack, everyone beats uj on you.T Jana said jlayfully.

Stewart looked at Shay, W'Hve taken several styles and systems in the jast. YuIitsu, Eung qu, pae Ewon Jo, pai zhi, and Oikido.T

WBouHre like Gruce 'ee"T Robert asked.

W o. Gruce 'ee founded Yeet Eune Jo, the way of the intercejting "st. 't is a hybrid of martial arts systems and life jhilosojhy. 't was in8uenced by ?ing zhun, pai zhi, pae Ewon Jo, Go7ing, qencing, and YuIutsu. Cis style cannot be comjared to any other style because it is a collection of techni!ues or movements.T Stewart e7jlained.

Wort of like Erav Faga.T Shay rejlied.

WBes, somewhat, but without the jhilosojhy.T Stewart said.

Yack8ojjed back on the couch, W?ellU 'U jreferU Mun qu, over any kind of martial arts.TK

WOye.T Red rejlied. WBe not very good with ye "st.T

9' jrefer not to get that close to someone whoHs trying to kill me.T Yack rejlied.

WHm sure Vicky told you what we do here.T Eevin said, trying to get the grouj back on track.

Steward nodded, WBes, she and pony both have "lled me in.T

WYack and the others could have used you in qrance a few weeks ago.T Ray said, referring to the incident with the man that Yack tased.

WOnd donHt forget, at the airjort too.T Eevin added.

What hajjened at the airjort"T Vicky asked, looking at Eevin and then at Yack.

WOthing. JonHt worry about it. 't was nothing,T Yack rejlied, looking over at Eevin.

Vicky looked at Stewart, WBou look juxxled. 's there something bothering you"T she asked.

Stewart looked at Vicky, W?hat about the other stu1"T he asked.

What other stu1"T Yack asked with a !uestioning e7jression.

WOrgan harvesting for one. Bou guysU ' meanU donHt we care about those jeojle too"T Stewart asked, directing his !uestion to no one in jarticular.

WHve heard of that.T icholas said. W?e have our hands full with Iust dealing with the se7 traPcking side of things.T

Stewart looked at icholas, Wphey are somewhat linked.T Stewart rejlied.

Wh what way"T Shay asked, shifting her weight forward in her chair.

WFany times, when a jerson outlives their usefulness as a se7 slave, their organs will be sold on the black market.T Stewart said.

WBouHre talking like a liver or kidney, right"T Vicky asked.

W̶hat and other jarts. Ceart, lungs, skin, you name it.T Stewart said. WzhilL drenHs organs are in high demand, they get toj dᴏllar for their organs.TK

phe grouj looked at each other and back at Stewart. WphatHs sick.T Shay said, looking over at Vicky.

W̶ouHre kidding, right"T Eevin rejlied.

W o, heHs right.T pony rejlied. WNnce they have outlived their usefulness, they will sell them as jarts on the ojen market. phey will get as much money out of them as they can and then Iust throw them away.T

W̶O heart will go for around 4$33,333, and a kidney for around 4533,333 on the black market.T Stewart rejlied.

W̶o, after these girls and boys are used as se7 toys for Mod knows how long, in the end, they are butchered, and their organs are sold"T Yim asked.

Stewart looked over at Yim, W ot all of them. Nnly the ones that have been able to stay healthy or if their organs are still usable.T

W̶ony, did you know about this"T Vicky asked.

pony looked down at the 8oor, WSadly, yes.T he rejlied.

W̶hy havenHt you said something about it"T Vicky asked, getting agreement from some of the others.

W̶here are many asjects of human traPcking. Se7, organ harvesting, labor, drug smuggling, and indentured servitude. ?e canHt address them all.T pony said, looking uj at Vicky "nally.

Shay sat back hard in her chair, causing it to slide back a coujle of inches, W o, but we can be on the lookout for the signs.T she said.

W̶ye, thatHs what we been doing. 'Hm sure weHve stojjed many from ending uj on some duineolcHs table.T Red added.

Yack looked over at Vicky. W e7t time you chat with the Sandman, ask him if he is aware of any activity like this from asir. ?e need to e7jand our ojerations to include these other issues.T he said, looking at the others in the grouj.

W̶certainly will.T she rejlied. She looked over at Ray, WRay, could you look into this and see what you can "nd"T

Wonsider it done. ' will also have my two internet friends look around and see what they can "nd too.T Ray said.

Wany of these victims come in across the southern border of the 6nited States.T Stewart said.

phe grouj all nodded in agreement. Wphose children who enter the country unaccomjanied by an adult or jarent are often julled into the human traPckL ing world.T Stewart said.

Vicky stood, WNk, looks like we have our work cut out for us. 'etHs say we break and go out by the jool.T she said.

pony cleared his throat to get everyoneHs attention, WGefore we all break and head back to the jool and start stuPng our faces...T

Red interrujted, WOye, and drink me some "ne Scottish ?hiskey.T he said with a big smile.

WBes, and before Red gets jlastered.T pony said, looking over at Red, who smiled and lifted his glass. W'Hve got an announcement to make.T he jaused, making sure he had everyoneHs attention. W' turned in my resignation to the qG' two weeks ago. So, ' guess you bums have me fullLtime now.T

phis was met with cheers from every member of the team. Wphis calls for a drink.T Red rejlied as he came over and hugged pony.

Shay walked over to Vicky, WJid you know this"T she asked.

WBes, he and ' talked about it before he turned in his resignation.T Vicky rejlied.

Why didnHt you tell me"T Shay asked, feeling a little hurt.

WCe asked me not to.T Vicky rejlied.

Well, you still could have told me.T Shay said.

Yack ajjroached the two, W' think this Stewart will "t in good.T he said, looking at Vicky and then at Shay.

WMlad you agree.T Vicky said. WYack, we need to get Jana and Stewart into that training camj we all went to.T she said.

Wow would be a good time.T Yack said. W'Hll contact Stan and see if he can get them in ASAP.T

WeHre going to need them on this zuba mission. 'etHs also send icholas, Red, Robert, and Yim too.T Vicky said.

What about Eevin, pony, Shay, and me"T Yack asked.

We donHt have time for you guys to take a coujle of weeks of training. ?e have to jlan this zuban trij. Gesides, ' think the four of you are solid enough right now. e7t time, you four can go.T Vicky said.

Yack looked over at icholas, W icholas, ' want you to focus on your longLrange shooting.T Yack said.

WMladly.T icholas rejlied with a slight smile.

Yackhanded icholas a folder with the layout of the comjound and surL rounding hills and area, WBou need to jrejare to take out "dgardo Santiago at the wedding if the ojjortunity arises.T

 icholas took the "le from Yack and brie8y looked at its contents. Wzonsider it done.T

Where is a hill that overlooks the comjound. Bou will need a sjotter on this trij. ?hat do you think about using Robert"T Yack asked.

Wthink Red would be better for this trij. zonsidering the terrain, Red, with his backwoods and tracking background, 'Hd like to have him at my side. 'f ' get a chance to take the shot, weHll need to get out of there as soon and as fast as jossible. Red would be the best chance of getting out of there alive.

Obout an hour later, Jana entered the conference room where Yack, Vicky, and Shay were working, WYack, can ' talk to you"T Jana asked.

Wure thing. ?hatHs on your mind, sister"T Yack said with a !uestioning smile.

Wheard you and Shay are going to the wedding to recover my sister.T Jana said.

VphatHs the jlan so far.T Yack rejlied.

W'want to go with you.T Jana said it in a more demanding tone than a re!uest.

Worry, Jana, ' donHt think that would be a good idea.T Yack rejlied, looking directly at Jana and shaking his head.

Jana walked over to Yack and stood Iust two feet away, WYack, 'Hm MN' M...T Jana said in a forceful tone.

W6.T Yack said calmly.

Jana took a stej towards Yack, now Iust inches away, W'Hm going to go in with you and get my sister.T She said slowly and "rmly.

Walm down Jana.T Yack rejlied.

WCOp... JN Hp BN6 p"" F" pN zO'F JN? ...T Jana yelled out.

Yack threw both hands uj in the air and took a stej back, Wzhill, Jana.T Yack said.

Shay stejjed over, jushed Yack back, and stood between him and Jana. She faced Yack and looked him in the eyes. WBou ass.T Shay said as she turned towards Jana.

What did ' do"T Yack said, with his hand still uj.

Wust go.T Shay rejlied.

Yack slowly turned, shaking his head, and walked out of the room. Os he ajjroached the door, he glanced over towards Vicky, who had been sitting at the table across from them. She Iust looked at him as he walked out and shook her head.

Shay guided Jana over to one of the chairs and sat her down. Shay julled uj another chair and sat across from Jana, and took both JanaHs hands in hers.

Wook, Jana, Yack is right.T Shay started. Jana tried to cut her o1, but Shay gave her hand a light s!ueexe.

WGut ' need to be there.T Jana rejlied, now crying.

Wack and ' will bring your sister home, or we will not comeback.T Shay said softly.

WGut.T Jana started.

WJana, youHre too close to this. Bour emotions might blow things. Bou donHt know how you or Eatie will react once you two see each other.T Shay said, looking directly into JanaHs eyes.

Jana looked away, as tears rolled down her face, W' Iust want her back.T

WOnd we will get her back, ' jromise.T Shay said.

Jana gave Shay a !uick nod, then turned and gave her a big hug, Wphank you.T Jana whisjered into ShayHs ear.

O week later, the team, minus Yack, Shay, pony, Eevin, Vicky, and Ray, was on their way to zharles FcEennyHs training camj. phey would sjend the ne7t three weeks training in basic and advanced weajons and selfLdefense tactics. Yack and the others continued to gather more data, as well as jlan the zuban mission.

phe jlan was to have Yack and Shay attend the wedding as sta1 workers. Ray would break into the security systems database and add their names to the sta1 list.

Yack walked into RayHs oPce. W?hatHs uj"T Ray said as he noticed Yack.

WHve got an idea.T Yack said as he julled uj a chair ne7t to Ray.

Ray leaned back in his chair, WShoot.T Rays said.

WØhis "dmundo 'uje dude.T Yack started.

WØhe guy whoHs throwing the wedding for asir"T Ray asked.

WØes, letHs fuck with him.T Yack said with an evil smile.

WHm listening.T Ray said.

Yack smiled, WBou think you can break into his banking accounts and move some money"T Yack asked.

WCave you forgotten who you are talking to"T Ray asked, showing a fake disajjointed look on his face.

W6, ' know you can do it.T Yack rejlied in a defensive voice.

WØust messing with you, man. zonsider it done.T Ray said. W?hat do you have in mind"T

WetHs move a large amount of his assets into asirHs accounts.T Yack said.

WOnd can you make it easy for that 'uje dude to trace it back to asir"T

WBou want him to think that asir stole his money"T Ray asked with a smile.

WØhat shouldnHt be a jroblem.T Ray rejlied.

WMreat...T Yack said.

WOnything else" Ray asked.

WŊo one of your deej dives into asirHs history and see what you can dig uj.TKYack said.

Ray leaned forward and grabbed his notejad, W?hat in jarticular will ' be looking for"T Ray asked.

WGank accounts, business dealings, jrojerties.T Yack started, WOnything you can "nd on him.T

WBou know zharles said that asir is o1 limits.T Ray said, jlacing his jen on the desk.

WeHre not going to do anything with the information you get. ' Iust want to be jrejared for later. Gesides, we donHt work for or take orders from zharles.T Yack said, shifting a little in his chair.

WMotcha. Onything else"T Ray asked.

WHm going to send the team down to zuba when they get back from their training. ' want them to scout out the area. phe jhotos and data we have on the target isnHt enough. ' want them to see it in jerson.T Yack said as he stood uj.

WMood idea.T Ray rejlied.

W' need you to jack uj a coujle of your drones and send them with the grouj.T Yack said.

Wōt a jroblem.T Ray rejlied.

WBou think youHll be able to control them from here"T Yack asked.

Ray sat there for a few seconds before answering, W'Hll send a signal booster. So, there shouldnHt be a jroblem.T

Yack gave Ray a thumbsLuj, WMreat.T Yack rejlied and turned to leave.

What about you and Shay"T Ray asked.

WeHll be going down a day or two later. ?eHll 8y into Cavana and get a hotel. phe others should have the area scouted out by then, and we can meet and work out the "nal details.

Wphe zuban Ombassador, what about him"T Ray asked as Yack e7ited the room.

Yack stuck his head back in, W?ell, icholas is going to take care of him at the wedding. Gut Iust in case. Mo ahead and "nd out where he hides his money.T

Wonsider it done.T Ray rejlied.

qor the ne7t two weeks, Yack, Shay, and the others continued to jore over the data and send the information to the grouj that was still at FcEennyHs training camj.

Ot the end of the two weeks, Eevin 8ew over and jicked the grouj uj and brought them back to Nmega. Nnce they landed, they all went into the conference room where Yack, Shay, and Ray were reviewing the information on "dmundo 'ujeHs comjound.

Red came busting into the conference room, W' need me a drink.T he yelled, breaking the silence of the room.

WBou always need a drink.T Shay rejlied, without looking uj from her jajers.

Red looked over at her and gave her a big smile, WOye, the trij back were a wee bit bumjy.T

Eevin followed the grouj as the rest "led in after Red, WNh, you big crybaby, we hit a little turbulence, and you almost lost it.T

WBe know ' dunt like to 8y.T Red rejlied as he found his bottle of whiskey.

Vicky entered a coujle of minutes later, W?elcome back, guys. Cow was the trij and training"T

WOye, the training0s "ne, but this "eIit,T Red jointed over at Eevin, Wneir killed us on the way back.T Red said as he joured himself another glass of whiskey.

Wgnore him.T icholas said, looking over at Vicky. WCeHll make uj any e7cuse to have a drink.T

Red raised his glass and gave icholas a wink and a smile.

WJana, how was the training”T Vicky asked, turning towards Jana, who had taken a seat ne7t to Shay.

Jana looked uj at Vicky, W’t was very interesting, ’ enIoyed the entire trij.T

WCow about you, Stewart”T Vicky asked, walking over to the conference table.

Stewart was standing Iust inside the door and rejlied, Wqascinating.T

WIust fascinating”T Yack asked, looking over at him.

WFr. FcEenny has a remarkably interesting and e7tensive training system.T Steward dryly said.

 icholas walked over to the wall, where an enlarged overhead jhoto of the "dmundo ’uje comjound was disjlayed.

W?hat do you think, icholas”T Yack asked as he walked over ne7t to icholas.

WIm thinking, based on the jhotos and information you sent me, that these areas here and here would be a good jlace to set uj my snijer hide.T icholas jointed out two areas on the maj. WGut ’ wonHt know for sure until ’ get down there and see it “rsthand.T

WWhat looks like a long distance. zan you make that shot”T Vicky asked as she Ioined the two, looking at the maj.

WPhis area here is about eight hundred yards, and this one is Iust short of a thousand yards.T ickolas said, jointing at the two areas on the maj.

WBou can hit the target from that distance”T Vicky asked, looking uj at icholas.

WWell, it dejends on the terrain and what is between me and the target. ’ wonHt know for sure until ’ get down there and see it in jerson.T icholas rejlied with an air of con“dence.

WDye, he can hit a 8y o1 a horseHs arse at that distance.TRed added.

icholas gave Red a wink and a smile as he took a draw of his drink. W' donHt have a jroblem with the distance. 'tHs hard to tell how thick the brush is from those aerial jictures. ' get there, and it may all be blocked by trees and bushes.T

Well, our jrimary target is JanaHs sister. Metting her out is the main thing. ? e can always go back and eliminate the Ombassador later.T Vicky said as she took a seat at the table.

What is the e7it jlan"T Robert asked, looking at Yack and then at Eevin.

WtHs going to be hard to e7ecute both e7tracting JanaHs sister and taking out the Ombassador, too.T pony said.

WCow so"T Yim asked.

Well, once you shoot the Ombassador, all hell is going to break loose. phat jlace will be locked down tighter than qort Eno7.T pony rejlied.

Yack looked at Yim and then at Robert, WphatHs why weHre going after JanaHs sister "rst. 'f we can e7tract her without anyone knowing it, then icholas will have a chance to do his thing.T Yack rejlied.

WGut wonHt you and Shay have jroblems once you arrive at the wedding"T Jana asked.

Wh what way"T Shay asked.

Weither one of you sjeaks the language down there. Os a matter of fact, none of us do.T Jana said with a concerned tone in her voice.

Steward cleared his throat, W"7cuse me.T he said.

Wes, Stewart will be key once we get down there. CeHll be in contact with all the teams, via ear mics, and heHll be able to helj if anyone needs a translation.T Yack said, glancing over at Stewart.

WStewart is going to be back here at Nmega during this mission"T Robert asked.

W6. CeHll be on the ground with us in zuba. CeHll go in with Shay and me to the wedding.T Yack rejlied.

Wf heHs at the wedding with the two of you, how is he going to be able to helj us"T Yim asked,

WCeHll jose as our driver.T Yack said, WCeHll stay back at the car so heHll be able to monitor everything and can resjond if one of us runs into a language jroblem.T

WWh, stick the Osian guy as the chau1eur.T Steward said, with a serious look on his face.

WhatHs going to jut you close to us, so if we need backuj, youHll be there.T Shay said.

Stewart looked at Shay and then at Yack, W?ell, as long as you donHt call me Eato, itHll be “ne.9

Wwould never say that.T Yack said with a smile.

CHAPTER ELEVEN

THE CUBA TRIP

The time of the mission anlyyr lvvide.I wt zls time to anlyice the .etliys of ln. vesuDe 'lnlCs yittye sistev ln. eyiminlte the bDpln lmplssl.ovI The telm zoDy. lvvide in bDpl in thvee seglvlte ,voDgsN lt .iRevent youltions ln. timesI

kiuhoyls ln. xe. zeve the avst telm to lvvideI Ther lvvide. tzo zeeJs pefove the othevs ln. zoDy. stlvt suoDtin, oDt the lvel zheve kiuhoyls zoDy. tlJe his shotI The ne-t telmN uonsistin, of TonrN xopevtN ln. MimN lvvide. l uoDgye of .lrs yltevI Ther lvvide. pr l .eegFsel ashin, polt oDt of éilmiN yovi.lI Ther enteve. bDpl lt bliplviKnNSzheve ther zoDy. setDg l uommln. gostI OedinN jhlrN MluJN 'lnlN ln. jtezlvt qez in the Vme,l Het ln. yln.e. lt the bienfDe,os livgovtI Ther hl. pvoD,ht in lyy the neuesslvr e"Digment thlt the telm zoDy. nee.I WiuJr ln. xlr vemline. lt Vme,l ?el."Dlvtevs to mlnl,e lyy the uommDniultions ln. uontvoysI

Theve zls l JnouJ lt the .oovN ln. xopevt syozyr zlyJe. odev to yooJ thvoD,h the geeghoye to mlJe sDve of zho it zlsI "1ho is it32 he lsJe.I

"wtCs MluJN noz ogen the stDgi. .oovI2 MluJ sli.I

xopevt ogene. the .oovN ln. MluJ enteve.N foyyoze. pr OedinN jhlrN jtezlvtN ln. 'lnlI

Tonr zls sittin, on the uoDuhN ”?i ,DrsI2 he sli.N yooJin, odev lt the ade uomin, thvoD,h the .oovI

Ys jhlr enteve.N she yooJe. lvoDn.N ”kiue hotey voomI2 she sli.I

”wtCs ulyye. ln L-euDtide jDiteI2 xopevt vegyie. ls he ye. the ,voDg inI

”Yn. it zls devr hlv. to an.N zith lyy the pi,zi,s uomin, in fov the ze.F .in,I2 Mim l..e.I

MluJ zlyJe. odev ln. slt .ozn ne-t to his Dnuye TonrN ”1hevelve xe. ln. kiuhoyls32 MluJ lsJe. ls he veluhe. fov some uhigs on the tlpye in fvont of the uoDuhI

”TherCve on the zlrI Ther shoDy. pe heve in lpoDt afteen minDtesI2 Tonr vegyie.I ”?ln. me some of those uhigsI2 Tonr sli. to MluJI

”4etCs see zhlt ze hlde so flvI2 MluJ sli. ls he stoo. ln. zlyJe. odev to one of the uomgDtev monitovs thlt zls set DgI

xopevt gDyye. Dg l sevies of levily ghotos thlt zeve tlJen of the L.mDn.o 4Dge uomgoDn. pr one of xlrCs .vonesI

MluJ yooJe. odev lt xopevtN ”?oz .oes it yooJ32 MluJ lsJe.I

”kiuhoyls thinJs he uln ,et l shotI 5Dt wCyy yet him ,o odev it zith roDI2 xopevt vegyie.I

jhlr zlyJe. odev ln. Hoine. MluJI Ys ther zeve yooJin, odev the levily ghotosN theve zls l JnouJ lt the .oovI

MluJ tDvne. tozlv.s the .oovI ”1ho is it32 MluJ lsJe.I

xopevt zlyJe. odev ln. yooJe. oDt the geeghoye to see zho zls theveI ”wtCs kiuhoyls ln. xe.I2 xopevt vegyie.I

Ys the tzo enteve.N jhlr tDvne. tozlv.s the gliv ln. smiye.I

”YreN poDt time roD yl.s ,ot .ozn heveI2 xe. smiye. ls he ,lde jhlr l hD,I kiuhoyls ,lde MluJN ’lnlN ln. Oedin l no. ls he zlyJe. odev ne-t to MluJI

”jo hoz .oes it yooJ32 MluJ lsJe. kiuhoyls ls he zlyJe. Dg ne-t to himI

”wCde i.entiae. tzo sgots zheve w uln set DgI 1eCve not entiveyr sDve zheve heCyy pe lvvidin,I 5Dt wCde ,ot l uyelv shot heve ln. heveI2 kiuhoyls gointe. lt tzo lvels oDtsi.e of the L.mDn.o 4Dge uomgoDn.I ”wCde lyso ,ot l uyelv shot of the gooy lvel ln. zheve the ze..in, ziyy pe hey.I2

MluJ no..e.N ”BveltI2

”1e .i. notiue l heldr gltvoy gvesenue in the lvel zheve zeCve gylnnin, on settin, DgI2 kiuhoyls sli. ls he gointe. oDt lvels on the mlg .isgylre. on the suveenI

”6oD thinJ thltCs ,oin, to pe l gvopyem32 MluJ lsJe.N ,ylnuin, odev lt kiuhoylsI

kiuhoyls tooJ l .eeg pvelth ln. e-hlye.N ”jhoDy.nCt peI2 he vegyie.I

”6oD .onCt seem so sDveI2 MluJ sli.N tDvnin, tozlv. himI

”1eCve l zee pit uyose to l goggr aey.I2 xe. sli. ls he zlyJe. Dg ne-t to MluJI

”?oz uyose32 MluJ lsJe.N zithoDt yooJin, lzlr fvom the monitovI

xe. gointe. to the suveen to the lvel zheve the aey. is youlte.I

”Thlt is lzfDyyr uyoseI2 MluJ sli.N yooJin, lt xe. ln. then lt kiuhoylsI

”élrpe ze shoDy. ulnuey thlt glvt of the missionI2 MluJ sli.N zith ulDtion in his doiueI

”YreN shoDy. pe aneN yon, ls ther .onCt hlde lnr gltvoys lvoor(around)I2 xe. vegyie.I

”Yn. if ther .o32 jhlr lsJe.I

S”Then zeCyy .ely zith themI2 kiuhoyls sli.I

MluJ yooJe. lt kiuhoylsN ”1e .onCt nee. to ,et into lnr ,Dnplttyes zith lnr .vD, ulvteysI2 MluJ sli.I

”4et me tlJe xopevt zith DsI ?e uln heyg zltuh oDv si-I2 kiuhoyls sli.I

MluJ tDvne. tozlv.s xopevtN zho zls sittin, lt the Jituhen tlpyeI ”6oD ,oo. zith thltN xopevt32 MluJ lsJe.I

”1hevedev roD nee. meI2 xopevt vegyie.I

”4et xlr Jnoz ze lve ,oin, to nee. liv sDggovtI w zlnt some of xlrCs piv.s qrin, odev roDI2 MluJ sli.I

”Teyy me zhlt roD hlde on this uomgoDn.I2 MluJ l..e.I

Mim pvoD,ht Dg ln odevhel. diez of the uomgoDn. on the monitovI

”kiue sgvel.N2 jhlr sli.N steggin, fovzlv. to ,et 1 pettev diezI

”The mlin hoDse sets pluJ oR the mlin vol. lpoDt 1 hDn.ve. rlv.sI Theve lve tzo entvlnuesN heve ln. heveI2 Mim gointe. lt the mlin glde. .videzlr ln. then lt 1 seuon. .videzlr lpoDt sedentrFade rlv.s lzlrI ”This .vide yel.s to the aey. zith ln entvr onto the mlin uomgoDn. heveI 1e thinJ this is zheve the ,Dests ziyy pe glvJe.N ln. shoDy. entev thvoD,h thlt ,lteI2

kiuhoyls yelne. inN ”wCde ,ot 1 uyelv shot lt this aey. ln. the entvr theveI2 kiuhoyls gointe. lt the ,lte yel.in, fvom the aey.I

”1e .i. 1 .vide prN ln. the zlyy lvoDn. the uomgoDn. is lpoDt afteen feet tlyyI2 Mim sli. ls he pvoD,ht Dg 1 stveet diez of the fvont of the uomgoDn.I

MluJ tiyte. his hel. syi,htyrN ”1hlt lpoDt ulmevls32 he lsJe.I

”ThltCs not 1 gvopyemI xlr hls thlt tlJen ulve ofI2 Mim vegyie.I

”boDy. his .vones ,et uyose enoD,h to see hoz mlnr ,Dlv.s32jhlr lsJe.I

”Too visJr qrin, them thlt uyose .Dvin, the .lrI ?e .i. tvr lt ni,htN pDt zlsnCt lpye to see lnrthin,I2 Mim vegyie.I

MluJ tDvne. ln. zlyJe. odev to the tlpye zheve xopevt zls sittin,N ”?ls he peen lpye to pvelJ into the seuDvitr srstem32 MluJ lsJe.I

xopevt yooJe. lt MluJ zith 1 gDccye. yooJN ”6oDCve tlyJin, lpoDt the ,velt ln. gozevfDy xlrI2

MluJ ylD,he.N ”jovvrI w Jeeg fov,ettin,I2

”’onCt zovvrN heCyy vemin. roD if roD fov,etI2 Mim 1..e.I

”ThltCs fov sDveI2 jhlr sli. ls she zlyJe. DgI

”1hltCs the gyln32 Mim lsJe.N yooJin, odev lt jhlrI

”’onCt yooJ lt meN lsJ MluJN this is his plprI2 jhlr vegyie. zith 1 syi,ht smiyeI

MluJ hl. HDst gDt uhigs in his moDthN ”Bet ’lnlCs sistev ln. tlJe oDt the Ymplssl.ovI2 ?e vegyie. ln. tooJ 1 szi, of zltev to zlsh them .oznI

”6e Jnoz onue the shootin, stlvtsN ther ,oin, to youJ .ozn this isyln.I2 xe. sli.I

”The tog gviovitr is ’lnlCs sistevI wf ze .onCt ,et the Ymplssl.ov this tvigN zeCyy ,et him some othev timeI2 MluJ vegyie.I

EG...

kiuhoyls yelne. pluJ in his uhlivN "Vnue ze snltuh hev fvom klsivN zhlt then32 kiuhoyls lsJe.I

"1e hel. to the Het ln. ,et the heyy oDt of heveI2 MluJ sli.I

Oedin yoɟe. lt MluJN "Thlt simgye32

"jDveI 1hlt uoDy. ,o zvon,3 wtCs l simgye ,vlp ln. ,oI2 MluJ vegyie. zith l smiyeI

"kothin,Cs thlt simgyeI2 Mim vegyie.I

Oedin zlyJe. odev to the mlg .isgylre. on the monitovI "Theve is l yot of .istlnue petzeen thlt uomgoDn. ln. the livgovt in bienfDe,osI2 he sli. ls he yooJe. lt the mlgI

"6oD hlde the Het vel.r fov tlJeoR zhen ze lvvideI2 MluJ sli.I

"ThltCs not ,oin, to pe l gvopyemI The gvopyem is ,ettin, edevrone oDt zithoDt pein, shot pr the youly ulvtey ov goyiueI This 4Dge feyyev hls l yot of gozev ln. uonneutions in bDplN not to mention the bDpln Ymplssl.ovI2 Oedin sli. ls he zlyJe. pluJ ln. tooJ l selt luvoss fvom MluJI

"1hlt is the pluJDg gyln32 Oedin lsJe.I

"Oedin ziyy qr Ds pluJ to the jtltes on the HetI2 MluJ sli.I "wfN fov some velsonN lnrone is uDt oR fvom the gvimlvr e-tvlution gylnI 1e flyy pluJ to the zlr roD lvvide.I 6oD mi,ht nee. to ylr yoz fov l .lr ov tzoI2 MluJ l..e. ls he yooJe. lvoDn. lt the othevsI

"MDst ,et mr sistevI2 'lnl sli.N ls telvs stlvte. voyyin, .ozn hev uheeJsI jhlr zlyJe. odev to 'lnl ln. gylue. hev hln.s on 'lnlCs shoDy.evsI "1e ziyyI 6oDCyy hlde roDv sistev home pefove roD Jnoz itI2

'lnl gDyye. jhlr in uyose ln. ,lde hev l hD,N "6oD gvomise32 'lnl sli. softyr into jhlrCs elvI

"6esN w .oI Vv w zonCt uome pluJI2 jhlr vegyie.I

Ther poth empvlue. ls 'lnl uvie.I The othevs feyy "Diet ls ther lyy yooJe. onI élnr zith telvs lyso voyyin, .ozn theiv fluesI

"w .onCt Jnoz zhlt w zoDy. hlde .one zithoDt roD ,DrsI2 'lnl sli. ls she yooJe. Dg lt hev nezyr foDn. flmiyrI jhlr smiye. ln. yooJe. lt 'lnlN "le lve flmiyrN ln. thltCs zhlt flmiyr .oesI2

MluJ zlyJe. odev to jhlr ln. 'lnlN "jtog zovvrin,N zeCyy pvin, hev homeI2 he sli.N gyluin, his hln. on 'lnlCs shoDy.evI

Yftev l fez seuon.sN MluJ tDvne. ln. zlyJe. odev to the levily diez of the uomgye- ln. sDvvoDn.in, lvelN .isgylre. on the monitovI

?e yooJe. lt the monitov fov odev l minDte zithoDt slrin, l zov.I The voom syozyr zent "Diet ls edevroneCs lttention tDvne. tozlv.s MluJI

kiuhoyls zlyJe. odev ln. stoo. ne-t to MluJN "1hlt lve roD thinJin,32 he lsJe.N yooJin, lt the monitov ls zeyyI

MluJ gointe. lt the glvJin, lvel ne-t to the uomgye-N "1hlt Jin. of shot .o roD hlde in this lvel32 he lsJe.N zithoDt yooJin, lt kiuhoylsI

"7vettr mDuh l uyelv shotN e-uegt fov l uoDgye of tveesN heve ln. heveI2 kiuhoyls sli. ls he gointe. oDt the tvees on the monitovI

"1hlt re pe thinJin, yl.32 xe. lsJe. fvom pehin. the plvI

"bhln,e of gylnsI2 MluJ sli. ls he tDvne. tozlv.s the ,voDgI

'lnl yooJe. lt MluJ zith l tevviae. yooJ on hev flueN "6oDCve not ,oin, to ,et OltieN lve roD32 she sli. ls l telv voyye. .ozn hev flueI

"koU w meln 6Lj82 MluJ vegyie.N yooJin, odev lt hevI

"1eCve ulnnin, the tlJe.ozn of the lmplssl.ovI2 MluJ sli.I "VDv onyr misF sion is to ,et OltieI 1e ziyy ,et the lmplssl.ov lnothev timeI2

'lnl smiye. in veyief ln. vln odev ln. ,lde MluJ l pi, hD,N "ThlnJ roD MluJI2

"MimN .i. xlr sen. lnr of those thin,s thlt ziyy gDt one of those tvluJevs on someoneCs ueyy ghone32 MluJ lsJe.I

"6esN he sent foDv of them zith the othev stDRI2 Mim vegyie.I

"1hlt .o roD hlde in min.32 jhlr lsJe. ls she tooJ l selt ne-t to MimI

"jtezlvtN jhlrN ln. w ziyy gose ls ze..in, zovJevsI Vnue ze ,et l uhlnueN jhlr ziyy ,et OltieI2

MluJ gointe. lt jhlr ln. jtezlvtN "jhlrN jtezlvtN ln. w ziyy eluh tlJe one zith Ds to the ze..in, glvtrI wf one of Ds ,ets uyose enoD,h to the lmplssl.ovN ze ziyy .oznyol. the tvluJin, thin, to his ghone so ze uln tvluJ him yltevI2

"joN then zeCyy Jnoz the ne-t time he disits the Znite. jtltesN ln. zeCyy Jnoz
zheve he isI2 Oedin vegyie.I

"L-lutyr82 MluJ sli.I "le ziyy tlJe him .ozn thenI2

"1hlt lpoDt Ds32 kiuhoyls lsJe.I

"6oDN xe.N ln. xopevt ziyy gvodi.e odevzltuh fov DsI wf thin,s ,o soDthN
roDCyy uodev oDv esulgeI2 MluJ vegyie. ln. zlyJe. odev to the tlpye ln. ,vlppe.
l hln.fDy of uhigsI

"1hlt lpoDt the esulge gyln32 'lnl lsJe.I

MluJ yooJe. lt 'lnlN "leCyy Jeeg it ls simgye ls gossipyeI leCyy e-it the slme
zlr ls ze ulme inI2

"YreN pDt zhlt if thin,s .onCt ,o simgyeN ther nedev .oI 1hlt then32 xe.
lsJe.N gointin, Dg lt the monitovI

"wf thin,s ,o soDthN OedinN roD ln. 'lnl ,et the heyy oDt of theveI2 MluJ sli.N
"Bet pluJ to the stltes ls flst ls roD ulnI2

Oedin shooJ his hel.N "5Dt zhlt lpoDt roD ln. the othevs32 Oedin lsJe.I

"6esN zhlt lpoDt Oltie32 'lnl lsJe. zith uonuevn in hev doiueI

"leCyy hel. in the oggosite .iveution ln. hel. to bliplviKnNSzheve Tonr ln.
Mim ziyy pe zlitin,I2 MluJ sli. ls he yooJe. odev lt MimI

"leCyy pe lpye to tvluJ roD fvom heve ln. heyg ,Di.e roD inI2 Tonr sli.I

"YreN ln. zhlt lpoDt kiuhoylsN xopevtN ln. me32 xe. lsJe.N "1heve lve ze
,oin,32

"wf roDCve not .isuodeve.N then roD ,Drs ziyy mlJe roDv zlr to the livgovt in
?ldlnl ln. e-it the zlr roD ulme inI2 MluJ sli.I "TonrN ze nee. to ,et xopevt
l tiuJetI2

"1iyy .oI wCde ,ot l hotey voom vesevde. nelv the livgovt fov roD ,Drs to stl,e
fvom pefove yeldin,I 6oDCyy lyy pe on .iRevent qi,hts oDt to .iRevent youltions
pluJ in the jtltesI2 Tonr vegyie.I

"?eyyoN ,DrsI2 Y doiue ulme odev the sgelJevI

"Byl. roD uoDy. Hoin DsN WiuJrII2 MluJ sli.I "leCve HDst ,oin, odev oDv e-it
gylnI2

”?oz is it yooJin,32 WiuJr lsJe.I

”wCyy ,o odev the .etliys zith roD ln. xlr yltevI2 MluJ sli.I

”xlrI2 MluJ sli.I

”wCm heve possI2 xlrCs doiue ulme in odev the sgelJevI

”?oz lve thin,s yooJin, on roDv en.32 MluJ lsJe.I

”Ldevrthin, is yooJin, ,oo.I wCde lutidlte. lyy roDv tvluJevsI 5iv.s lve uhlv,e. ln. vel.rI2 xlr vegyie.I

”1hlt lpoDt the uomgoDn.32 MluJ lsJe.I

”wCde ,ot uontvoy of the seuDvitr ulmevls ln. uommDniultions of the uomF goDn.I2 xlr vegyie.I

“Ray, this is Tony. Jim and I will be monitoring the local traffic from the onFsite uommln.I2

”?er TonrN ,oo. to helv roDv doiueI2 xlr sli.I

”WiuJr ln. w ziyy pe monitovin, edevrthin, fvom Vme,lI2 xlr sli.I ”1eCyy pe roDv pluJDg ln. e-tvl eresI2

”1hen ziyy klsiv pe lvvidin,32 MluJ lsJe.I

”?eCs suhe.Dye. to yln. lt bienfDe,os livgovt in lpoDt tzo hoDvsI2 WiuJr sli.I

”bienfDe,os32 MluJ lsJe.I

”6esN thlt is zheve ther lve suhe.Dye. to yln.I2 WiuJr vegyie.I

”Thlt mi,ht ulDse l gvopyemI2 MluJ sli.I

”1hr is thlt32 WiuJr lsJe.I

”leyyN thltCs zheve ze gyln on e-tvlutin, ’lnlCs sistev Oltie fvomI2 MluJ sli.I

”1 e ziyy pe yln.in, soonN lvihlN2 klsiv sli. in YvlpiuN yooJin, odev lt OltieI

jhe .i. not vegyr ln. HDst uontinDe. yooJin, oDt the zin.ozI

klsiv yooJe. lzlrN "To.lr ze ziyy vestI Tomovvoz ze ziyy glvtr ln. the
ne-t .lrN roD ziyy pe mr pvi.eI2 he sli. lyoD.N pDt Oltie .i.nCt vegyr ln. HDst
uontinDe. yooJin, oDt the zin.ozI ?e stoo. ln. stlvte. to zlyJ to the pluJ of
the gylneI

Yftev l moment of siyenueN Oltie sli. softyr in ZJvlinilnN "w ziyy nedev pe
roDv pvi.eI2

klsiv stogge. pvieqr zithoDt tDvnin, pluJ tozlv.s hevI Yn,ev lggelve.
luvoss his flue ls he uontinDe. tozlv.s the pluJ of the gylneI

He took a seat across from his assistant, Yasser Ziad, and looked out the
zin.ozI "1hlt is pothevin, roDN klsiv32

Ys he stlve. oDt the zin.ozN klsiv .i.nCt vegyr lt avstN "Ynrthin, w uln .o32
Ɑssev lsJe. in YvlpiuI

" lvihlI2 klsiv vegyie.I

"1hlt noz32 Ɑssev lsJe.I

"?ev .isope.ienueI2 klsiv vegyie. softyrI

"ƌesN she is l hlv. one to pvelJI2 Ɑssev sli.I

klsiv yooJe. odev lt ɑssevN "'o roD vesgeut meN Ɑssev32

1ith l sDvgvise. yooJ on his flueN "ƌesN klsivI 1hlt Jin. of "Destion is thlt32
Ɑssev lsJe.I

"'o roD felv me32 klsiv sli. uoy.yrI

Ɑssev yooJe. lt klsiv zith l sDvgvise. ln. shouJe. yooJ on his flueN " elv
roD32 Ɑssev lsJe.I

klsiv yelne. fovzlv. tozlv.s ɑssevN " lvihlCs tvlinin, ln. uondevsion hlde
peen roDv vesgonsipiyitrI wf she hDmiyiltes me in fvont of L.mDn.oN 4DgeN ln.
othevsI2 klsiv glDse. ln. pvieqr yooJe. lzlrI 1hen he yooJe. pluJ lt ɑssevN
his .emelnov hl. totlyyr uhln,e.N theve zls gDve hltve. in his eresI "ƌoD ziyy
glr .elvyrI2 klsiv sli. syozyrI

Ɑssev yooJe. lt klsiv in totly shouJ ln. zls sgeeuhyessI

"'o w mlJe mrseyf uyelv32 klsiv lsJe.N stlvin, .eegyr into ɑssevCs eresI

6lssev fvoceN then yooJe. .oznN not zlntin, to mlJe ere uontlut zith klsivI
"6esIII w Dn.evstln.I2
   "BVV'82 klsiv e-uylime.I "Then w hlde nothin, to zovvr lpoDt32
   "koN klsivI 7elue pe Dgon roDI2 6lssev vegyie. softyrI
   klsiv slt pluJ in his uhlivN "Yn. Dnto roDI2 klsiv sli.N zith l syi,ht smiyeI

">
X   l rN zhlt is the stltDs of klsivCs gylne32 MluJ lsJe. him odev the
     miuvoghoneI
   "?oy. on l seuon.I2 xlr sli.I Yftev l fez seuon.sN heve tDvne. zith the
stltDs of klsivCs qi,htN "?eCs suhe.Dye. to yln. lt bienfDe,os in ln hoDv ln.
afteen minDtesI2
   "ThlnJs mlnI2 MluJ sli.I
   "Ynrthin, eyse roD nee.32 xlr lsJe.I
   "kothin, vi,ht nozI Oeeg Ds Dg.lte. if lnrthin, uhln,esI2 MluJ sli.I
   "1hlt noz32 jhlr lsJe.I
   "OedinN roDN ln. Tonr hel. to bienfDe,osI 5e theve zhen he yln.sI in. oDt
zhoCs zith him ln. mlJe sDve Oltie is theve ln. VIOI2 MluJ sli.I
   "wCm ,oin, tooI2 'lnl e-uylime.I
   "kot sDve thlt zoDy. pe l ,oo. i.elI2 MluJ vegyie.N yooJin, odev lt 'lnlI
jhlr stoo. ln. zlyJe. odev ne-t to 'lnlN "wtCyy pe VIOIN wCyy ,o tooI2 jhlr
sli.I
   MluJ yooJe. lt jhlr ln. 'lnlN "VIOI aneI Oeeg me Dg.lte. on zhlt roD an.
oDtI2 MluJ sli.I "jhlrN roDN ln. 'lnl tlJe Dg gosition lt the Vme,l MetI TonrN
roDN ln. Oedin gosition roDvseydes lt the e-itI Thlt zlrN if jhlr ln. 'lnl ulnCt
,et l uyelv diez of theiv lvvidlyN then roD tzo ziyy hogefDyyr pe lpye to ,et l disDly
on Oltie ls ther yeldeI2

"VJN soDn.s ,oo.I wCyy ,et the tvDuJI2 Oedin sli. ls he zlyJe. tozlv.s the
. oovI "wCm tlJin, one of the di.eo ulmevlsN ln. hogefDyyr roDCyy pe lpye to
zltuhI2 Oedin l..e.I

"jhot,Dn82 jhlr shoDte.I

Ys she zlyJe. glst MluJN he ,vlppe. hev lvmN "Oeeg 'lnl oDt of tvoDpyeI2
MluJ zhisgeve.I

jhlr smiye. ln. yooJe. Dg lt MluJN "1hlt uoDy. she ,et into32
MluJ uouJe. his hel. to one si.eN "MDst zltuh hevI2 he sli.I

"'onCt zovvrN w ziyyI2 jhlr vegyie.N voyyin, hev eresI

"é vIYyF?l.i.N ze ziyy pe yln.in, in ten minDtesI2 The ltten.lnt sli.N
in YvlpiuI

klsiv yooJe. Dg lt the ltten.lnt ln. no..e.I ?e yelne. pluJ in his uhliv ln.
uyose. his eresN "ássevI2 he sli.I

"áesI2 ássev vegyie.I

"xemempev zhlt w sli.I2 klsiv sli.I

"áesN sivI2 ássev vegyie. ln. yooJe. lzlrI

"ws the polt vel.r ássev32 klsiv lsJe.I

"áesN sivI2

"?lde the giyot vefDey the Het ln. vetDvn home ls ze gylnne.I2 klsiv sli.I
ássev anlyyr yooJe. odev lt klsivN "áesN sivI2

1 hen jhlr ln. the othevs lvvide. lt the bienfDe,os livaey.N Oedin ln.
jhlr stlre. nelv the Het zhiye Tonr ln. 'lnl stoo. zltuh nelv the e-it
of the livgovtI

”w thoD,ht MluJ toy. roD to Jeeg ’lnl oDt of tvoDpyeI2 Oedin sli. ls ther z ltuhe. klsivCs Het mlJe its lggvoluh ln. yln.I

jhlr yooJe. odev lt OedinN ”w thinJ w vemempev him slrin, somethin, lpoDt thltI2 she sli. zith l smiyeI ”jheCyy pe aneN sheCs zith TonrI2

”w hoge soI2 Oedin sli.N ls ther zltuhe. klsivCs Het syozyr tl-i to l stog HDst aftr rlv.s fvom the Vme,l HetI

”Ther HDst gozeve. .oznI2 Oedin sli. odev his vl.ioI

”bogrI2 MluJ vegyie.I

”bogrI2 xlr vegyie. ls he ln. WiuJr monitove. edevrthin, fvom Vme,l hel.“DlvtevsI

”bogrI2 Tonr vegyie.I

”le hlde l disDly of the HetN ln. ther lve lpoDt to e-itI2 Oedin infovme. edevroneI

Ys ther lyy zlite. fov the HetCs ouuDglnts to e-itN MluJ zlnte. to uheuJ in zith jhlr lpoDt ’lnlCs stltDsI joN he mDte. lyy the uommDniultions e-uegt fov jhlrCsI ”?oz is ’lnl hoy.in, Dg32 he lsJe.I

”jheCs .oin, aneI2 jhlr vegyie.I

”Boo.N .onCt yet hev fvelJ oDt zhen she sees hev sistevI2 MluJ sli.I

”’onCt zovvrN sheCyy pe aneI2 jhlr sli.I

The HetCs ouuDglnts stlvte. e-itin, the Het ls tzo dehiuyes lggvoluhe.I

”Ther lve e-itin, nozI2 Oedin sli.N Dg.ltin, the othevsI

”ws Oltie zith them32 MluJ lsJe.I

”6esI2 jhlr sli.N ls Oedin hey. Dg l di.eo ulmevl ln. tvlnsmitte. edevrthin, pluJ to the othevsI

”le hlde l uyelv disDlyI2 MluJ sli. ls edevrone theve ln. pluJ lt Vme,l zltuhe. in lntiuigltionI

The avst one oR the gylne zls 6lssevN ”1ho is thlt32 MluJ lsJe. ls he stegge. fovzlv. tozlv.s the monitovI

”That is Yasser Ziad, Nasir’s right-hand man.” Ray reported.

ke-t oR the gylne zls OltieN ln. foyyoze. uyoseyr pehin. zls klsivI

”1e hlde uonavmltion thlt Oltie is zith him ln. yooJs to pe oJI2 jhlr sli.I

”?oz is ’lnl hoy.in, Dg32 MluJ lsJe. l,linN sgelJin, onyr to jhlrI

”1eyyUI sheCs .oin, aneI2 jhlr sli.I

”jhlrN zhltCs zvon,32 MluJ lsJe.N stiyy onyr zheve jhlr uoDy. helvI

”kothin,82 jhlr sli.N pDt not devr uondinuin,yrI

”jhllllrN zhltCs Dg32 MluJ lsJe.I

”1eyyN sheCs zith TonrI2 jhlr sli.N veueidin, l ,ylnue fvom OedinI

”1?YT wk T?L ?L44 wj j?L ’VwkB 1wT? TVk632 MluJ reyye. odev jhlrCs elvgieueI

”jheCyy pe aneI2 jhlr sli.N pDt not devr uondinuin,yrI

”w thoD,ht w toy. roD to Jeeg ln ere on hevI2 MluJ sli. in l notFsoFgyelslnt toneI

”w thinJ w dl,Deyr vemempev roD slrin, somethin, lpoDt thltI2 jhlr sli.I

”’onCt zovvrN sheCs zith Tonr lt the e-itI2

”1hr is she lt the e-itI w thoD,ht roD ln. she zeve ,oin, to stlr on the gylne zhiye Tonr ln. Oedin zeve ,oin, to pe lt the e-it32 MluJ lsJe.I

”1eyyN ze uhln,e. thin,s DgI Oedin nee.e. to pe lt the Vme,l HetN in ulse someone stlvte. lsJin, “DestionsI ?e uoDy. teyy them thlt he zls uheuJin, on the HetI2 jhlr e-gyline.I ”ThltCs zhr Tonr ln. ’lnl szituhe.I2

”VJ aneI TheveCs nothin, ze uln .o lpoDt it nozI w HDst hoge she .oesnCt pyoz this entive ogevltionI2 MluJ vegyie. ln. ogene. the uhlnney so edevrone uoDy. helvI

jhlr zltuhe. ls the thvee zlyJe. tozlv.s the zlitin, dehiuyesI ”VJN Oltie is ,ettin, in the fvont glssen,ev seltI klsiv is pehin. hevN ln. 6lssev is pehin. the .videvI2 jhlr veylre.I

”1hlt Jin. of dehiuye lve ther in32 Tonr lsJe.I

”OedinN roD Jnoz zhlt thlt is32 jhlr lsJe.N yooJin, odev lt himI

Oedin yooJe. thvoD,h the pinouDylvsN ”wt yooJs yiJe l ve. ov. P-P jDgev Duty F250 diesel Raptor. The second vehicle is a black Ford F250 Dually with l yift JitN roD ulnCt miss itI2 Oedin sli.N yettin, the othevs Jnoz zhlt to yooJ fovI

”bogr thltI2 Tonr vegyie.I

”ThltCs one pl.lssFyooJin, tvDuJI2 jhlr sli. ls the tzo .vode oRI

’lnl yooJe. lt Tonr zith l uompinltion of e-uitement ln. felv in hev eresI

Tonr gylue. his vi,ht hln. on ’lnlCs shoDy.evN ”Yve roD VJ32

”wCyy pe ane zhen w ,et Oltie pluJI2 ’lnl vegyie.N ls l telv voyye. .ozn hev uheeJI

The flint soDn. of the tzo dehiuyes veluhe. TonrCs ln. ’lnlCs elvsI ”Ther ziyy hlde to stog heve pefove ther tDvn to hel. tozlv. L.mDn.o 4DgeCs uomF goDn.I2 Tonr sli. ls he yooJe. tozlv. the lggvoluhin, dehiuyesI

’lnl tooJ l .eeg pvelthN in ln eRovt to tvr ln. gDyy hevseyf to,ethevI ”’lnlN zhen ther stogN tvr not to velutI Oeeg roDv hel. .ozn ln. .onCt mlJe ere uontlutI wf Oltie sees roDN she mi,ht tvr to esulgeI2 Tonr sli.I

’lnl yooJe. Dg lt him ln. zige. lzlr the telvsI ”Yn. zhr .onCt roD zlnt hev to tvr32 ’lnl lsJe.I

” ov oneN ze hlde no zelgonsI TzoN ther hlde Ds oDtnDmpeve.I jtiuJ zith the gylnI2 Tonr sli. ls the tzo dehiuyes gDyye. Dg ne-t to themI

’lnl stoo. theveN fvocenN ln. syi,htyr fluin, lzlr fvom the tzo dehiuyes ls ther stogge.I ”jtlr ulymI2 Tonr zhisgeve.I ”Oltie is aneN wCm yooJin, vi,ht lt hevI2

’lnl shifte. hev eres tozlv. Tonr ln. then tDvne. hev hel. syi,htyr tozlv. the yel. dehiuye ls it stlvte. to gDyy lzlrI Yt thlt momentN Oltie yooJe. odev lt the tzo geogye stln.in, theve on the stveet uovnevI ’lnlCs ln. OltieCs eres met ls the dehiuye syozyr gDyye. lzlrI

OltieCs eres zi.ene. ls she veuo,nice. hev sistev ’lnl stln.in, theve HDst l fez feet lzlrI ’lnl moDthe. the zov.sN ”w yode roDI2 ls Tonr ,vlppe. hev ln. stlvte. zlyJin, in the oggosite .iveutionI Oltie gylue. hev hln. on the zin.oz ln. zltuhe. ls ther .vode glst hev sistevI

” lvihlN zhlt is it32 klsiv sli. ls he yelne. fovzlv.I

”kothin,8 Theve zls l qr on the zin.ozI w zls tvrin, to Jiyy himI2 Oltie sli. in l notFsoFgoyite toneI

EP...

klsiv yelne. pluJ in his selt ln. yooJe. odev lt 6ssevN ,idin, him l stevn yooJI 6ssev yooJe. lzlr ls the velyicltion of his fDtDve zls in .oDptI

Chapter Twelve

THE NIGHT BEFORE

Nasir and the others arrived at Edmundo Lupe's compound and were met by two of Lupe's bodyguards.

"This way." one of the guards said to Nasir, Yasser, and Katie as they exited the vehicle. They followed him through the gate and into the vast courtyard.

"My friend!" Lupe yelled as he greeted Nasir. "Welcome to my humble casa."

Lupe and Nasir embraced each other as Lupe said, "Who do we have here?"

Nasir looked back at Yasser and Katie, "You know Yasser."

"Yes, of course, welcome. Glad to see you again, Yasser." Lupe said as he shook Yasser's hand. "And who is this lovely young lady?"

Nasir turned and looked at Katie, "This is my bride-to-be, Fariha."

Lupe stepped forward and extended his arms to embrace Katie, "It's an honor to meet such a beautiful bride and an honor to host this most joyful occasion."

"That makes one of us." Katie replied harshly as she stepped back to avoid Lupe's embrace.

Rage and embarrassment loaded Nasir as he looked at Katie and then at Yasser.

No one spoke for what seemed like an eternity. Cntil Lupe Bnally broke the silence, "Pome. Let me show you your accommodations." Lupe turned and started towards the house, and Katie followed. Nasir stood there looking at Yasser, not saying a word, but the look said everything. Yasser knew it was over for him and that his future would soon be over. Nasir turned and followed Lupe and Katie, followed shortly by a defeated Yasser.

Lupe stopped beside a tall, dark wooden door, "This will be your room for tonight." Lupe said to Nasir as she opened the door into a large, spacious bedroom. "I hope this will meet your needs, my old friend. I know it's nowhere near as nice as your palace. Hut I hope it will su8ce.

Nasir Bnally looked at Lupe and gave him a half-hearted smile, "Yes, it will be Bne." As he stepped into the room.

Lupe smiled and gave him a slight nod, "Jery good. Now, if Fariha and Yasser will follow me, I will show the two of you your accommodations for the night. The three started down the long hallway when Nasir stuck his head out of his room, "I'm expecting three special guests. A Mr. Pharles zascal and two associates."

Lupe stopped and turned, "Why yes, Pharles and Mr. zost arrived about an hour ago.

"Hill Vavis was not with them?" Nasir asked, looking somewhat concerned.

"Yes, he arrived before them, maybe two hours ago. The last I had seen of him, he was walking the grounds." Lupe said.

"I'll let them know you have arrived as soon as I get Fariha and Yasser settled." Nasir nodded, "I will send for them later." he said, slowly closing his door.

(Two days before.)

A black sedan pulled up to the building, and the driver exited. qe walked over to the door and paused brie1y before entering the code to open the door. There was an audible click as the lock disengaged, allowing him to enter the building. qe slowly walked down the hallway and paused before entering the open door on his left.

Jicky was hard at work on her computer and didn't notice the intruder standing at the door. Ray was retrieving a cold drink out of the small refrigerator over in the corner of the room. Ray turned back toward his desk and saw the man standing in the doorway. qe stopped in his tracks and dropped the water bottle on the 1oor.

"Hutter Bngers." Jicky said as she looked up from her computer. Ohe paused and cocked her head slightly to one side as she saw Ray looking past her toward the door.

"What is it?" she asked, turning towards the door. A look of total surprise was on her face as she yelled out, "qunter! What in the hell are you doing here?"

"You need to work on your security." qunter said as he walked toward Jicky. They both embraced as Jicky said, "What are you doing here? Why didn't you call and let us know you were coming?"

qunter looked over at Ray, who was still standing there with his mouth open, "I just came by to pick up some things, before heading down to Puba." he placed a suitcase on the table.

"Ch, uh, what do you need?" Ray asked, still fro'en in place.

qunter opened the suitcase, "And while you are at it, scan all this stu5 for any tracking devices that may have been planted."

"Oure thing." Ray replied. "What else do you need?" Ray asked, walking over to the table.

"A cell phone, a tracker, an earpiece, a couple of guns. You know, the standard travel necessities." qunter said as he took a chair at the conference table.

"Oure thing. Give me a few minutes." Ray replied as he rushed o5 to get the items qunter had re0uested.

"Where is everyone else?" qunter asked, looking over at Jicky.

"Puba." she replied.

"Going after Katie?" he asked, grabbing Ray's water bottle and taking a swig.

Ohe nodded, "And Ambassador Oantiago."

"Oantiago?" qunter replied, placing the water bottle down on the table.

"That's the plan." she said." Katie is the primary target. If they get a chance, they'll take out Oantiago too."

"Gutsy plan." qunter said, looking up at Ray as he returned with qunter2s items.

"You know Sack." Ray said.

"qe knows that Katie is the primary target. qe's not going to screw things up and risk Katie's rescue." Jicky said, leaning back in her chair.

"Let's hope so." qunter replied.

"qere are the things you asked for." Ray said as he placed the items on the table. "I'll let you get the weapons you want. I know how personal those things can be."

"That's Bne." qunter said as he looked over the items. "I'm assuming the belt has the tracker in it?" he asked, looking up at Ray.

"Yes, just the same as the one you had before." Ray replied.

"And that didn't work out very well, did it?" qunter said, looking at Ray, with a slight smirk. "What is this?" qunter asked, picking up a small three-by-two-inch rectangle object about a 0uarter inch thick, "What is this gadget?" he asked, showing it to Ray.

"Uh yes. That will transfer a bug onto someone's phone so that I can track them." Ray said as he pulled up a chair next to qunter. "All you have to do is turn it on here." Ray showed qunter the small switch on the side, "And get close enough to the other phone. It will automatically download the bug."

"Sust how close do I have to be?" qunter asked.

"Within twelve inches or so." Ray replied.

qunter looked at Ray, "Oo, I've got to hug them for this to work." he said, shaking his head.

Ray smiled, "No, just stand close to them."

"For how long?" qunter asked, looking at the device in his hand and then at Ray.

"At least sixty seconds. Maybe more." Ray said.

qunter glanced over at Jicky, "Maybe? Maybe more?" he replied.

"Ninety seconds for sure." Ray added sheepishly.

qunter leaned back in his chair, "Let me get this straight. I've got to basically slow dance with these guys in order to plant this tracking thing on their phones?" qunter said harshly.

Jicky laughed, "It'll be Bne qunter, nobody's going to notice two guys dancing together nowadays."

qunter looked over at Jicky, "I don't need any help from you."Q

"Sack and Ohay will try to bug the ambassador's phone. If they fail, then we'll need you to try." Jicky said and smiled, "While you're at it, see if you can bug Pharles's phone too."

qunter nodded, "I'll see what I can do."

"Look, qunter, just get the unit close enough and it will be Bne." Ray said.

qunter nodded, "Uk, Bne, I'll Bgure something out. I also need something I can use to dump Nasir's computer onto. Pan you get me something?"

Ray stood and walked over to his desk. qe reached into one of his drawers and pulled out a box. "qere, just plug this into one of the COH ports. It'll start automatically." Ray said as he placed the COH drive next to the other things on the table.

qunter looked down at the drive, "And how long will this take?"

"It depends on how much data is on his computer. Maybe Bve or ten minutes." Ray said.

qunter picked the COH drive, "qow do they work?" qunter asked, looking at it in his hand.

"Sust plug it into the COH port and it will start automatically." Ray replied.

"Why did Pharles let you o5 his leash?" Jicky asked, getting qunter2s attention.

qunter looked over at Jicky, "qe had to let me free at some point."

qunter held up the COH drive, "Get me Bve of these COH computer things. I don't know how many I'll need." qunter stood and headed to the weapons vault. After a few minutes, he returned.

Jicky turned her chair towards qunter as he entered the room, "When are you heading out?" Jicky asked.

"Now." he replied.

"qere, I boxed everything up for you." Ray said as he handed him a small box.

qunter leaned over and kissed Jicky on the cheek, "I'm heading down there now. I start o8cially as Nasir's head pimp for North America." qunter said. "I've been invited to the wedding."

"Well, aren't you special?" Jicky said with a slight smirk.

"You know it." he replied. qunter headed towards the door. qe stopped just before exiting. "Keep me updated on things. I'll be in contact as often as I can."

Jicky smiled, "You know I will. I'll call Sack and Bll him in on your visit."

"Tell him I'll be at Lupe's tomorrow and contact him as soon as possible." qunter said.

Jicky stood and walked over to qunter and gave him a hug, "Oure thing. Uh, and qunter, good seeing you again. Keep in touch when you can." she said.

qunter nodded, turned, and walked out the door. As he walked down the hallway, he yelled back, "Ray, get this damn security system upgraded."

q unter walked through the garden area of Edmundo Lupe's casa, stopping occasionally to check out the surrounding area. "Uk, Sack, sounds like a good plan. I'll do whatever I can on my end."

"We don't want to do anything to blow your cover. Jicky Blled me in on everything. Red told me to tell you that's a nice suit you are wearing." Sack said.

"What?" qunter replied as he looked around.

Sack laughed, "Red, Nicholas, and Robert are up on the hill about four hundred yards away. Nicholas has his cross hairs on you now."

qunter turned towards a large clump of trees, way up on the hill overlooking the property. qe took his right hand, placing it on his right cheek, and raised his middle Bnger.

Sack laughed, "Nicholas said, back at you."

"Tell him that I hope he can shoot better than he did last time." qunter replied as he turned back toward the main house. "Got to go, kid." he ended the call, placed the cell phone in his pocket, and headed toward the main house.

qe saw Nasir, Edmundo Lupe, Pharles zascal, and the Puban Ambassador, Edgardo Oantiago, sitting at a table together next to the Ulympic-si'ed pool. qe smiled and waved as Nasir motioned him over to the table.

"This is my new associate, Hill Vavis." Nasir said as qunter approached.

"You have such a beautiful place here, Mr. Lupe." qunter said, smiling and nodding to the others.

Lupe took a long draw from his Pohiba Hehike HqK 3″ cigar, "I've been very fortunate. Hut please call me Edmundo." he said, taking his cigar and pointing it towards Edgardo Oantiago. "And this is the Puban ambassador to the Cnited Otates, Ambassador Edgardo Oantiago."

qunter nodded towards Oantiago and smiled, "Nice to meet you, Mr. Ambassador."

"zlease call me Edgardo. We're all friends here." Oantiago said as he took a drink of his Madeira wine.

qunter smiled and nodded, "Is that a Hehike you're smoking?"he asked.

Oantiago smiled, "Why yes, it is. You know your cigars. zlease be my guest." he slid a box of cigars over toward where qunter was standing.

"Where are my manners? zlease, Hill, pull up a chair and join us." Edmundo Lupe said. "I believe you know the others."

qunter nodded at Nasir and Pharles as he sat next to Lupe.

qunter sat next to the Puban Ambassador and took one of the Pohiba Hehike cigars out of the box.

Nasir lifted his drink in a toast, "Hill will be overseeing my tra8cking trade in North America." Nasir said. "qe comes highly recommended by Pharles."

Ambassador Oantiago leaned over toward qunter and softly said, "Next time I'm in America, you need to Bx me up with some fresh young samples."

qunter reluctantly smiled, "I'll see what I can do." he said.

Edmundo laughed, "Yes, Edgardo likes them young."

"Edmundo." qunter said, trying to change the subject.

"Yes, Hill." Edmundo replied as he tapped the ashes from the end of his cigar.

"qow much property do you have here?" qunter asked.

"Oee the top of that far hill?" Edmundo said, pointing to the right.

"Oure." qunter replied.

Edmundo then pointed to the far left at a distant pasture on top of a hill. "You see that green pasture up on the hill there?"

"Yes." qunter replied as he turned back towards Edmundo.

"My property line is just past there, about two hundred yards. All in all, about eight hundred acres."

qunter nodded, "Jery impressive, what do you grow?" he asked.

"This and that." Edmundo replied, waving his hand back and forth in a dismissive gesture.

qunter nodded, "It must be hard to keep the locals out." qe said, turning back towards the hillside.

"I have patrols with dogs that keep them out. Anyone who's caught trespassing will not live to regret it." Edmundo replied in a callous voice. "They will be increasing their patrolling of the hillside and property tonight and tomorrow."

Nasir stood and looked over at qunter, "Hill, come walk with me." he said.

qunter stood and followed Nasir, "Oure."

They both walked a little before the two said anything. qunter stopped and admired a bed of perfectly formed red roses. Nasir stopped a few feet away, not looking over at the roses qunter was admiring.

"The view here is breathtaking." qunter said as he looked over his shoulder towards Nasir.

"Yes, very colorful." Nasir replied, not looking at qunter.

qunter turned and faced Nasir, "What did you want to talk about? I know you didn't ask me for a walk, just to admire the 1owers."

Nasir turned and faced qunter, "There will be an associate arriving later this evening. You'll be working with him in the Otates. qe'll bea valuable resource for you, as you build the network there."

qunter nodded, "I normally work alone."

Nasir turned and started walking towards a bench, "Pome and sit. Let's enjoy the beauty around us.

qunter followed Nasir and took a seat next to him. qunter leaned back on the bench and placed his right arm on the back of the bench.

"I need you to work with this person. qe can help in many ways that will make your job much easier." Nasir said.

"I'll talk with him tonight and see what he has to o5er." qunter replied.

Nasir smiled, "Fair enough. I'm sure you'll Bnd that he'll be a great resource to you."

qunter pointed towards the decorations being Bnali'ed for the wedding, "Tell me about this wedding." qunter said.

Nasir looked at the decorations, "What would you like to know?"

"I assume that it's nothing like the weddings we have in the Otates." qunter said.

Nasir leaned forward and placed his elbows on his knees, "qave you ever been married before, Hill?" he asked.

qunter laughed, "Unce, for a very short time. Ohe didn't like me being away so much. Ohe had an a5air with a friend of mine."

"Not much of a friend." Nasir replied.

"No." qunter said softly.

"Any children?" Nasir asked.

"No, thank God." qunter said. "Tell me about your wedding and customs."

Nasir leaned back, "Jery well. I performed what we call the Oalat al-Istikhara when I met Fariha. It's anQextremely powerful prayerQin Islam that is performed by Muslims when they are facing a decision or a choice in their lives and seek guidance from Allah. The prayer is essentially seeking Allah's guidance for the best possible outcome in a decision or situation. In this instance, the wedding. Once this was completed, I o8cially announced the marriage." Nasir said.

"qow did your family take it?" qunter asked.

"What do you mean?" Nasir replied.

"Fariha, she's not a Muslim." qunter said.

"My family was not happy at Brst. My brother said it would never last. I told them Allah had blessed my taking Fariha as my wife." Nasir said.

qunter looked at Nasir, "Will Fariha be your Brst wife?"

Nasir laughed, "No, I have two other wives."

"Fariha will make your third wife?" qunter asked.

"Yes."

"qow do the other two wives feel about this?" qunter asked, with a curious look on his face.

"They have no say in the matter." Nasir replied sharply.

"Fariha is what, seventeen?" qunter asked, but knew the answer.

"No, she is Bfteen." Nasir replied.

"That's a little young." qunter said.

Nasir gave qunter a look of irritation, "Ohe will give me many children."

qunter looked at Nasir, "What about the other wives?"

"I have grown tired of them. They are good to have around ifI need something that Fariha cannot provide. They have not provided me with as on." Nasir replied harshly.

qunter nodded, "Uk, continue with the wedding ceremony."

"Next comes the Mangni. This symboli'es the formal ring ceremony and engagement, where close friends and family gather to celebrate the start of the union. In this Muslim wedding tradition, wedding sweets, clothes, andQjewel-ryQare often gifted to the happy couple from either side of the family. We did this several months ago with my family in :atar." Nasir said.

íFariha's family is ok with this marriage?" qunter asked.

"Fariha has no family. Ohe is an orphan." Nasir replied.

Nasir continued, "Next would be the qaldi ceremony. This isa cherished tradition in the Muslim culture, in which qaldi, which is a paste, is applied to the face, neck, hands, and feet of the bride and groom. The paste is known to have beautifying e5ects and antimicrobial capabilities, comprising a gram of 1our, turmeric, sandalwood, water, and oil. We will do this tomorrow morning before the wedding."

"Oounds interesting." qunter replied.

Nasir smiled, "Tonight is the Haraat. This marks the arrival of the groom and his family and friends at the wedding venue, where the marriage ceremony will occur. It is a lively and celebratory event, Blled with music, dancing, and merriment. We will celebrate tonight, my friend."

"Oo, I get to meet some of your family?" qunter asked.

"Yes, my brother and his family, sister, and cousins. Then tomorrow, the wedding ritual is the Nikah, where the marriage is solemni'ed by the chosen Imam. Vuring the Nikah ceremony, the Hride á Groom are often covered by a translucent wall between them, either of cloth or 1owers." Nasir said.

qunter nodded.

"This ceremony usually begins with a recitation from the :uran or a brief sermon by the Imam. This often includes reminders about the signiBcance of marriage in Islam."

"After that, the proposal or Ijab and the acceptance :ubool, as they are called, are key elements of the Nikah. The Groom's side initiates the proposal by stating the Groom's intention to marry the bride. The bride's side, Yasser will Bll that role, accepts the proposal on her behalf, expressing her willingness to marry the Groom." Nasir said.

"The couple must then say the beautiful words ¿:ubool qai' three times, giving their consent to marry." Nasir continued. "The Mehar, commonly known as the Mahr, symboli'es the wedding contract which must be signed by the couple. This is one of the steps carried out in the Nikah, as blessings are received by the couple and their families. As this occurs, prayers are read out from the :uran. Are you a religious man, Hill?" Nasir asked.

qunter laughed, "Not really. In my line of work, I don't think God would bless it or approve."

Nasir nodded, "That's unfortunate." Nasir paused for a second before continuing, "Traditionally, the Mahr symboli'es a payment which is agreed upon before, to be paid from the Groom to the Hride. Hut we will forgo this part." Nasir said.

qunter nodded his head, "I see. Oort of like pre-divorce payment." qunter replied and laughed.

Nasir looked at qunter with a pu"led expression. "Remember when I said the couple was split between a cloth or 1owers?" Nasir asked.

qunter nodded, "Yes."

"Well, the Arsi Mushraf occurs after the ceremony, and is essentially the Brst look between the couple. The term itself is a combination of two wordsň "Arsi," which means mirror, and "Mushraf," which means blessed or honorable. The Arsi Mushraf ceremony involves the use of a mirror, and it holds cultural and symbolic signiBcance. qow the Arsi Mushraf is carried out will di5er amongst families, as well as the traditions that have been passed down." Nasir leaned back in the bench, "qow we will perform the Arsi Mushraf is with Fariha and myself, sitting next to each other, with the mirror placed between us, at the perfect angle where we can see each other in the re1ection of the mirror." Nasir said.

"Is this the end of the ceremony?" qunter asked.

"No. The Rukhsaat ceremony is a heartrending and emotional moment in the wedding festivities, marked by the bride's transition from her childhood home to her new life as a wife with her new partner.QCltimately, the Rukhsaat symboli'es the start of the couple's new chapter."

"The Walimah, which is what you would call the reception, isa joyful celebration that marks the public announcement of the marriage and the couple2s union. It's an opportunity for everyone to come together and celebrate the newlywed couple's happiness. With an endless supply of food, dances, and celebrations, the Walimah will be truly a grand a5air!" Nasir said.

"With plenty of li0uor?" qunter asked with a big smile.

"No. True followers of the Koran and Islam do not partake in alcohol of any kind." Nasir replied.

qunter shook his head, "Visappointing."

QNasir laughed, "I'm sure Edmundo has some available so you can sneak a drink."

qunter smiled, "Ur two."

Nasir stood, "We must get back. The Bnal arrangements are being made, and our guest will be arriving soon."

Ohay, Sack, and Otewart piled into their vehicle and headed to Edmundo Lupe's casa.

"We just can't walk in and start serving drinks and food." Otewart said as they closed the doors.

"Three of the scheduled workers called in sick today." Sack replied. "A temporary agency made the last-minute arrangements for us to take their places."

"Oo, three just happened to get sick at the same time?" Otewart asked, not believing it.

"Yep." Ohay replied. "It's surprising what money will buy."

"And the temporary agency?" Otewart asked.

Ohay looked back at Otewart, "Jicky, is the temp agency."

Twenty minutes later, they pulled up to the side gate of Edmundo Lupe's casa. They were met by two men who appeared to be guards.

"You see any weapons on these two?" Sack asked, as the three looked out the vehicle's windows at the approaching men.

Une of the guards motioned towards Ohay to lower her window, "Nothing visible." Ohay replied. "Hut I bet you twenty dollars they are carrying." she said as she rolled down the window.

"Estaciona tu auto all..., al lado del ñrbol." The guard said to Ohay, as she just stared back at the guard, without saying a word. "A little help, Otewart," she whispered, smiling back at the guard.

Otewart whispered back, "qe's telling us to park our car over there next to the tree."

Ohay smiled, nodded at the guard, and looked over at Sack. "You heard the man. zark over next to that tree."

Sack nodded and waved at the guard. qe slowly pulled the vehicle over and parked next to the tree.

"There, that wasn't so hard now, was it?" Otewart said.

"Ohut up and get out, you two." Sack said lightheartedly. "Time to get down to business."

The three exited the vehicle and slowly walked toward the gate and one of the guards.

"You ready for this?" Ohay asked, not directing her 0uestion to either one of them.

"As ready as I'll ever be." Otewart replied anxiously.

"Oure thing." Sack said as he walked slightly ahead of the others.

Otanding about six foot six and weighing around two hundred and ninety pounds, the guard at the gate stepped in front of them and put up his hand for them to stop. "¡Puñl es tu negocioa0u...?" he said with a stern voice in Opanish.

Otewart, who was lagging behind about ten feet, "qe's asking you what your business is here." he said softly over his mic so only Sack could hear him through his earpiece.

"We're here to work." Sack replied, not sure the man understood what he was saying.

The man tilted his head to one side and looked over at the other two who stood beside but slightly behind Sack.

Sack looked around at the two other men and then back at the man standing at the gate, "Tell OoBa Fernñnde' we are here."

This seemed to register with the guard, who nodded and motioned for the three to follow him. Unce inside, the three followed the guard over to a table Blled with food. "Oeéorita Fernñnde'(. You have three people here to see you." he said in Opanish.

OoBa turned and smiled. Ohe threw both hands up in the air as she started walking towards them. "Wonderful! It's about time!" she shouted out in Opanish.

The three stood there without saying a word, just smiling. Finally, Sack introduced the three to her, "The agency sent us. This is Oharon Otory, Sie Yang, you can call him Say, and I'm Vavid Martin."

OoBa stood there looking at the two of them and shook her head in disgust. "Americans?" she asked, in a deep Opanish accent.

Sack smiled, "Yes."

"¡qablas espa)ol? she asked.

Sack smiled again, "No."

OoBa motioned for them to follow, "ZNo puedo creer 0ue la agencia me haya enviado a tres imbéciles que no pueden hablar el idioma!" (I can't believe that agency sent me three imbeciles that can't speak the language!) she said as she turned and walked towards the serving tables.

Sack leaned over towards Otewart, "What did she say?"

Otewart smiled, "Ohe said you are very handsome and to follow her."

"Uh, ok." Sack replied as the three followed behind her.

"I don't think that's what she said." Ray said over the team's earpieces.

Sack stopped and threw up his arms, "Then what did she say?"

Ohay pushed Sack forward to catch up with OoBa, "Von't worry about it."

OoBa stopped next to a table with a pile of assorted si'es of white serving jackets. She looked at them and shuffled through the pile until she found three jackets that would come close to Btting them. Ohe tossed each one a jacket. Ohe then pointed at Sack and then pointed to a work station behind one of the serving tables. Ohe did the same to Ohay.

"I guess you and I are working these two serving stations."Ohay said as she began putting on her jacket.

Sack started putting on his jacket, "I guess so."

OoBa pointed at Oteward and motioned for him to follow.

"Well, I think I'm working somewhere else." Otewart said as he followed OoBa.

"qave fun." Sack replied.

Ohay looked over the food on her station, "We've got to Bnd out where Katie is."

Sack looked around as the crowd started lining up at his station. qe pressed his transmit button on his hidden mic. "Otewart, where are you?"

"Ohe put me in the kitchen, I'm making pastries and cupcakes." Otewart replied, somewhat disappointed.

"We need to Bnd out where Katie is." Sack said.

"qow? It's not like we can just walk around and check the rooms." Otewart replied.

Sack looked at the line forming in front of him and noticed a familiar face. They both made eye contact with each other. Sack gave him a slight nod, and qunter returned the gesture without being noticed.

"I see you've Bnally found your calling. What do you recommend here, kid?" qunter asked as he looked at the assorted foods on the serving table.

"qell, I don't know what half of this shit is." Sack replied, just loud enough so only qunter could hear. "qave you seen Katie? We need to Bnd out where she is."

qunter slowly shook his head, "I'll try to Bnd out. Give me a few minutes." qunter said as he turned and walked away with his plate of food.

"qow may I serve you?" Sack asked the next person in line.

qunter walked over to where Nasir was standing and talking with a small group of people. As he approached, he stopped about ten feet away and waited to be asked to join them.

Nasir turned and noticed qunter standing there with a plate of food in his hand. "zlease come, Hill, join us. I would like for you to meet my brother qam'a."

"It's an honor to meet the brother of Nasir." qunter stuck out his hand for qam'a to shake.

qam'a grabbed qunter2s hand and gave it a Brm shake. "I understand that you'll be working with my brother to expand his operation in the C.O."

qunter smiled, "That's what I hear."

qam'a smiled, "That is good to hear. qis last associate, over the C.O. operations, disappeared without a trace. I hope you have better luck." he said, looking over at Nasir.

Nasir placed a hand on qunter2s shoulder, "I'm sure he will do just Bne." he replied.

"We are taking bets on how long Nasir's marriage will last, with this young woman, Fariha. Would you like to get in on the action, Hill?" qam'a asked, laughing as he turned and looked at Nasir.

"What's the wager?" qunter asked.

"Fifty." qam'a replied.

"Fifty?" qunter said. "I'll take Bfty that the marriage will last a long time." qunter said as he pulled out his wallet and removed two twenties and a ten.

qam'a laughed, "That's Bfty thousand."

qunter looked at Nasir, who was giving his brother a disgusted look, "No, thank you, I think I'll pass. Hy the way, where is your beautiful bride-to-be?" qunter asked.

Nasir turned away from his brother and looked at qunter, "In her room."

qunter looked towards the main house, "Will we be seeing her this evening?"

"You'll have to ask Yasser." Nasir replied.

qunter, Nasir, qam'a, and Edmundo continued to talk for another Bfteen minutes, until qunter spotted Yasser exiting the main house.

"Excuse me, gentlemen." qunter said as he turned and headed towards Yasser. qe walked over to where Yasser was standing. "Excuse me, Yasser, you have a second?"

Yasser smiled, "Yes, Hill, what can I do for you?" he replied. "May I o5er you a drink?"

qunter looked at the drink in Yasser's hand. "What are you drinking?" he asked.

"It's tamarind fruit juice. Would you like one?" Yasser asked.

qunter looked at the dark brown li0uid, "Never tried it."

Yasser lifted his glass slightly and looked at it, "It's a mouth-watering tart drink. Think of concentrated lemonade with a dash of sugar. It's made with crushed tamarind, water, sugar, and lemon juice."

"Oounds delicious." qunter replied.

Yasser turned towards the bar and poured qunter a glass of tamarind. "qere you go Hill, enjoy."

qunter took the glass and took a small sip, "Not too bad, very tart."

Yasser smiled, "Tamarind juice has manyQhealth beneBts. It is anti-in1amma-tory and helps maintain healthy blood pressure."

"Interesting. I'll have to remember that." qunter said, lifting his drink in the air.

Yasser smiled, "You'll have to try some of our other drinks. I think you will like the taste and the health beneBts too."

"I will. Uh. I've not seen Fariha. Is she ok?" qunter asked.

"Yes, I believe so. I checked on her a few minutes ago." Yasser replied.

"qas she eaten anything?" qunter asked.

Yasser glanced over towards one of the serving tables, "I don't believe so. I don't think she's eaten anything since we arrived."

"Ohe needs to eat something. Ohe's got a big day ahead of her." qunter said.

Yasser nodded, "Ohe's a very stubborn girl."

qunter laughed, "Aren't they all?í

Yasser also laughed, "Yes, but she is more than most. Nasir will have his hands full with this one."

"I think I'll have one of the servers prepare a meal for her and take it to her." qunter said as he glanced over toward one of the serving tables.

"Good luck my friend. Hetween you and me, I think she would rather starve to death than go through with this marriage." Yasser said, in a faint voice.

"You don't say." qunter replied.

"You didn't hear that from me." Yasser cautioned.

qunter turned his drink up and downed the remainder of his drink, "Not a word." qunter replied. "If you will excuse me." he said, placing his empty glass on the table.

"Good luck." Yasser said.

"Uh, I forgot to ask, what room is she in?"

"Cp the main staircase and turn to your right. qer room is the third door on the right." Yasser replied.

qunter walked over to the serving table where Ohay was working. qe stood there for a second, looking at the food that Blled the table.

Ohay gave qunter a big smile, "Pan I help you, sir?" she asked.

"I see you've found your true calling." qunter said with a smile.

Ohay reached for one of the plates, "Heats getting shot at." she replied.

qunter nodded, "I've found out where Katie's room is." he said, looking over the food selection on the table.

Ohay looked over at Sack, who was preparing a plate of food for someone in line at his table. "Where?" she asked.

qunter looked around to make sure no one was within earshot, "Oee the double doors across from you?"

Ohay nodded as qunter pointed at a lobster tail. "Go through those doors and you'll see the main staircase. Go up the main staircase and turn to your right. qer room is the third door on the right."

"Uk." Ohay said as she placed the lobster tail on a plate. "What else would you like, sir?"

"zrepare a plate for her and take it to her. From there, you are on your own. I'm assuming you have a plan to get her out of here without being noticed?" qunter said, pointing at something he did recogni'e.

"Uf course, we have a plan." Ohay said.

"What is that stu5?" he asked, pointing at another item on the table.

"The hell if I know." she said, placing a double helping of it on his plate. "Anything else, sir?" she asked.

"No, I think that will do it, thank you." qunter said, he took his plate, turned, and walked over towards the table where Nasir and the others were sitting.

Ohay tapped her earpiece to communicate with the others. "Uk, I've got Katie2s location. I'm going to prepare her a plate of food and take it to her." she said over her mic. "Are we all ready?" she asked.

"Zeus, Deacon, Red copy and ready. Base copy and clear, Tony replied. Eagle and Grave Vigger ready. Robin qood and Mother are ready on our end, Ray replied from Umega head0uarters. Popy all." Sack replied.

"What's your plan?" Sack asked Ohay.

"I'm going to take her a plate of food, and then we're going to walk out to the car and leave." Ohay said as she started putting assorted food items on a plate.

"That's your plan!" Sack replied.

"What do you want me to do?" Otewart asked over the earpiece.

Sack thought for a second, "As soon as she lets us know she is heading out with Katie, you head towards the car and make sure the area is clear."

"What are our rules of engagement?" Nicholas asked from his overwatch location, high up on the hillside.

"If we don't encounter any resistance, keep 0uiet. If you detect any hostile threats, do what you have to do to neutrali'e the situation." Sack replied.

"Popy." Nicholas replied.

"Sack, this is Jicky. Is this plan going to work?" Jicky asked, with a genuine concerned tone in her voice.

Sack looked around to see if he could see any of the guards, "I don't know Jicky. Ask me again in ten minutes."

After Ohay prepared a plate of food for Katie, she headed towards the door leading into the main house. Ohe grabbed one of them as she passed the table with an assortment of servers' jackets and kept walking. Ohe entered the main house and went up the stairs to the second 1oor. Ohe found the room where Katie was staying. "Uk, guys, I'm outside her door, everyone stand by." Ohay whispered over her mic.

Sack looked around the area to see if anyone had noticed Ohay leaving her station. qe made eye contact with qunter, who was sitting about thirty feet away. qe gave qunter a slight nod and looked away. "Uk, guys, be ready." he said softly.

Ohay took a deep breath and knocked on the door. There was no reply from inside. Ohe knocked again, but this time harder. A voice from inside responded this time. "Go away!"

Ohay placed her head close to the door, "Upen the door." Ohay whispered.

"I said(GU AWAY!" Katie replied.

Ohay leaned against the door and tried the doorknob, but the door was locked. "Katie, we're here to get you out." Ohay said.

"Who are you, and how do you know my name?" Katie asked. This time, Ohay could tell she was just on the other side of the door.

"Katie. Upen the door, and I can explain." Ohay pleaded.

"Tell me who you are Brst." Katie demanded as she started to cry.

Ohay took a deep breath, "Katie(your sister Hohdana sent us to rescue you. I'm with Umega."

Chapter Thirteen

THE GREAT ESCAPE?

Shay could hear Katie unlock the door. Katie opened the door a couple of inches, just enough so that she could look at Shay. "Bohdana is here?" Katie asked as a tear rolled down her face.

"Yes." Shay replied in a low voice, "Now let me in."

Katie opened the door, and Shay slipped in. She quietly closed the door and locked it. Katie grabbed Shay and gave her a big hug. "Thank you." Katie said as the tears started to Wow.

"'eOre not out of the woods yet. 'e still have to get you out of here and safely out of the country." Shay told Katie. "IK, guys, DOm in." Shay said over her mic.

"D want to speak to her." 'anaHs voice over ShayOs earpiece came.

Shay removed her earpiece and placed it into KatieOs ear. "Ik, say something." Shay said.

"Kello." Katie said softly.

"атриноя, д умлтщт, бя іьщшекоьпящн ок чяюмв ргяся сящя!м(,Ҝatryna, D thought D would never hear your voice again(Б 'ana shouted into the mic.

"Тясутот? 1н ук?")Bohdana? 'here are you?Б Katie replied, and a big smile appeared on her face. Now, the tears started to Wow at both ends of the conversation. Pven Shay began to shed a few tears as she listened and watched Katie.

'ana switched to Pnglish, "DOm not far away. You do whatever Shay tells you to do. 'e will be together very soon." 'ana said.

"Ik." Katie replied.

"Be careful." 'ana said, as the tears continued to Wow.

"'ana." Katie said softly.

"Yes." 'ana replied.

"D love you." Katie whispered.

There was a moment of silence over the earpiece, "D love you, too. Now do whatever Shay tells you and weOll be together very soon."

"D will." Katie said softly, trying to get control over here motions.

"Now give the earpiece back to Shay." 'ana instructed.

Shay took the earpiece and placed it back into her ear. "You ready, Katie?" Shay asked.

Katie nodded her head.

Shay handed her the serverOs jacket that she had taken oF the table, "Gut this jacket on."

Suddenly, there was a knock at the door, "7ariha. You must come out now. Nasir demands it." Yasser said from the hallway.

Katie looked at Shay, "'hat do D do?" she whispered.

Shay looked over at the door, "0et rid of him." Shay whispered back.

"0o away(" Katie said and looked at Shay.

Yasser tried to open the door, but it was locked, "Ipen the door(" Yasser demanded.

"D said, go away(" Katie repeated her demand.

"Df D must get someone to unlock this door, D will. Now open this door(" Yasser demanded again.

Katie looked at Shay with a terriMed look on her face. "'hat do D do?" she whispered to Shay.

"DOll unlock the door." Shay said, taking KatieOs hand, and led her to a spot about eight feet from the door. "Stand here. 'hen D unlock the door, tell him to come in." Shay whispered to her. Shay walked over, unlocked the door, and stood against the wall ne t to the door. Ince she was in position, Shay nodded to Katie.

"IK, itOs unlocked." Katie said and looked over at Shay. Shay nodded, pulled a syringe out of her pocket, and removed the safety cap.

Yasser opened the door and stood there in the doorway. "You must come and join Nasir and the festivities."

Shay was waiting behind the door so that Yasser couldnOt see her. She nodded at Katie and motioned for her to get Yasser to come in.

Katie stood there motionless for a second, "You must come in and help me decide what to wear." Katie said, with a bit of hesitation in her voice.

"Jery well. But the door must remain open." Yasser stepped into the room and over towards Katie. Ke was now just two feet in front of Shay. "Gut the blue." That was all that Yasser said before he felt a stick to the side of his neck, and everything went dark.

Shay helped Yasser down to the Woor and quickly closed the door.

"'hat now?" Katie asked, looking down at Yasser, who was lying on the Woor at her feet.

"'e leave before someone else comes." Shay replied.

"Shay, whatOs the status?" Rack asked softly over the mic.

"0ive us about two minutes." Shay replied.

Rack keyed his mic again, "Stewart, start making your way out to the car." Rack said.

"Lopy." Stewart replied. Vbout thirty seconds later, Rack saw Stewart slowly making his way out of the main house and towards the side gate. Rack looked towards the entrance and saw the giant guard still standing there. *He must be six feet six and well over two hundred and eighty pounds.* Rack thought to himself.

"2eus, are you guys set?" Rack asked.

"'eOre ready. 'e have a clear shot of the gate and parking area from this position." Nicholas replied.

"Lopy. Eemember, do not engage unless you see an imminent threat." Rack reminded the overwatch team.

"Vye, we hear ya. 'hat bout the Vmbassador?"¿ Eed asked.

"Negative. 'eOll get the Vmbassador later. óetOs focus on getting Katie out and safe." Rack said.

"Vye." Eed replied in a disappointed tone.

"Eobert, howOs our si looking?" Nicholas asked, not taking his eye from the scope of his weapon.

Eobert was about ten feet away, looking for threats that might sneak up on them from behind. "Vll clear." Eobert whispered.

Rack looked around the patio area and saw Kunter sitting with Nasir and the others at the table. "Pagle, you ready on your end?" Rack asked.

"'eOre fueled and ready. óet us know when youOre about ten minutes out. 'eOll have the engines hot and ready for immediate takeoF as soon as you arrive." Kevin replied.

Rack looked around to make sure no unnoticed surprises had arrived, "Lopy." he replied.

"Eobin Kood to Stryker, weOre ready on our end. 'eOre monitoring all units, and two Cother Kawks are in the air. 'eOll be ready to jam all electronics and security cameras on your command." Eay said.

"Lopy." Rack replied. "Shay, all units ready."

Shay looked at Katie, "You ready to see your sister?" she asked.

Katie smiled, "YouOre damn right D am."

"Stryker, weOre on the move." Shay said. Shay grabbed KatieOs wrist and walked towards the door. She slowly opened it and looked out into the hallway to make sure no one was there. "IK, stay close, weHre going to just walk right out through the patio, through the gate, and into a waiting car." Shay softly said, looking over her shoulder at Katie.

"'hat if weOre seen?" Katie asked.

"Rust keep walking and follow my instructions." Shay replied. The two quiZ etly walked down the hallway and down the stairs. They paused brieWy at the door leading onto the patio.

Shay took a deep breath and pushed the door open. The two casually walked out onto the patio and along the wall towards the gate.

Stewart walked through the parking area and approached their vehicle, "Stryker, we have a problem." Stewart said.

"'hatOs the problem?" Rack replied with great concern in his voice.

"'eOre blocked in." Stewart said. "Iur car is blocked in by another vehicle. D canOt get it out." Stewart said with a slight panic in his voice.

"ñY dénde estz ese peque3o alborotador? ñGor qu4 dejé su puesto?")Vnd just whereOs that little troublemaker at? 'hy did she leave her station?Б Rack turned and saw SoMa 7ernznde5, yelling at the top of her lungs, approaching him. Pveryone on the patio turned to see what was going on.

Pdmundo óupe stood up from the table, "'hat in the hell is going on?" he said aloud, mostly to himself.

Nasir was sitting with his back to the commotion. Ke looked at Pdmundo and then heard someone yelling. Ke turned and looked over his right shoulder to see what was happening. Ke saw SoMa 7ernznde5 yelling and storming towards the serving tables. Covement caught his eye just past SoMa and moving towards the gate. Vt Mrst, it didnOt register who he was looking at. Vnd then it hit him. "7ariha(" he yelled out, "'hat are you doing? 'here are you going?"

Katie heard Nasir call her, and she stopped in her tracks. She looked directly at him and fro5e. Shay had KatieHs hand, and she stopped when Katie stopped. Shay turned towards Katie to see why she had stopped. Shay pulled on KatieHs arm, "Lome on." Shay said and started pulling Katie along.

"7ariha Stop(Lome back here at once." Nasir yelled as he stood.

Katie smiled, Wipped Nasir the bird, and ran towards the gate right behind Shay.

Vbout ten feet from the gate, Shay came to an abrupt halt. 6ooking back at Nasir, Katie didnOt see that Shay had stopped. She ran into Shay, almost knocking her down. "'hy did we stop?" Katie asked as she turned and saw a giant standing between them and the door.

The guard smiled and put up his hand, "ñJas a alguna parte, peque3a?")0oing somewhere, little one?Б he asked, as he stood between them and their escape.

Rack watched as Shay and Katie stopped at the gate, "0uyOs things are going south fast." he said over his mic.

"Jiper, if you can get that guy to take two steps towards you, D will have a clear shot." 2eus said o ver his mic.

"Negative." Rack replied. "Kold."

"Lopy." Nicholas replied with a hint of disappointment in his voice.

Shay stood there, not moving or taking her eyes oF her opponent. She smiled, "D donOt know what you just said 0oliath." she said.

The big man tilted his head slightly to one side and smiled. Shay moved into a Mghting stance and looked at the man. This made the man laugh as Shay slowly inched her way towards the towering giant.

Ke laughed aloud, "Te aplastar4 como a un peque3o insecto.")D will crush you like a little bug.Б The man said. No sooner had he gotten the words out of his mouth. Ke was struck on the right side of his head. Ke staggered to his left as he grabbed the right side of his head. Vs he regained his balance, he was struck again, on the left side of his head. Ke dropped down to his knees.

Shay walked up to him and with her right hand struck the man under his chin, driving his head back suddenly. She stepped aside, and the giant man fell forward, landing faceZMrst on the walkway.

Shay looked through the gateway and saw Stewart standing there smiling. "'hat did you hit him with?" Shay asked as she stepped on the manOs back and walked through the gate. Katie looked down at the unconscious man as she walked around him and through the gate.

Stewart smiled, "Baston Mghting sticks." he replied.

Lonfusion was growing as the patio crowd wondered what was happening. "Stop them(" Pdmundo yelled, pointing at Shay and Katie running through the garden gate.

Two of PdmundoOs men started running towards the escaping Shay and Katie. Vs they neared, Rack overturned his serving table as the two men apZ proached. 7ood Wew all over the Woor, causing the two pursuers to slip and fall. Rack looked over at SoMa, "D quit." Rack said. "Ih, and the other two quit, also." Rack turned and ran towards the open gate. SoMa stood there with her mouth wide open, unable to say a word.

Shay and Katie ran past Stewart, and he fell in behind them. They ran towards the car to retrieve their weapons bag.

"Iur car is blocked in, and we need a new one." Stewart said as they headed towards their car.

"D heard, but we need to get the weapons bag." Shay replied as the three slowed to a fast walk towards where they had parked their car.

"DOve already taken the bag out when D retrieved my bastons." Stewart replied. "DOve hidden the bag over in the bushes."

"0et the bag. DOve got my eye on our new ride." Shay replied. Shay and Katie walked past their car towards a red 7ord 8 8 Super 'uty7áUx diesel Eaptor. V man was standing ne t to the truck and noticed the two approaching.

"ñGuedo ayudarte, peque3a?")Lan D help you little one?Б the man asked, as he stepped forward.

"Stewart, a little help here." Shay whispered.

Stewart had retrieved the bag and was heading to catch up with Shay and Katie. Ke heard the conversation between Shay and the man over his earpiece. "KeOs asking what you want." Stewart said, now about Mfty feet behind them.

"The keys to the truck." Shay said as she got closer to the man.

Ke looked at the two standing in front of him, tilting his head slightly. Not understanding what Shay said, he raised his right hand to stop them.

Vs soon as Shay got close enough, she reached over the top of his e tended hand and grabbed it. She gave her hand and his a sudden twist to the right and down. Lausing severe pain to the manOs wrist, elbow, and shoulder. Vs he bent over, Shay gave him a kick to the face. Lausing the manOs head to jerk back slightly. The man lost consciousness and fell faceZMrst to the ground.

"0et in(" Shay told Katie, as Shay looked through the manOs pockets for the keys.

"'hat are you doing?" Stewart said as he ran up ne t to Shay.

"Borrowing us a ride." Shay replied, still looking through the pockets of the unconscious man.

"7ound them." Katie yelled as she leaned out of the passengerZside door. "They were in the ignition, letOs go." Katie screamed as she saw more men heading their way.

"0et in." Shay shouted at Stewart and ran to the driverOs side. Shay reached up above her head and opened the driverOs side door. Vs the door opened, a step appeared underneath the truckOs door. "Nice." Shay said to herself as she climbed into the truck cab.

Rack ran towards the gate. Vs he approached the gate, he stepped on the back of the giant guard, as he tried to get up. The guard grunted as Rack stepped on his back and drove him back to the ground.

Rack stopped outside the gate and looked around for Shay and the others.

".Vlto(")Stop(Б a man shouted just behind Rack. Rack turned and saw two men about ten feet away, pointing guns right at him.

Rack raised his hands in the air, "V little help here, guys."

"Standby, 2eus is here." NicholasHs voice came over RackOs earpiece.

The two men slowly approached Rack, pointing their handguns at him.

They stopped about si feet from Rack. They both motioned for him to get down on the ground. "Now would be a good time." Rack whispered into his earpiece.

"Eange, seven hundred MftyZthree yards. 'ind is right to left at about Mve miles per hour. 7ourteen degrees down angle." Eed whispered as he looked through the range Mnder.

Nicholas made slight adjustments to his scope. "0ot it." Nicholas replied.

"Send it." Eed said.

Nicholas slowly took the slack out of the trigger. The riWe kicked, sending the riWe round towards the intended target. Pven though Nicholas was Mring a suppressed riWe, there was still a slight, noticeable pop sound. Rust a fraction of a second after the bullet left the barrel, it struck one of the men in the upper right shoulder. The man fell to the ground, and the other man looked down at him in shock. V second later, another bullet struck the other man, and he also fell to the ground.

Rack turned and fro5e as he saw a large truck rapidly approaching him. The truck came to a sliding stop just three feet away.

"0et in(" Stewart yelled from the back seat and pushed the door open.

"Ye a better get a move on Rack." Eed said, "ThereOs a group of angry lads heading ye way."

Rack looked back at the gate and saw about Mve men coming through it. Ke grabbed the open door and climbed in, closing the door behind him.

N icholas Mred another shot, this time striking a tree near the men advancZ ing toward Rack and the others. Vs soon as bark Wew from the tree, all the men took cover behind nearby vehicles.

Several people pointed towards the tree line up on the hill. "Sniper(" SomeZ one yelled, as shouts and screams were heard throughout the property.

Nasir stepped through the open gate, just as the truck sped past the crowd and towards the road. Ke saw Katie sitting in the front passenger seat as the truck passed. Gure rage Wowed through his entire body. Several of PdmundoOs men ran toward their vehicles to pursue the Weeing truck.

Pdmundo, Kunter, Pdgardo, and several others came running up ne t to Nasir as the truck e ited the property and sped down the road.

Three vehicles sped past the group as they pursued the Weeing truck. "'e will catch them, and my men will kill them all." Pdmundo proclaimed.

"No(" Nasir said sharply, "D donOt want any harm to happen to 7ariha." Nasir said as he watched the three pursuing vehicles head towards the road.

"But Nasir." Pdmundo started, but was cut oF by Nasir.

Nasir looked at Pdmundo, "D want 7ariha brought to me, unharmed. D will deal with her myself."

"'hat about the ones who took her?" Pdmundo asked.

"Df you can, bring them to me, dead or alive, D donOt care. But no harm will be done to 7ariha. 'o D make myself clear?" Nasir said as he turned and walked back into the garden.

"D have alerted the local authorities." Pdgardo Santiago, the Luban VmbasZ sador, said.

"Cake sure they know that no harm will happen to 7ariha. 'o D make myself clear?" Nasir demanded.

Pdmundo walked up ne t to Nasir, "'hat about the sniper?" he asked.

"'o as you wish." Nasir replied.

NasirOs brother approached, with his arms spread wide to embrace him. "DOm sorry, brother, but D told you this would happen."

Nasir pushed his brother away, "D donOt want to hear anything out of you." Nasir said, proceeding over to one of the tables and taking a seat.

Kunter walked up to Pdmundo, "'hat are you going to do about the sniper?" Kunter asked, hoping to get as much information from him as he could.

"D will do what D do with all who trespass on my land without permission." Pdmundo replied.

"'hich is?" Kunter asked.

"Kunt them down and kill them." Pdmundo replied. Ke picked up his phone to call his head of security, but the phone didnOt work. Eay had successZ fully jammed all the cell phones in the area. "'amn it(" Pdmundo uttered. Ine of his staF members walked past, and Pdmundo grabbed him. "0otell Santiago to release the dogs." Pdmundo said and pushed the staF member away.

"'ogs?" Kunter asked.

"Yes, D have four of the best tracking dogs in all of Luba."Pdmundo said with pride in his voice. "That sniper will not get away."

"'hat do you plan on doing with the sniper when you catch him?" Kunter asked.

Pdmundo turned and faced Kunter, "Cy dogs are trained to kill their prey. There will not be much left of that sniper once they catch him." Pdmundo laughed.

Up on the hillside, Nicholas, Red, and Robert watched as Shay and the others sped away, with three vehicles in close pursuit behind them. "6etOs pack up and get the hell out of here." Eobert said as he started gathering up some of the equipment.

Vbout a thousand yards away, they heard the barking of dogs that sounded like they were heading their way.

"7orget the equipment, it will only slow us down." Nicholas said as he looked towards the sound of the approaching dogs. "Those dogs are coming for us, we need to get the hell out of here("

Eobert looked at Nicholas and then at Eed, "'hat about the guns?" Eobert asked.

"Keep ye handgun." Eed said. "The other stuF will only slow you down."

"Eay, this is 2eus. 'eOre bugging out. 'eOve got guards and dogs tracking us. 'eOre heading for the primary e traction point." Nicholas urgently said over his mic.

"Negative, 2eus, primary e traction is a noZgo. 'eOve got cops and local military swarming all over this place. The airfield is locked down to all traffic." Kevin replied over his mic.

Nicholas looked at the others, "Lopy that." Nicholas replied. "IK, guys, secondary e traction, weOre hooMng it to the coast." Nicholas told the others.

"Vye, weOll need to split up." Eed suggested.

"0ood idea. 'ivide and conquer." Eobert said.

"Try to avoid law enforcement the best you can." Nicholas said, "Unless you want to spend the rest of your life in a Luban prison cell."

"Good luck, guys, see you in the good old U.S.A. in a couple of days." Robert said as the three parted and headed in diFerent directions.

Rack lay on the Woor of the truck. The truck was bouncing and weaving as it Wped down the road. Rack looked up and saw Stewart looking down at him. Stewart reached down to help Rack up into the seat ne t to him. "'id we all get out safe?" Rack asked, looking out the rear window at the three vehicles pursuing them.

"Yes, weOre all out, including Katie." Stewart replied.

"0 ood!" Jack replied. "Wait a second.... Who's driving?" Jack asked as he looked around.

"Ce, who else?" Shay said as she looked back at Rack.

Rack leaned forward, "STIG TKP LVE(" Rack yelled as they were bouncing down the road, hitting every possible pothole on the road.

"Rack, we canOt stop. Those other vehicles are gaining on us fast." Stewart said as he looked back at the approaching vehicles.

Rack glanced at Stewart, "D donOt care. Stop the car." Rack repeated.

"Df those guys catch us, thereOs no telling what they might do to us." Katie said, totally confused about why Rack wanted to stop the vehicle.

"YouOve never ridden with Shay driving, have you?" Rack said, looking Mrst at Katie and then at Stewart. They both shook their heads.

"DOll take my chances with those guys back there." Rack said as he motioned with his head.

"Sit down, put your seatbelt on, and shut up." Shay said, looking up at Rack in the mirror.

The truck continued to speed down the country road, not slowing down at intersections and passing slower cars.

"Shay, let me drive." Rack demanded.

"No, and shut up. DOm trying to focus on the road." Shay shouted back at Rack.

"You can hardly see over the steering wheel, much less seethe road," Rack replied, sitting back in his seat and fumbling with the seatbelt.

"Rack, what is going on?" Jicky asked over the mic.

"ShayOs driving. SheOs going to get us all killed." Rack replied.

"Lalm down Rack, and let Shay drive." Jicky replied.

"Plus, we've got two.... No three vehicles chasing us." Jack replied to Vicky.

"6et Shay drive, you worry about those three vehicles.

"Rack, weOve lost contact with Nicholas, Eed, and Eobert." Jicky replied.

"'hat do you mean youOve lost contact?" Rack yelled into his mic at Jicky.

"Their last report said they were being pursued by a team of men and dogs. They dropped all their gear so they could travel faster." Jicky replied.

"Shit('hat about their cell phones? Lan Eay track them?"Rack asked.

"DtOs spotty at best. ThereOs no reliable reception where theyOre heading." Jicky replied.

"'hat about the Ret? Lan they make it there?" Rack asked, as Shay hit a bump and the four bounced around in their seats.

¿"Kevin said the airport is locked down and swarming with cops," Jicky replied. "Their best bet is to make it to the hotel and lay low for a couple of days until things cool oF." she said, with noticeable stress in her voice.

The three split up, and soon they were out of sight of each other. The thick brush and tropical forest provided them with some cover from anyone looking for them, e cept for the dogs.

The sounds of the pursuing dogs kept getting louder and louder as they approached. Ke stopped occasionally to get his bearings and to catch his breath. Ke estimated that the dogs were about two hundred yards behind him and were catching up fast. Ke turned and pushed on, tripping over roots and rocks as he battled to stay ahead of the men and the dogs.

Ke could hear the dogs and men running through the brush in close pursuit. Ke stopped again and looked around, but all he saw were trees in all directions.

Ke could see a clearing through the trees and a small farmhouse beyond that. Ke could make up some time if he could make it to the clearing. The farmhouse was about three hundred yards away. 'ith luck, he could make it. Ke pushed aside small trees and bushes, creating his own trail as he fought his way towards the clearing and possible safety.

Ke reached the clearing and paused a second to listen for the approaching men and dogs. Vll he heard was the wind blowing through the trees. Kave they given up their pursuit, he thought to himself. Vt Mrst, he cautiously started walking towards the farmhouse, looking in all directions. But no sign of the dogs or the men. Ke increased his stride towards the farmhouse and safety.

Ke heard the rustling sound of the leaves about a hundred feet away. Ke fro5e and turned towards the sound. Ke didnOt see anything. 'asit his imagination? 'as it a small animal or maybe a bird? The hair on the back of his neck stood up. Ke turned and started towards the farmhouse. Ke only took a couple of steps, and then he fro5e.

Between him and the farmhouse stood a massive Eottweiler just Mfty feet away. 'as that dog from the farmhouse, or was it one of the dogs pursuing him?

Ke heard a sound to his right and slowly turned his head. Inly to see another Eottweiler standing there, this one about thirty feet away. Ke looked back at the Mrst one and noticed it was now also about thirty feet away.

Ke heard the snarl to his left and turned to face a sleek and powerful 'oberZ man Ginscher inching its way closer to him. "Ya no tienes adénde huir.")You have nowhere to run now.Б came a voice from behind. Ke turned and saw four men standing at the edge of the woods.

Ke lifted his hands in surrender, knowing there was no way to escape. "You win." he said.

The four men just stood there looking at him. Ke glanced to his left and then to his right and noticed the dogs were now sitting, but not taking their eyes oF of him.

Ine of the men reached into his pocket and pulled out a whistle. Ke smiled and placed the whistle into his mouth and blew. The three dogs immediately started charging at full speed.

꒐ ith Shay behind the wheel, the 7ord Eaptor bounced down the rutted road. Rack and Stewart kept their eyes on the vehicles close behind them. "Gaved road ahead." Shay yelled, as all of a sudden, the truck stopped bouncing as it hit the pavement. Shay pressed down on the accelerator, kicking the5.2-liter Supercharged Shelby GT500-based V-8 engine into full power and increasing their speed, leaving the pursuing vehicles behind.

The truck was cruising at one hundred and twenty miles per hour. "Shay, you have a small group of houses about two miles ahead." Eay said over ShayOs earpiece.

"0otcha." Shay replied.

"You need to slow down." Eay warned.

"'hy?" Shay replied, not letting up oF the accelerator.

"ThereOs a sharp left just two miles ahead. YouOll never make it at that speed. Dƒou donOt make that turn, youOll Wy oF the road and down an embankment." Eay cautioned.

"Shay, DOve got an idea." Rack said.

"'hat?" Shay yelled back.

"D want the three cars behind us to get closer." Rack replied.

"'KVT('hy?" Shay said, not taking her eyes oF the road.

"Vbout a hundred yards from the turn, D want you to slowdown." Rack said, leaning forward between the two front seats.

"'hat are you going to do?" Shay asked, glancing up into the mirror to see Rack.

"Trust me." Rack replied as he sat back in his seat. "Stewart, hand me the weapons bag." he said, pointing at the bag at StewartOs feet.

Stewart grabbed the bag and placed it between him and Rack. Rack un5ipped the bag, reached in, and took out two smoke grenades. "Stewart, open the back window." Rack said, motioning towards the sliding glass in the back window.

"Ik, Rack, here we go, DOm slowing down now." Shay yelled as the truck started rapidly slowing down. This caused everyone to slide forward a little in their seats until their seatbelts stopped their forward motion.

Rack tossed the two smoke grenades into the back of the truckOs bed. Soon, smoke Mlled the air behind their truck, blinding the vehicles that had closed in behind. Shay turned sharply, barely making the sharp turn, and sliding sideways on the road.

Two of the vehicles that were behind them Wew oF the road and down the embankment. The third one slid to a stop, just short of going over the edge. Shay stomped on the accelerator and picked up speed, now reaching one hundred miles per hour.

"Shay, we just overheard on the radio that the Luban police have set up a roadblock ahead." Tony said, over her earpiece.

"Key Tony, long time no hear." Rack replied.

"'eOve been monitoring the local police, and they are waiting for you about Mʋ miles ahead." Tony said. "They have the roadblocked." he added.

"'onderful. 0ot any good news for us?" Rack asked.

"'e just heard over the police radio that a capture order is out on Katie. That no harm is to come to her." Tony said.

Rack looked at Katie, "'hat about us?" Rack asked.

"'ell, thereOs a kill order on you guys." Tony replied.

"Vnd on top of that, we still have that car following us from behind." Stewart said, looking back towards the pursuing vehicle.

"They are trying to bo us in." Shay replied.

"Tony, Eay, a little help here." Rack said into his mic.

¿"Vccording to the satellite map, no other roads e ist between you and the roadblock." Eay replied.

Rack pointed, "D can see a road to our left about three hundred yards." he said.

"D see it." Shay said, glancing to her left.

Katie raised in her seat and tried to look for the road, "ThatHs a cliF(ThereOs no way we can make it down there." she said, in a near panic.

"Lome on, Eay, talk to us." Rack yelled into his mic.

"Kold on. Bringing up a topographical map of the area." Eay replied.

"YouOre about one mile from the roadblock." Tony said.

"The car behind us is closing fast. 'eOve got to do something, like right now." Stewart yelled.

"Vhead, D think we can make it." Shay yelled out.

Rack looked through the front windshield where the ground rapidly sloped down from the road. "'hat are you talking about?" he replied.

Shay pointed at a narrow path oF to the right, "There(" Shay said, "Dt looks like it leads down to the road below.

"ThatOs a goat path(" Stewart yelled as he looked over ShayOs shoulder.

"The roadblock(" Katie yelled as she pointed ahead. Rust within sight sat about half a do5en police cars, blocking the road ahead. They could barely make out several people behind the cars, pointing guns in their direction.

Shay slammed on the brakes, and the truck slid sideways to a stop. "DOm going for it." Shay yelled.

Stewart leaned forward in his seat, "0oing for what?" he asked, not really wanting to know the answer.

Shay pointed, "The trail."

"P cuse me, but donOt we get a vote?" Rack asked, with an iety in his voice.

"Nope, hang on." Shay said as she eased the truck towards the embankment.

Vs Shay inched the truck oF the road and headed down the steep emZ bankment. Vs they started down the hill, the vehicle pursuing them came to a screeching halt, right where they had just gone down.

The truck with Katie and the Imega team rapidly started picking up speed. The truck and its occupants bounced viciously up and down and side to side. The truck became airborne several times as it bounced over ruts and washedZout areas of the steep hillside.

Shay did her best to steer the outZofZcontrol truck, as the careening truck chose its own way down the hill.

"Shay, if we live through this, DOm going to kill you myself(" Rack screamed out over the noise of the truck crashing down the hill.

The car in pursuit tried to follow them down the steep hill, only to lose control and roll over on its top.

The police at the roadblock jumped into their patrol cars and headed to where they saw the two vehicles veer oF the road and down the embankment. Vs soon as they arrived, the officers jumped out of their cars. They watched, in shocked surprise, as the truck reached the bottom of the hill and onto the road.

The truck came to a hard jolt as it hit the road and stopped. Shay looked over at Katie and then towards the back at Rack and Stewart, "Ds everyone ok?" Shay asked, concerned with everyoneOs condition.

"Shay(Rack(Vnybody(" Tony shouted over their earpieces. There was no response, "Lome on, guys, talk to me."

"D think weOre all ok." Rack replied, answering both Shay and Tony.

"That wasnOt a very smart move." Jicky said, noticeably upset.

"'eOre Mne, everybody. Now get us the hell out of here." Shay said to calm the concerns of the others.

There was silence for several seconds until Eay Mnally replied, "IK, guys, D donOt know what direction youOre pointed in or what condition your vehicle is in. But you need to head north for about Mfteen miles.

"D have no idea which way is north, south, up, or down at the moment." Shay replied.

"0o left at the bottom of the hill you just came down." Eay replied.

"That was no damn hill(Dt was a cliF(" Stewart replied, still trying to calm his nerves.

"'hat about the police at the roadblock?" Rack asked.

"TheyOre going to have to backtrack for about ten miles. You should be clear right now." Eay replied.

Shay checked the condition of the truck, and it looked to be drivable. The engine was still running, all four tires were still on and inWated. "'here will this road take us?" Shay asked.

"To the coast. DOm sending you the 0GS directions to the marina where the boat that Tony and the others arrived in is docked." Eay said.

"Kow are they going to get out?" Shay asked.

"'onOt worry about us. 'eOll lay low for a few days and Wyout on a commerZ cial Wight." Tony replied.

"Kave you heard anything from the others?" Rack asked.

"Kevin and 'ana are still stranded at Lienfuegos airport. 'eOve lost contact with Nicholas, Eed, and Eobert." Tony replied.

"Shay, you donOt have anyone chasing you right now, so drive slowly and try not to bring any attention to yourself. YouOve only got about Mfteen miles." Jicky said.¿

MAY DAY, MAY DAY

"They got away." Edgardo Santiago said as he placed his cellphone in his pocket.

"SON OF A BITCH!" Edmundo Lupe shouted. "They beat one of my people. Shot two others and wrecked three of my vehicles. No four, my precious truck.... It's ruined." Edmundo said as he paced the ?oor.

Nasir turned towards Edgardo, the Cuban Ambassador, "Is Fariha still, oké" Nasir asked, with slight concern in his voice.

"They made it past the police roadblock." Edgardo replied. "Last report is that they are headed towards CaibariWn," he added, with a noticeable irritation in his voice.

"1hat is in CaibariWné" Nasir asked.

"It's a small seaside town. Nothing is there but houses and marinas." Edgardo replied.

"That's how they plan on escaping." Nasir replied. "Can you send more police to intercept themé"

"They were all at the roadblock. It will take them twenty minutes, or more, for them to catch up to them." Edgardo replied.

Edmundo's phone rang, "Ges." Edmundo listened intently to the person on the other end. "jood. Leave him." he ended the call and returned the phone to his pocket. He walked over to where Nasir and Edgardo were standing. "jreat news my friends." Edmundo said as he approached them.

Nasir watched as Edmundo approached, "I could use some." Nasir replied.

Edmundo smiled, "The sniper. He has been captured." Edmundo said.

Hunter walked up qust as Edmundo was giving the news of the capture of the sniper. "The sniper was capturedé" Hunter asked, trying to remain calm on hearing the news.

"1onderful, bring him here. 1e must Mnd out who he is working for." Nasir replied.

"I'm sorry, that will not be possible." Edmundo replied.

"1hy is thaté 1e must 0uestion him." Nasir asked.

"-y dogs are trained not to take prisoners. I'm afraid that the sniper is dead. -auled to death by the dogs." Edmundo replied, somewhat pleased by the outcome.

Hunter's heart sank, "1hat do you mean, mauled to deathé" he asked, trying to keep his composure.

Nasir turned towards Hunter, "Gou sound displeased that the sniper is dead." Nasir said, looking at Hunter with a 0uestioning look on his face.

Hunter paused for a second without responding, "It's qust that we needed him alive so we can 0uestion him."

"-y men said there was evidence that he was not alone, perhaps two others were with him." Edmundo said. "They are currently getting reinforcements and going after the others. 1e will soon have them also."

"1hen they are captured, have your men bring them to me...alive." Nasir demanded.

"Vo we know the name of the man your dog capturedé" Hunter asked, wanting to know, but also not wanting to know, which one of his friends had been killed.

Edmundo looked at Hunter, "No. There was no identiMcation on the body."

"1here is the bodyé" Edgardo asked.

"It's in a Meld on Yecardo Esposito's property." Edmundo replied.

"Have someone send me the address. I'll have someone go and retrieve the body." Edgardo said.

"Leave it for the bu ards." Edmundo said sharply.

"No, I will have it taken to the local morgue. 1e will see who claims the body." Edgardo said. "Then we will detain that person and Mnd out who they are, and why they did what they did."

"1E 'NO1 1HG THEG VIV IT!" Shouted Nasir. "They wanted Fariha! And I want to know who's involved."

Edmundo turned towards Nasir, "1hen we catch them, we will gladly turn them over to you for 0uestioning. 1hen you are Mnished, you will turn them back over to me so I can properly deal with them."

"Jery well. If there is anything left to return." Nasir harshly replied.

A man walked up and whispered something into Edmundo's ear. "Jery well, I'll inform Nasir. Show the gentleman in." Edmundo replied to the man. The man nodded and walked away.

"Nasir, you have a late guest to the party." Edmundo said, "-y man is showing him in."

Hunter had walked over to the bar and ordered himself a drink while trying to Mgure out a way to get a message to Jicky, without blowing his cover.

Nasir looked towards the gate and saw the guest enter. Nasir motioned for the man to come. They talked brie?y before Nasir called over to Hunter to qoin them.

"Bill, come here, I want you to meet an associate of mine. He's from the States. Gou'll be working with him once you start your work there." Nasir said as Hunter walked over.

The man reached out to shake Hunter2s hand, "It's a pleasure to meet you. Nasir has told me a lot about you. -y name is Yoger Basiliano." he said, as he took Hunter2s hand.

It was everything Hunter could do to hold it together. First hearing about the death of one of the team members and friend. And now, meeting and working with the man who has been trying to track down and Mnd the Omega group.

Hunter smiled, "It's nice to meet you."U he said, with a slight hesitation in his voice.

Nasir stood between them, "Yoger is a valuable asset. He's one of your FBI very special agents." Nasir laughed.

"It appears I missed all the fun." Yoger said, looking around and seeing the table and food all over the ground.

"It seems that Fariha has been taken." Nasir replied in a matterzofzfact tone.

"By whoé" Yoger asked.

Nasir put his right hand on Yoger's shoulder, "I do not know. But with your help, we will Mnd out."

Yoger nodded and turned towards Nasir, "I will be more than happy to help and bring the resources of the FBI to your aid."

"First, we must check out the video and get pictures of everyone involved." Yoger said, pointing at one of the video cameras mounted on the side of the house.

Edmundo walked up as the three talked, "jood evening. -y name is Edz mundo, and welcome to my humble casa." Edmundo said, with a big smile.

"Thank you. I need access to your surveillance recordings." Yoger said.

"1hat foré" Edmundo asked. "And who are youé" he added, with concern.

"He works for me." Nasir replied, "He's with the American FBI."

Edmundo looked surprised, "Gou have American FBI agents on your payz rollé"

Nasir smiled, "Ges. They come in handy sometimes."

Edmundo looked down and shook his head, "Pnfortunately, my friend, the cameras went out qust before the party started."

"Von't you Mnd that a little oddé" Yoger asked.

Edmundo shrugged his shoulders, "It happens."

The Cuban ambassador approached, "-y men are catching up to the basz tards, they should be in contact in ten minutes."

"-y orders still stand. No harm had better come to Fariha. Vo I make myself clearé" Nasir said in a demanding voice.

"-y men understand and will do everything possible to return her to you safely." Edgardo replied.

"And when we capture them. 1hat of the ones who took heré"Edgardo asked, looking at Nasir.

Nasir thought brie?y, "E3ecute them all, and bring me Fariha. I will deal with her myself."

Hunter stood by, not saying a word, listening to the conversation. He thought about losing nearly the entire Omega team in one day. The thought sent cold chills up his spine.

A loud crash came from near the house. Everyone looked on as Gasser stumz bled and crashed into tables and chairs. "Stop them, they are taking Fariha!" he yelled, dropping to the ground. He fought to stand and stumbled again as he approached Nasir. Once he reached Nasir, he fell to both knees, "Nasir, you must stop them, they are taking Fariha!"

Nasir looked down at Gasser as he knelt before him, "Gou incompetent fool!" Nasir shouted. "They have already taken her and have gone." Nasir said and then spat on Gasser.

"4lease, Nasir, it was not my fault, they drugged me."Gasser pleaded.

Nasir looked away, "Gasser, you have failed me for the last time." Nasir looked at Hunter, "Bill, remove this... this incompetent fool from my sight."

Hunter reached down, grabbed Gasser under his arm, and helped him to his feet, "1hat do you want me to do with himé" Hunter asked.

"'ill him and put his body with the others when they are captured." Nasir ordered.

Surprised, Hunter asked, "Gou want me to kill himé"

"Vid I not make myself clearé" Nasir glared at Hunter. "He has failed me for the last time. The ne3t time I hear his name uttered, it better be that he is dead." Nasir said.

"Ges, sir." Hunter replied and pulled Gasser along as they walked towards the house. "I'm going to lock you in your room until I Mgure out what to do with you." Hunter said as he pushed Gasser along towards the main house.

"Rack, I've ordered 'evin and Vana to leave as soon as they can get clearz nce." Jicky said. "I told them to ?y into -iami and wait."

"jood idea. Any word from Yed and the othersé" Rack asked, hoping that J icky could make contact with one of them.

"Nothing yet." Jicky replied, not wanting to tell them what they had interz cepted over the radio.

"Let us know as soon as you hear from them." Rack said.

"1ill do." Jicky said.

"Rack. Yay here. I've got you about two miles from the marina. Gou need to step on it. The police from the roadblock are closing fast. They qust radioed that they are about Mve miles away." Yay hurriedly said.

Rack leaned forward towards Shay, "Gou heard the man, step on it."

Shay ?oored the accelerator without being told twice, and they raced towards the marina. "Stewart, you need to help me with these signs." Shay yelled, "I can't make out what any of them say."

Stewart leaned forward and looked between the two front seats, trying to Mnd a sign pointing them to the marina.

Yay was still tracking them via j4S, "It should be right upon your right." Yay said.

Stewart pointed towards a sign ahead, "Ges, there's the sign, CaibariWn -az rina." Stewart said. "Turn ahead."

Shay turned sharply into the marina, s0uealing the tires and sliding the truck slightly sideways as they entered the entrance.

"Tony, where did you park the boaté" Rack yelled into his mic.

Tony had been monitoring the conversation and tracking their progress, "It should be up and to your left. It's a blue and white deepzsea Msher."

"juy's, qust heard over the radio that the cops are about half a mile from the marina. Gou better hurry and get the hell out of there." Yay said over their earpieces.

'atie pointed, "There's a left." she said, as they approached a sharp left turn.

Shay turned the wheel, and the truck turned sharply left, sliding on the wet pavement.

"NO!" Stewart yelled, "That's the boat..." he was interrupted by a sudden deceleration that threw them forwards. later covered the truck a sit came to an abrupt halt, "boat ramp." he Mnished saying.

"1ay to go Shay." Rack said as water started pouring into the truck.

"1hat happenedé" Jicky asked, sounding concerned.

"Gou know, Shay, she thought she could drive back to Florida." Rack replied, undoing his seat belt and checking on 'atie, "Is everyone oké" he asked.

Stewart unbuckled his seatbelt, "I got a busted lip when my face hit the back seat. Other than that, I'm good."

"jood here." Shay replied.

'atie was trying to open her door, "I'm ok, I think." she said, in a panic.

Rack forced his door open, "Let's get out of here."

They could all e3it the sinking truck through Rack2s door and started to wade towards dry land. As they almost got to shore, "There's the boat." Rack said, hurrying his pace towards the boat.

Rust then, they heard a voice out in the water, "Necesitas ayudaé" 6Vo you need helpé7 the voice came from a boat pulling up.

Everyone stopped and turned towards the voice. E3pecting to be facing guns pointed at them by the local police.

"Si." Stewart replied and started wading over towards the boat. The others saw what he was doing and followed.

The boat was a black over grey, brand new (8 Nighthawk, atopzofzthezline Cigarettezstyle boat. It measured fortyzone feet in length, powered by four ()K hp -ercury racing engines, and had a top speed of Dx mph.

The four of them climbed aboard the boat, "jracias." Stewart said, as Rack and the others looked around at the beautiful boat. The man began 0uestioning Stewart about what had happened. After Stewart e3plained to the man that Shay was learning to drive, they were trying to get to her father's boat. Shay walked over ne3t to the man and pushed him over the side of his boat.

"1hy did you do thaté" Stewart yelled.

"1e need his boat." Shay replied. "1e couldn't outrun a rowboat in that boat Tony wanted us to escape in. At least in this, we'll have a chance." she said, pointing over towards the boat they were supposed to have taken.

Shay turned, grabbed the boat2s steering wheel, and looked down, trying to Mnd the gas pedal.

Rack placed his hand on the seat behind Shay, "Hold on, girl, you're not about to drive this thing."

Shay looked up at him, "And why noté"

"Have you ever driven a boat beforeé" Rack asked.

"1ell, no, but it can't be that hard." she replied, not wanting to give up and let Rack drive.

"juys." 'atie said. "juys!" she said again, trying to get thei   r attention.

"1haté" Rack said as he turned and looked at 'atie.

She pointed towards the boat ramp. There stood the boat's owner, standing ne3t to four car loads of police, all pointing their guns at them.

"jot to go." Rack yelled, turned the wheel towards open water, and pushed the throttle almost all the way forward. The boat accelerated suddenly, causing Stewart and 'atie to fall backwards onto the boat2s deck.

"-ove!" Rack yelled over the scream of the four engines. Rack wedged his way into the seat and took control of the boat. They hit áK -4H coming out of the marina, causing a large wake. The wake slammed into several other boats, which were tied up to the dock, and caused them to bang violently against the pier and each other.

"Hold on." Rack yelled as he pushed the throttle all the way forward. The Cigarette boat rocketed across the water and soon reached its top speed as it headed into open water.

"1hat do you mean they got awayé" Edgardo Santiago, the Cuban ambassador, yelled. This got the attention of Nasir, Hunter, and Edmundo. Temporary relief Mlled Hunter as he heard the news. He walked over towards Nasir and the others to see what he could Mnd out.

"E3cuse me -r. Lupe." Yoger said, "I qust checked your camera system, and it looks like someone had temporarily qammed them. They are all working Mne now." he said, looking at Edmundo and then at Nasir.

"And so were the cell phones." Edgardo replied.

Yoger turned his attention to Edmundo, "-ight I ask if you had a photogz rapher here today, to take pictures of the festivitiesé"

"1hy yes." Edmundo replied, not sure why he had asked.

"-ay I see the picturesé" Yoger asked, looking a little e3cited, "The phoz tographer may have gotten a picture of the ones involved intaking Fariha." he looked around to see if he could spot the photographer.

Edmundo motioned for one of his assistants to come over to him. Once the assistant got near, Edmundo told him to Mnd the 4hotographer and bring him to Yoger. The assistant turned and headed o¿ to Mnd the photographer for Edmundo.

Edmundo smiled and looked at Yoger, "Gou will have your answer soon." Edmundo said.

Nasir stood there fuming, as the thought of them getting away made him even angrier. He looked at Edgardo, "1hat are you going to do about this nowé" Nasir demanded.

The Cuban ambassador was not accustomed to being talked to this way. He looked at Nasir and put his hand up. "I'm doing everything I can. I'm going to make a couple of calls. I've got some favors that I can call in." Edgardo said, obviously not pleased with the entire situation.

"Something had better happen 0uickly, Nasir demanded. If they make it to the P.S. mainland, I may never get her back." The Cuban ambassador walked away fuming at the way he had been spoken to.

Yoger had walked up behind Nasir, "Sir, I think we're in luck." as he held the digital camera up, and turned it so that Nasir could see the picture. "Is this one of the people that took Farihaé"

"Ges, yes!" Nasir replied as he looked at a picture of Rack standing behind the serving table.

"How about this oneé" Yoger pulled up a picture of Shay as she led 'atie towards the garden gate.

"Ges, her too." Nasir replied.

"Here's a better picture of her." Yoger now had a picture of Shay working behind her serving station.

"Jery good!" Nasir said, now more e3cited that they now have pictures of two of the people responsible for taking Fariha. "Can you identify themé" Nasir asked.

"In time, I think I can. I'll have to run them through the FBI database." Yoger said.

The ambassador walked about thirty feet away, out of earshot of the others. Yeaching into his pocket, he pulled out his cell phone and scrolled through his contacts until he found the one he was looking for. He pressed the send button, and the phone on the other end started ringing.

1ithin three rings, someone picked up. "Fuer a de Vefensa AWrea de Cuba, Capit"n -artóne , Qen 0uW puedo ayudarleé" 6Cuban Air Vefense Force, Capitán Martinez how may I help you?) "Este es el Embajador Edgardo Santiago. Permítame hablar con el General de División Ruiz". (This is Ambassador Edgardo Santiago. Let me speak to jeneral de Vivision Yui .7. Pn momento, por favor. 6One moment, please.7 came the reply from Captain -artine .

After several seconds, jeneral de Vivision Yui came on the line. "Edgardo, how are youé 1hat an honor to hear from you, my friend." the general said, switching to English.

"I need your help." Edgardo said.

"But of course. 1hat can I do for youé" the general asked.

"I need a boat stopped. It qust left CaibariWn -arina about Mfteen minutes ago, heading for the P.S. I need it stopped." Edgardo said with a sense of urgency in his voice.

"I will see what I can do." jeneral Yui replied.

"Thank you." Edgardo said and started to disconnect the call.

"Rust one thing. 1hen you say stopped, please clarify what you mean." jeneral Yui said.

There was silence at the other end, as Edgardo pondered his ne3t reply. "If you can stop them and turn them back to CaibariWn -arina. I want no harm to the occupants of the boat." Edgardo said.

"And if they refuseé" jeneral Yui asked with a tone of interest in his voice.

Edgardo thought for a second about how Nasir had spoken to him, "If they refuse to stop and return, then sink the boat and make sure there are no survivors." he replied, "Am I clearé" he added.

"Ges sir, consider it done." jeneral Yui said, I'll make a phone call and get back to you as soon as I Mnd out something."

"Jery good. Thank you, my friend." Edgardo said and ended the call. He turned and walked back over to Nasir and the others. They were all looking over the pictures that Yoger had brought them. They all went silent when he approached the group, as Nasir turned towards him.

"1ellé" Nasir asked in a sharp tone.

Edgardo smiled, "Consider the matter handled. They should be in custody within the ne3t hour and a half."

A smile came across Nasir's face, "Thank you." he said, giving Edgardo a slight nod.

"I contacted a friend in the Cuban Air Vefense. He is going to have them intercepted and brought back to the marina.

"-aybe I won't have to run these pictures through our FBI database after all." Yoger said.

"Let's hope not." Edmundo said and lifted his drink in a toast.

As soon as Hunter heard the news, he knew what it meant. He looked around and saw Charles sitting near the bar. Hunter made his way over to him and pulled up a chair ne3t to him.

"Bill, how goes the hunté" Charles asked.

"Vepends on whose side you're on." Hunter said, still very concerned for his friends.

"How may I be of serviceé" Charles asked.

Rack, Shay, Stewart, and 'atie were speeding as fast as possible in the getaway boat they "borrowed" from a Cuban marina. Rust a mile from international waters, Stewart made his way to Jack, "I think we're being followed." Stewart said, looking back and pointing.

Rack turned and looked at Stewart, "1hat are you talking abouté"

Shay, standing close to them, looked in the direction Stewart was pointing. She saw two small dots in the sky, about two hundred feet o¿ the water. Two dots that were getting bigger by the second. "Rack, I think we have a problem."

Two Yussian 'Az)K 1erewolf attack helicopters came within view. They were ?ying straight towards them on an intercept course. Once the Yussian attack helicopters came within three hundred yards, one of them Mred several warning shots across the bow of the boat.U

"1hat the HELL!" Rack shouted. "Are they really shooting at usé" he said in a terriMd voice.

"Looks like it." Stewart replied, looking at the two helicopters closing in on them on both sides.

'atie made her way from the front of the boat to where the others were standing. "1hat are we going to doé 1e cannot outrun them." 'atie said in a panic.

Rack looked around and found the boat's radio. He picked up the microz phone, "MAY DAY, MAY DAY!" Jack called over the radio. "We are being fired at by two Russian helicopters! MAY DAY!".

"Captain to the bridge." Came the call over the loudspeaker.

After a few seconds, Captain 1illiam jregory entered the bridge, "Captain on deck." Came the call from one of the Petty Officers, "What do you have?" the captain asked.

"Sir, we're receiving a -ay Vay call." the Senior Chief said, turning towards the captain. "They say they're being shot at by two Yussian helicopters." The Senior Chief said.

"What the hell?" Gregory said.

After Rack made several -ay Vay calls, a reply came back over the speaker, "This is Captain 1illiam jregory on the PS Coast juard Hamilton. Yepeat your transmission."

Jack spoke into the microphone again, "MAY DAY, MAYDAY! We are being fired at by two Russian helicopters! MAYDAY!".

The captain looks over at his radar person. "Vo you have anything on radaré"

"I have two, repeat two aircraft heading threezMvez ero degrees, speed onezMvezsi3 knots, Sir."

"Anything on the vessel making the -ay Vay callé" the captain asked.

"Negative. The two aircraft qust passed into international waters, Captain."

"This is the PS Coast juard Cutter Hamilton, calling the watercraft in distress, give us your location and registration." the captain said.

"Hell, I don't know what direction we're heading.... North towards the Pnited States, I hope!" Rack replied. "Gou can call us the PSSS crewed, if you don't help." Rack screamed into the radio.

"Copy that. -ake your heading ThreezMvez ero degrees. 1e should be in your vicinity in xK minutes." the captain replied.

"1e'll be Msh food by then. Gou think you can hurry it up someé" Rack pleaded.

The captain turned towards his radio operator, "Contact Night Hawk." the captain said. Night Hawk was a Boeing Ez5 Sentry A1ACS aircraft, commonly known as Airborne 1arning and Control System. This aircraft served to proz vide detailed information on enemy units and the battle situation. It was the eye in the sky for Allied troops. They identiMed the enemy troops, guided allied resources to their location, and directed attacks.

"This is Captain jregory of the PS Coast juard Cutter Hamilton. 1e are receiving a distress call for a watercraft out of Cuba. They are reporting that they are under attack by two Yussian helicopters." the captain said, relaying the information to the A1ACS ?ight crew.

"Ges, Sir, we are picking up two airborne aircraft that appear to be engaging a small fastzmoving vessel." the reply came back from the A1ACS crew. "1e've identiMed the two airborne craft as Yussian 'Az)K attack helicopters."

"Thank you." Captain jregory replied, "Vo we have any aircraft in this sectoré"

"That's affirmative." came the reply.

Captain jregory turned toward the helmsman, "All ahead ?ank." the capz tain ordered to the helmsman. He then turned toward the Chief and ordered, "Chief, sound general 0uarters." he said, and instantly alarms started sounding over the ship and the Chief announced over the intercom, "General Quarters, General Quarters, man your battle stations, this is not a drill. Repeat this is not a drill." echoed throughout the ship.

The crew all stopped what they were doing and headed towards their assigned battle stations. 1ithin seconds, the ship was ready for whatever lay ahead of them. The only 0uestion was, will they make it on timeé

"Night Hawk calling juardian Angel, how do you copyé" the radio operator said.

"Loud and clear, Night Hawk, do you have traffic for us?" came the reply.

"That is affirmative, Night Hawk, we have two Russian KA-50attack helicopters attacking a fastzrunning watercraft out of Cuba. The watercraft is identiMed as a PSzregistered vessel." the A1ACS operator said.

"Night Hawk, we copy." he replied. "Send us the coordinates." The juardian Angel commander re0uested.

"Copy juardian Angel, your heading is One Seven One, range Two Eight Five -iles. Gour lane is clear." the Night Hawk controller replied, giving the juardian Angel pilot the direction and distance to where Rack and the others were Mghting to survive.

"I copy, a heading of One Seven One, range Two Eight Five -iles." the juardian Angel commander replied, verifying the direction and distance.

"That's affirmative." the Night Hawk controller said.

-ako Three and Four, break right and approach from the 1est. -ako Two, follow me down to the deck. 1e're going to see how close we can bu those two Yussians." The commander of juardian Angel instructed the other three.

-ako One and Two dropped to qust two hundred feet above the water and pushed their Fz8á Mghter qets past nine hundred and twenty -4H, hitting -ach one point two within seconds. -ako Three and Four stayed at Mve thousand feet and about ten miles to the right of -ako One and Two. They both matched their airspeed to -ako One and Two, staying ten miles right of their target.

The -ako commander switched radio fre0uencies to the one that Rack had been calling his -ay Vay distress call on, "juardian Angel calling PS vessel in distress, do you copyé"

Rack looked down at the radio, not knowing what to do.

"This is Lieutenant Re¿erson of the D5rd Fighter S0uadron, calling the Pnitz ed Stateszregistered vessel that is under attack. Vo you copyé" Re¿erson said.

"Geah, what's upé This is the PSS Screwed. 1e need a little help, please." Rack yelled over the radio as he igz agged the boat, trying to keep from being shot by the approaching helicopters.

"This is Lieutenant Re¿erson of the Pnited States Air National juard Mghter wing. I need you to listen carefully." Lieutenant Re¿erson said.

Rack switched the radio over to the speaker so that everyone could hear. "I'm all ears, I hope you2ve got a plan to get us out of this messé" Rack replied with some urgency in his voice.

"I need you to turn your boat around one hundred and eighty degrees. And give it full throttle." Re¿erson said.

Rack looked over at Shay, "VO 1HATé" Rack shouted into the microphone. 'atie and Stewart were watching the two Yussian helicopters behind them. 1hen they heard what Re¿erson had said, they both turned and looked at Rack.

"1hen I say e3ecute, turn your boat around one hundred and eighty degrees. And then give it full throttle." Re¿erson repeated.

"Isn't that heading right back towards Cubaé" Rack shouted.

"Ges, but it will cause the two helicopters to slow and swing around. That will put some distance between you and them. They will have to regroup behind you." Re¿erson said.

"And then whaté" Rack asked.

"1hen I say now, I want everyone to cover their ears." Re¿erson said.

"If you say so." Rack replied, "I hope you know what you're doing."

"Trust me." Re¿erson replied, *I hope so too.* he said to himself. "By the way, what's your nameé" he asked.

"Fish food if you don't hurry up, but you can call me Rack." Rack replied.

"Hold on, Rack, we'll be there real soon."

"1here are youé" Rack asked as he and the others looked around.

"1e're about one hundred and twenty miles from you." Re¿erson replied.

"1haté How long is it going to take for you to get hereé" Rack asked, looking at the others.

"1e should be there in about eight minutes." Re¿erson replied.

"How fast are you guys goingé" Rack asked, somewhat shocked.

"Let's qust say we've got the pedal to the metal." Re¿erson replied.

Stewart glanced back at the two helicopters and back at Rack, "They're travz eling roughly nine hundred miles an hour. jive or take." Stewart said.

"Gou're the boss." Rack said to Re¿erson.

After a few minutes, Re¿erson returned over the radio, "1eare approaching at your one o'clock, in MftyzMve seconds." Re¿erson said.

Rack and the others scanned the hori on for the approaching Mghter qets. 'atie pointed, "There they are." They could barely make out two tiny dots heading towards them.

"HOLV ON!" Rack yelled to the others.

"O'... On three, I need you to e3ecute. One...Two... Three e3ecute, e3ecute. e3ecute!" Re¿erson said.

As soon as he said three, Rack turned the boat hard to the right, causing Shay and the others to slide suddenly to the left, as the boat rapidly turned and headed in the opposite direction. The sudden turn caused the two Yussian helicopters to ?y right over them and come to a standstill. Once they Mgured out what was going on, the two helicopters slowly turned, and their pursuit was on again.

Rack and the others were now several hundred yards ahead of the two hez licopters, which were now trying to catch up to their prey. Their boat hit its ma3imum speed of ninetyztwo miles per hour again.

"-ako Two, I have the two tangos at ten miles and closing. Tango one on the right is appro3imately Mfty feet above the water, and Tango two on the left is appro3imately eighty. Their current speed is ten miles per hour and increasing." -ako One said, relaying the information to his wingman.

"Copy that." -ako Two replied.

"-aintain current speed. -ake altitude one hundred twentyzMve feet above the deck. As soon as we cross over the top of them, you pull hard up and roll to the right. I'll do the same to the left." Re¿erson said.

"Copy that." -ako Two replied.

-ako Three and Four held at Mve thousand feet and slowed their air speed to subsonic.

"Rack, NO1!" Re¿erson said over the radio. Then Re¿erson started the countdown for his wingman, "Contact in three... two...one." as soon as Re¿erz son said one, the two Fz8á Mghter qets crossed over the top of the two Yussian helicopters. As soon as they did, they both pulled back on their controls and shot straight up into the sky.

The two Yussian pilots saw the two Fz8ás as they crossed qust above their helicopters. For a split second, they were both distracted. And then the sonic boom and shock wave hit the two Yussian helicopters. This caused them both to spin out of control temporarily. One helicopter hit the water and sank a few feet until the pilot regained control.

The other helicopter dipped down, almost crashing into the water as well. It barely missed the other helicopter as it ?ew over it.

"This is Lieutenant Re¿erson of the Pnited States Air National juard Mghter wing, out of Naval Air Station 'ey 1est, Florida. Calling the two Yussian 'Az)K attack choppers Mring on a Pnited Stateszregistered vessel in internaz tional waters." Re¿erson said as the two Fz8ás climbed to two thousand feet in a matter of seconds.

"No answer from the Yussians, Sir." Lieutenant Re¿erson's wingman, -ako Two, replied.

The Yussian helicopter, which had gone into the water, slowly lifted out of the water and turned towards the speeding boat in an attempt to qoin the other helicopter in its pursuit.

"Sir, we are within Mring range, and I have a lock." -ako Three said as a loud tone sounded inside -ako Three's Fz8á's cockpit. This indicated that the qets2 AI-zD Sidewinder missiles were locked on both helicopters.

"This is Lieutenant Re¿erson calling the two attacking helicopters, we have missiles locked on you. 1ould you like to engageé" Re¿erson asked over the radio.

The two Yussian attack choppers peeled o¿ away from Rack and the others, setting a course back into the closest Cuban airspace.U

"I didn2t think so." Yeplied Lieutenant Re¿erson. "-ako Oneto -ako Three and Four. -ake sure our two Yussian friends make it back into Cuban waters safely."

"Yoger that." replied the pilot of -ako Three.

Re¿erson switched his radio back to the distress channel that Rack was on, "This is Lieutenant Re¿erson calling the PSS Screwed." Re¿erson said.

"1e copy." Rack replied over the cheers of the others.

"-ake your heading ThreezMvez ero degrees, you should be within range of the PS Coast juard Cutter Hamilton in appro3imately ten minutes." Re¿erson said.

Rack and the others looked up as two Fz8á Mghter qets circled overhead, "Thank you so very much." Rack replied.

"Gou're welcome." Re¿erson said as he and -ako Two turned and headed towards Homestead Air Yeserve Base.

"Hey, can we buy you and your guys a beer when we get backé" Rack asked.

"That's not necessary. jlad we could be of assistance." Re¿erson replied as the two qets formed up and did a lowzlevel ?yover about two hundred feet above Rack and the others in the boat.

Shay looked towards the back of the boat, as the two qets headed o¿ out of sight, "Rack, we have a problem." she said, with a bit of concern in her voice.

Rack looked over at Shay, "1hat now, a Yussian submarineé" Rack replied.

"No, but we'll soon be one, we're taking on water." she said.

Stewart worked his way over to the left side of the boat. He leaned over and saw two large holes, big enough to put your Mst through. "Rack! 1e've got two holes over here on the side, qust above the water line. I'm sure they passed through and went out the bottom." he yelled as he made his way back over to Rack.

'atie yelled in a panicked voice, "1hat are we going to do nowé"

"Everyone, get a life qacket on, I'm going to make it as far as we can." Rack yelled as he reached for the microphone. "-ay Vay, -ay Vay, this is PSS Screwed. 1e're taking on water fast. I don't know how much longer we can stay a?oat."

"This is Captain jregory on the PS Coast juard Hamilton. -aintain your current course. 1e will be rende vousing with you in 8K minutes." jregory said.

Captain Gregory turned to his First Officer, "Launch the rescue helicopter." he ordered, and turned as he raised his binoculars and started scanning the surface for the boat.

The ship's alarms started sounding as the First Officer ordered the rescue crew and the rescue helicopter into the air. It only took three minutes for the crew to get the -Hzá) Volphin helicopter o¿ the deck of the Coast juard ship and heading toward Rack and the others. Flying at 89x.)knots or x8K mph, it didn't take long for the helicopter to be hovering over the sinking boat.

The boat that Rack, Shay, Stewart, and 'atie were in had already stopped and was almost underwater when the helicopter arrived. Two rescue swimmers qumped from the hovering helicopter and assisted the four, one at a time, into the rescue harness and up into the helicopter. 1ithin Mfteen minutes of arriving, they had all four on board the helicopter and were heading back to the Hamilz ton.

Once aboard, the captain told the ship's medic to check them all out. He wanted to make sure none of them had any serious inquries. Once that was completed, then let him know their status, and then send Rack to his 0uarters.

jregory was sitting at his desk, reviewing the ship's status reports, when there was a knock at his door, "Enter." Captain jregory said.

The door opened slightly, "Gou wanted to see meé" Rack asked as he stuck his head through the opening.

"Ges, enter." he said as he stood and motioned for Rack to enter.

Rackapproached his desk as he looked around the small cabin office. "I want to thank you for saving us. I didn't think we were going to make it." Rack said.

"1e were qust doing our qob." jregory replied. "Rack," jregory started, as he walked around his desk and stood in front of Rack, "Gou, sir, have some powerful connections. I don't know who you and your friends are. I was told by my boss to give you whatever you want and not to ask any 0uestions." jregory took a step closer towards Rack, "I don't like not knowing the people on my ship. And especially why they were being pursued by two Yussian 'Az)K attack helicopters. I've been told to get you stateside as soon as possible. jo gather your friends, and the four of you will be escorted to the deck. Gou and your friends will be ?own to Homestead Air Force Base. There you'll have transportation home. 1herever that is." jregory turned and walked over behind his desk, "Gou are dismissed. Now gather your friends and get o¿ my ship."

"Ges sir." Rack turned and headed towards the door.

"Oh, and I hope whatever you were up to, you were successful. I'm sure there's going to be maqor blowback from the Cubans. I hope it was worth it." jregory said as Rack turned to close the door.

"Ges, I think it was." Rack smiled and closed the door. TwentyzMve minutes later, Rack, Shay, Stewart, and 'atie were all in the Hamilton's -Hzá) Volphin helicopter, heading to Homestead Air Force Base. Once they landed, Rack told them he was going to Mnd a phone, since they all lost theirs somewhere during the escape, and call a ta3i for them. They would head to -iami International Airport and catch a ?ight home.

They hadn't walked Mfty feet from the -Hzá) when a military vehicle pulled up ne3t to them. The rear passenger side tinted window rolled down. "Need a rideé" came a voice from inside the vehicle. Rack and the others stopped and peered into the window.

"'evin!" Shay yelled, "1hat in the hell are you doing hereé"

"1ell, I thought you might need a ride home, so I ?ew over to pick you up." 'evin replied.

"How did you get permission to land at this military baseé" Rack asked, looking around at all the military aircraft.

"Our friend the Sandman. Jicky told me that he made a few calls, and here we are." 'evin replied, shaking Rack2s hand, "Gou guys get in, our qet is fueled and ready." 'evin slid over in the seat so that Shay, Stewart, and 'atie could get in, while Rack got in the front passenger seat.

The driver, an Air Force Airman, pulled o¿ and headed towards the Omega qet, which was parked on the other side of a row of hangars. No one talked on the way to the qet, they didn't want the Airman to know what had happened and what they had been up to.

Once they were dropped o¿ and their ride drove away, "Any word from the othersé 1e all lost our cell phones, and I've not had a chance to contact Jicky." Rack asked 'evin as soon as the vehicle was within a short distance.

"Nothing. Rim and Tony are staying behind and waiting for Nicholas, Yed, and Robert to arrive." Kevin said, "They had to get away as fast as they could. The last thing we heard was that some of Edmundo Lupe's guards and dogs were tracking them." 'evin said as he and Rack walked to catch up with the others.

"1here's Vanaé" Rack asked, looking ahead at 'atie and the others as they approached the qet.

"She's inside, waiting for 'atie." 'evin said.

Rack alled out, "Shay, Stewart, you two come over here fora second."

The three turned towards Rack, "'atie, you go ahead and get in the qet, we'll be in shortly." Rack said as the other two headed back towards Rack and 'evin.

"1hat's upé" Stewart asked, as they neared Rack.

"Vana is on the qet. I wanted to give Vana and 'atie a little time together before we all boarded.

"1ell, tell me, how was your trip from Cubaé Vid you guys have any probz lemsé" 'evin asked.

Rack stopped and turned towards 'evin, "Let me tell you."

Chapter Fifteen

GOT THEM!

The cell phone vibrated in his pocket, Edgardo Santiago, the Cuban Ambassador, reached in and saw the number. It was his contact in the Cuban military, General de Division Ruiz. "You have good news for me, Ruiz?" Edgardo asked eagerly.

There was a long pause at the other end before Ruiz spoke. "No, I do not have good news for you."

"Explain." Edgardo demanded as he turned and walked away from the others.

"Let me start by saying that none of this was my fault."Ruiz said in an apologetic tone.

"Yes, yes of course. What happened? Did they catch them?" Edgardo asked impatiently.

After a slight pause, "No, they got away." Ruiz said softly.

Edgardo looked at Nasir, who was standing about thirty feet away. He turned and started walking away, so that Nasir couldn't hear, "What do you mean, they got away?" Edgardo said, not believing what he had just heard.

"My men said they were attacked." General Ruiz replied.

"By who! The three who took the girl?" Edgardo shot back.

"No, sir, the United States Military." Ruiz said.

"What do you mean, the United States Military?" Edgardo asked.

"My men told me that they were attacked by over ten American qghter jets." Ruiz replied.

"And where did these jets come from?" Edgardo asked.

"They told me they came from the American Peet." Ruiz 3uickly replied.

"American Peet?" Edgardo said, not believing what he was being told.

"Yes, an American aircraft carrier and about qve other warships. They were lucky to get out of there alive." General Ruiz said matter-of-factly.

"Yes, yes, I'm sure." Edgardo said, not believing a word. "Thank you anyway for all your help." Edgardo said and ended the call. He turned and slowly walked toward Nasir, who was eagerly awaiting the news of Fariha's capture.

"Well?" Nasir asked as Edgardo approached.

"I'm sorry, Nasir, they got away." Edgardo said apologetically.

"WHAT DO YOU MEAN THEY GOT AWAY, YOU FOOL!" Nasir shouted.

Edgardo pointed his qnger at Nasir, "Don't you dare raise your voice to me! I'm the Cuban Ambassador!" Edgardo qred back at Nasir as he stood face to face with him.

Nasir stepped to within twelve inches of Edgardo, "I don't give a shit who you are, you incompetent idiot." Nasir said, looking him eye to eye.

"Gentlemen, Gentlemen, please stay calm. I'm sure there is a reasonable explanation." Edmundo said as he stepped to the side of the two men. "Vlease, Edgardo, explain how this could have happened." Edmundo pleaded as he placed a hand on both men's shoulders.

Edgardo stood there looking at Nasir, "As I was about to say. General Ruiz told me that the two helicopters he sent to retrieve them came under attack by the American Navy." Edgardo replied, without looking away.

"Are we talking about one ship? Two ships?" What?" Nasir asked, shaking his head.

"The General said there was an entire Navy Fleet, Stealth qghters, Destroyers, and an Aircraft Carrier. His two helicopters had no chance, they were lucky to get out of there alive." Edgardo replied.

Hunter and Charles were standing about thirty feet away and overheard the entire conversation. Hunter looked over at Charles, "Did you have anything to do with this?" Hunter whispered to Charles.

Charles smiled, "I made a call." he said, as his phone rang. "Excuse me for a second," he said to Hunter as he answered the call. After a few seconds, he ended the call and turned back to Hunter. "You'll be pleased to know that your friends are safe, but a little wet, onboard the Coast Guard Ship Hamilton. They will soon be Pown to Homestead Air Force Base, where Kevin will be waiting to transport them home."

Hunter closed his eyes, "Thank you. I owe you one." Hunter said softly, trying to hold back the tears.

"Don't mention it. 5ust make sure you destroy Nasir's sex tra6cking business." Charles replied and lifted his drink in a toast.

"Now we need to get the other two out and somehow retrieve whoever's body." Hunter said, solemnly.

"I'm sure the other two will make it out safely." Charles said, trying to reassure Hunter.

Without looking at Charles, Hunter nodded. "Look at those three over there arguing. They look like three little kids, trying to blame each other for their screwup.

Charles nodded, "What are you going to do with Yasser?" he asked.

Hunter turned and looked at Charles, "I don't have a clue. Nasir wants him dead." Hunter took a sip of his drink and placed it on the table. "I've got him locked in his room with one of Edmundo's men guarding the door."

Charles took a long draw of his drink and sat it back down on the table, "I have an idea." Charles said.

Hunter turned and faced Charles, "Do tell."

It was getting dark as he stopped to rest. It had been several hours since he and the others had split up. "Wonder how the others are making out?" he said to himself. He looked around at his surroundings. Nothing but thick trees and brush. He cautiously knelt next to a river that measured about fifty yards across. He scooped up some water and poured it over his head to cool himself off. He then scooped another handful and slowly sipped it, while looking around. Off in the distance, he could hear the barking of dogs, "I wonder if that's the same dogs that had been after them." he thought to himself.

He heard a rustle in the bushes behind him and a low hissing sound. He turned, and about fifteen feet from him was an enormous crocodile. He grabbed a stick that was lying about three feet away. The stick wasn't that big, about five feet long and about one and a half inches in diameter. It wasn't much of a weapon to defend himself, especially against a ten-foot hungry crocodile.

They both stood there, waiting for the other one to make the first move. The crocodile, sizing up his dinner, decided that it was time to eat and prepared to charge forward.

He took his stick in both hands as the crocodile opened its mouth wide. As soon as the crocodile got closer, he shoved his stick down its open mouth and about six inches down its throat.

The crocodile closed its mouth around the stick and shook its head violently. He held on to the stick with both hands as the crocodile tried its best to pull the stick free. As soon as the crocodile opened its mouth again, he shoved the stick again, causing the stick to go even farther down the crocodile's throat.

At this point, the crocodile had had enough and retreated into the thick brush from where it came, still with the stick lodged in its throat.

As soon as the crocodile vanished, he took that opportunity to backtrack down the path that he came from and down another path away from the water and thick brush.

After almost two more hours of making his way through the trees and overgrown vegetation, he came to a clearing on the side of a hill. He could see lights in the distance. He stopped and collapsed to the ground from exhaustion. He laid there for almost an hour, trying to regain his strength.

After resting, he got up and started towards the lights, which appeared to be the lights of a small town.

Walking a few hundred yards and stopping. He listened for any sounds of the dogs that had been pursuing the three of them. He had stayed close to the roads as he made his way towards what he hoped was the hotel where Tony and 5im were waiting. He was concerned for the other two. Not knowing if the others had been captured or made it to safety.

He had forgotten about Shay and the others, as he was focused on his own survival. He found a fallen tree and decided to stop and rest for an hour. As he sat, all he could hear was the birds singing and talking with one another. He examined his arms and legs, where he had gotten several cuts a little while ago. He had been walking down the road when he heard a vehicle approaching, not knowing if it was the men who were pursuing him or just a local heading into town. He dashed into the thick brush to avoid being seen, which resulted in several cuts for his e¡ort.

He looked around to make sure that the vehicle was gone and that no others were coming. I think it's better if I stay o¡ the road and travel in the brush. It would be harder, but safer. He thought to himself as he started pushing his way through the brush.

After just over an hour, he came to a clearing. About a hundred yards away, he spotted a small farmhouse and a run-down barn o¡ to the side. That would be a good place to rest up until dark. Then he would try walking the road again. He made his way down towards the run-down barn, trying to stay out of sight of the farmhouse. He would move from tree to tree, keeping an eye on the farmhouse and the dirt road that ran in front of the house.

Finally, after twenty minutes, he made it to the back side of the barn. He peered around the side of the barn at the farmhouse. Nothing, no one in sight. He slowly walked around the side of the barn towards the front. He paused again and looked towards the house. He still didn't see anyone. He looked around for a minute and decided it was clear to slip around the corner and into the barn.

He opened the door, just wide enough for him to slip in, and slowly closed the door behind him. He would stay there until it got dark, then head out again.

A s he got closer to the town, he started recognizing buildings. He remembered several of the buildings from his earlier recon of the area. It was the town where they had stayed and set up a command post.

The 3uestion was, are Tony and 5im still there? He knew that in his condition, he would draw attention if anyone were to see him. He sat on a nearby stump to rest and thought about the others. Had they made it back before him? Were they still avoiding the dogs and the men chasing them? Were they captured? All these images ran through his mind. After about thirty minutes, he decided to push on and take his chances.

He slowly worked his way to the qrst row of buildings that bordered the outer part of the town. He stopped and looked around the corner of the building. He could see Pashing blue and red lights several blocks away. 5ust beyond the Pashing lights, he saw the hotel that they had been staying in.

"I hope Tony and 5im are still there." he said, under his breath. He slowly moved closer, trying to keep to the shadows. Suddenly, a dog, just twenty feet away, started barking and growling. He froze and looked toward the ten or so men standing next to their police cars. Had they heard the dog? Will someone come and investigate what the dog was barking at? He looked around to make sure no one was approaching. So far so good.

He walked past the still barking dog and around the corner of the next building. As soon as he was out of sight of the dog, the dog stopped barking. Relieved that the dog didn't alert the police, he cautiously walked down the alleyway behind the buildings.

There, just a hundred yards away, stood the hotel. Now, just make it past the group of police o6cers without being seen. But there was a problem, a qfty-foot problem. He had to cross a dimly lit street. The group of o6cers was now about seventy-qve yards away. He slowly walked across the street. He tried to act as normal as he could, hoping that if they noticed him, they would think he was just a local resident crossing the street on his way home. As soon as he crossed the street, he felt home free.

"Ðetengan a la polic'a!" 8Halt Volice!9 came a voice from the darkness from behind.

He froze in his tracks. Now what? He thought to himself. He had just another hundred feet to the room.

The police o6cer slowly moved towards him from behind, "Identiqcaci...n por favor." 8Identiqcation, please9.

He raised his hands, but didn't turn around. "Identiqcaci...n por favor." The o6cer repeated. He could sense that the o6cer was standing just about two feet directly behind him, a big mistake on the o6cerés part.

He took a deep breath and 3uickly spun to his left. He struck the o6cer on the left side of the o6cer's face with his left hand. This caused the o6cer to stagger to the right. He was now facing the o6cerés back and acting 3uickly, before the o6cer could recover and call for help. He placed his left arm around the o6cer's neck and put him in a sleeper hold. He grabbed the o6cerés right shoulder with his left hand to give him more leverage. And with his right hand, he reached around and covered the o6cer's mouth.

Within twenty seconds, the o6cer started to lose consciousness due to the lack of blood going to his brain. Typically, a person will regain consciousness within seconds once the chokehold is removed. However, the longer the chokehold is applied, the longer the person will remain unconscious. But too long, and it could cause brain damage or even death.

After holding the chokehold on the o6cer for about forty-qve seconds, he released his hold and eased the o6cer to the ground. He looked around to see if the other nearby o6cers noticed the 3uick confrontation. Feeling that he was in the clear, he lifted the still-unconscious o6cer. He placed the o6cer over his right shoulder and 3uickly walked to the door of the room.

Three knocks sounded on the door, and Tony and 5im looked at each other. Tony lifted his hand to motion for 5im to stay 3uiet. He stood and walked 3uietly over to the door and looked out the peephole.

"Son of a Bitch." Tony said as he opened the door. "Nicholas! Get in here." Tony whispered, and he opened the door wider so Nicholas could pass.

"What the hell happened?" 5im asked as he rushed over to help lower the unconscious o6cer to the Poor.

"Grab me a syringe of that knockout juice." Nicholas said as he checked the o6cer's breathing and pulse.

Tony walked over with the syringe and injected the o6cer with the M00 drug, "Whose your friend?" Tony asked.

"I ran into him down the street. I didn't want to leave him there, for his friends to qnd him." Nicholas said. "Any word from the others?" he asked, looking qrst at Tony and then at 5im.

"No, nothing. You're the qrst one from your team we've heard from." 5im said, handing Nicholas a bottle of water.

Nicholas took the top o¡ and took a long draw of water. "What about 5ack and his team? Did they make it?" Nicholas asked.

"Yes, they are in Miami. We lost contact with them when they hit the water. We didn't hear back from them until they reached Miami." Tony said.

Nicholas looked at Tony with a puzzled look, "What do you mean, they hit the water?" Nicholas asked.

"Well, Shay was driving andQ" 5im started.

Nicholas laughed, "What did she do, try to drive that truck they escaped into Miami?" Nicholas replied.

They all three laughed, "After we lost contact with them, I walked down to CaibariZn Marina. That was where we last heard from them. Once I got there, it was packed with police. From what I saw and could put together, Shay drove the truck down a boat ramp and into the water." 5im said, trying to keep from laughing.

Nicholas laughed, "So, she did try to drive to Miami."

"Well, they stole a boat from this man who tried to help them." 5im said. "After that, we assume they had no problems between there and Miami."

"Unbelievable." Nicholas replied.

"Yep." Tony said, "You hungry?" he asked, walking over to the kitchen.

"You damn right I am. What do you have?" Nicholas asked as he followed Tony into the kitchen.

C harles made a couple of calls and then gave Hunter a slight nod. Hunter nodded back and walked over towards the three men, still arguing over who had screwed up the capture of 5ack and the others.

"Excuse me, gentlemen, may I have a word with you, Nasir?" Hunter asked.

"By all means." Nasir replied and turned and followed Hunter. After they got out of earshot of the others, Hunter stopped and turned back towards Nasir.

"You said that you wanted Yasser dead, right?" Hunter asked, looking at Nasir and then glancing over at Edgardo and Edmundo.

Nasir was noticeably irritated by the question, "Yes, did you not understand my orders?" Nasir shot back.

"Yes, yes, I totally understood your orders." Hunter replied.

"Then what is the problem? Do you not have the stomach to carry out such a trivial order?" Nasir said.

"No, not at all." Hunter said.

"Then do as you were told." Nasir said and started to turn and walk away.

"I have a better idea." Hunter said, causing Nasir to stop and turn back towards him.

"And what would be better than death?" he asked.

Hunter smiled slightly, "Life in prison." Hunter replied.

Nasir folded his arms in front of his chest, "Explain."

"If we kill him, that is the end of his suffering. However, if he's spending life in prison, then he'll spend the rest of his life, knowing how he disappointed you, and have to suffer the indignity of life in prison." Hunter said.

Nasir pondered the idea for a second, "And where do you propose Yasser spend this time at?" Nasir asked, now seeming open to the idea.

"Combinado del Este, here in Cuba." Hunter replied.

"Combinado del Este, why here? There are much worse prisons." Nasir asked.

"Because Cuba is where he failed you. Also, he would be a foreigner and in the minority in the prison population. On top of that, being a Muslim in a country that is mostly Catholic. He will not do very well in that prison." Hunter explained.

Nasir studied Hunter for several seconds before replying, "Very well. Make the arrangements. I'm sure Ambassador Santiago can help you out with making the arrangements." Nasir said that the two of them turned and headed back towards the others.

"Edgardo, my assistant here has a re3uest for you." Nasir said as he and Hunter walked up.

Edgardo smiled, "Yes, how may I be of assistance, Bill?"

Hunter smiled, "I would like for you to make some arrangements for Yasser to spend some time in Combinado del Este."

Edgardo cocked his head to one side, "Combinado del Este?" he asked.

"Yes." Hunter replied.

Edgardo smiled and looked at Nasir and then back at Hunter, "And for how long would this visit be?"

"Life." Hunter replied.

Edgardo smiled and looked back at Nasir, who nodded in agreement with Hunter. "4ery well. I will make the arrangements." he replied, as he reached into his pocket and retrieved his phone.

"Oh, and one other thing." Hunter said.

"We don't want to ever hear from him again, as a matter oj act, if he were to spend the rest of his life in solitary conqnement, that would be suitable." Hunter said.

"4ery well. I'll make the arrangements and have someone pick him up." Edgardo said.

"Thank you." Hunter said, "If you will excuse me, I'll get Yasser ready for his new home." Hunter walked towards the main house, and as he passed Charles, he gave him a slight nod.

"One last thing." Nasir said as Hunter started to walk away.

Hunter turned towards Nasir, "Yes, what is it?" he asked.

"I want Yasser's family brought here." Nasir said.

Hunter, not sure what Nasir had in mind, asked. "His family?"

"His wife and two daughters." Nasir replied.

"Once they are here, what do you want me to do with them?"Hunter asked.

"Take them to visit Yasser in his new home." Nasir replied with an evil smile.

"Is that all?" Hunter asked.

"No. Once he sees them, execute each one of them in front of him." Nasir said, now with a serious look on his face.

"Execute them?" Hunter asked, shocked at the re3uest.

"Yes. In front of his very eyes. I want him to live the rest of his life with the images of his wife and daughters being executed before his very eyes." Nasir said.

"4ery well." Hunter said, "I'll have them brought to Cuba as soon as possible." he said as he turned and walked away.

"One last thing Bill." Nasir said.

Hunter stopped and looked back over his shoulder at Nasir, "Yes, what is it?"

"I want them beheaded." Nasir said.

"What?" Hunter said as he turned towards Nasir and faced him.

Nasir looked right into Hunter's eyes, "You heard me. I want them beheaded in front of Yasser. And I want you to be the one to do it."

Hunter stood there without saying a word for several seconds. "Is there a problem?" Nasir asked.

"No. No, as you wish." Hunter replied, "Is there anything else?" Hunter asked.

"No, that should do it. After that task is completed, meet Roger in the States and help him qnd those who took Fariha." Nasir ordered.

Hunter just nodded and walked away.

A few hours later, Edmundo received a call. As soon as he got o¡ the phone, he went and found Nasir, who had been sitting by the pool with Hunter, Charles, Roger Basiliano, and a few of the remaining guests.

"Great news." Edmundo shouted as he approached Nasir.

Nasir leaned forward in his chair, "What is it? Have you found Fariha?" Nasir asked excitedly.

Edmundo waved his hand back and forth, "No, no, they've captured one of the snipers.

"Are you sure?" Nasir asked.

"The local police found him hiding in a barn." Edmundo replied, still showing excitement in his voice.

"But are you sure he's one of the snipers?" Roger Basiliano asked.

"He's not from around here. He was all scratched-up and his clothes were all ripped and dirty." Edmundo replied.

"He could just be some local homeless person trying to get out of the weather." Hunter said, trying to shed some doubt on the capture.

"No, they are sure he's the one." Edmundo said, trying to reassure the others.

"Great news! Where is he?" Nasir replied.

"He's being held in a small village about an hour and a half drive from here." Edmundo said as he took a seat next to Charles.

"I'll send some men there to bring him to us." Edgardo said.

"NO!" Nasir said, looking directly at Edgardo. "You've screwed up enough. I'll send Roger there to get him and bring him back."

Edgardo tried, in vain, to suppress his anger, "Fine, suit yourself." he said.

Nasir turned back towards Edmundo, "Tell your people that there will be a man from the FBI to come and pick him up in about two hours." Nasir said.

"4ery well." Edmundo replied.

Nasir pointed at Edmundo, "And make sure they don't hand him over to anyone else. Am I clear?" Nasir said.

"4ery." Edmundo replied. He turned and placed a call to the station that was holding the alleged captured sniper.

Nasir stood, "Roger, go down there and bring this person backQ alive." Nasir ordered.

"I'll need transportation." Roger said.

"Not a problem. You can take one of my SU4s, and two of my men will go with you." Edmundo said.

"Mind if I tag along?" Hunter asked.

Roger looked at Hunter, "Not at all, Bill, it seems we'll be working together soon, this will give us time to get to know each other." he said, as he excused himself to gather a few items for the trip.

"I'll meet you out front in about ten minutes." Hunter said to Roger.

Hunter went to his room and called the team down at CaibariZn. He informed them that another one of the team had been captured. He told them of the plan that Roger Basiliano, he, and a couple of Edmundo's men would head there to retrieve him and bring him back. They would arrive in about two hours. 5im told Hunter that they were about forty-qve minutes away from that town. And they would devise a plan to rescue their team members before he and Roger arrived.

Forty minutes later, they pulled up to the small town's police station and went inside. "Hello, I'm Roger Basiliano with the United States FBI." He Pashed his badge and placed it back into his pocket. "I'm here to take custody of the prisoner that Mr. Lupe called you about."

"4ery well, sir, I will get him for you." the o6cer replied in very broken English.

"Is there anything I need to sign?" he asked the o6cer.

"Yes, sir, if you would sign here and here, then he's all yours." the o6cer replied and handed him a pen.

After all the paperwork was signed and the prisoner was turned over, they all left.

About an hour later, Roger entered the police station, "May I help you?" the o6cer asked, looking up from his paperwork on his desk.

"Yes, my name is Senior Special Agent Roger Basiliano with the United States FBI. This is my associate, Bill Davis. We're here to pick up a prisoner that Mr. Lupe called you about."

H is phone rang, "Yes, Nasir here." Nasir listened intently before ending the call.

"Is that good news from Roger?" Edmundo asked and took a drink of wine.

Nasir placed the phone on the table and stood. He walked around and stood behind Edmundo. "Yes, it was Roger." Nasir replied through gritted teeth.

"Are they on their way back with their prisoner?" Edmundo asked.

"Apparently, there was some sort of a mix-up." Nasir said, shaking his head.

Edmundo turned and looked up at Nasir, "What do you mean, a mix-up?" Edmundo asked.

As Nasir went around and took a seat next to Charles, "They released the prisoner to the wrong Roger Basiliano." he said, just barely loud enough for them to hear.

Charles leaned forward and looked at Nasir, "What do you mean they released him to the wrong Roger Basiliano?"

Nasir sat back in his seat and looked at Charles, "About thirty minutes before Roger and the others arrived, another person claiming tobe FBI Agent Roger Basiliano arrived. He presented an FBI identiqcation, and they released the prisoner to him." Nasir said as he rubbed the side of his head.

Edmundo placed his hand on Nasir's arm, "I'm sorry." he said.

"Is there anything I can do?" Edgardo asked.

Nasir looked qrst at Edmundo and then at Edgardo. He glanced down for a second and then up at Edgardo, "Apparently." Nasir paused for a second, "No one on this god forsaken island is competent enough to do anything but FUCK THINGS UV!"

Nasir stood and looked over at Charles, "Charles, can you Py me out of this hell hole as soon as possible?" he then turned and looked at Edmundo, "If you want anything done right, then you have to do it yourself."

Charles nodded, "Of course, Nasir. I'll call and have my jet ready to go as soon as possible. Give them a couple of hours to fuel and prepare the jet."

"4ery well. I'll be in my room till then. Have Bill and Roger come to my room as soon as they arrive." Nasir stood and walked towards the main house.

Tony knocked three times on the door to signal to Nicholas that it was them. Nicholas opened the door and greeted them. He smiled when he saw him, "Well, it took you long enough."

"Aye, I thought I would take the scenic walk." Red replied, and the two embraced. "Where's Robert?" Red asked, looking around the room.

"He's not made it back yet." Tony replied.

5im laughed, "That city boy probably got himself lost in the woods. I'm sure he ended up somewhere on the other side of this island."

"Well, we'll hold up here until we hear from him. I sent Hunter a text for him to call whenever he's clear." Tony said as he walked into the living area and took a seat.

"What are we going to do with this cop?" Nicholas asked, motioning with his head towards the bedroom where they had him tied up.

"What cop?" Red asked, looking around at the others.

"Nicholas thought he'd invite a friend to the party." 5im said.

"What are we going to do with him?" Nicholas asked.

"We can't release him. He'll run straight to his friends and bring the entire Cuban police force back." Tony said.

Nicholas nodded in agreement, "Well, taking him with us is out of the 3uestion too."

"Killing him is not an option, we don't kill cops." 5im said.

"Here is what we'll do. When we leave, I'll pay for an extra day's stay. We'll keep him tied up and drugged. Once we're safe back home. We can call the authorities and let them know where he's at." Tony said.

"How are Shay and the others?" Red asked as he headed for the kitchen.

"They made it back safe." 5im replied.

"Despite Shay's driving." Nicholas replied.

"What are you talking about?" Red asked as he was preparing something to eat in the kitchen.

They spent the next forty-qve minutes telling each other what had happened to each other, when Tony's phone rang.

"Hello, this is Tony. Hunter, what's going on?" he said, as he listened to Hunter. He informed Hunter that Red and Nicholas made it back. A little bruised and battered, but safe. Tonyés expression changed, and he looked over at 5im, "Ok, I'll let the others know. He slowly placed the phone in his pocket and walked over to where the others were sitting. "Red, come in here." he yelled to Red, who was still in the kitchen.

Red walked in with a plate piled high with food, "What's up?"

Tony didn't say anything as he looked down at the Poor.

"What is it?" Nicholas asked, leaning forward in his chair.

"That was Hunter." Tony said, looking up at 5im.

"Yes, we gathered that. What did he say?" Red asked.

"It's Robert." Tony started.

"What about Robert?" 5im said, with concern in his voice.

Tony took a deep breath, "He'sQ. he's dead."

"WHAT!" 5im shouted, not believing what Tony just said.

Tony repeated to everyone what Hunter had told him, "I'm sorry, 5im, I know you and Robert were very close."

"Where is the body?" 5im asked.

"Hunter said he's being kept at a morgue in an area hospital, about qfty miles from here," Tony replied.

"Let's go get him." Red said, looking at Tony.

"No, that's what they want. They've set up a trap for anyone who tries to claim the body." Tony replied.

"Well, we can't just leave him here!" 5im shot back.

"We're not. Hunter said they have a plan." Tony replied.

"Who is they?" 5im asked.

"Him and Charles." Tony said. "Hunter wants us to lay low for a couple of days, and Red and Nicholas head to the airport. Red will go to the airport in Havana tomorrow, and Nicholas to 4aradero Airport the day after. 4icky has already booked Pights back to the States for each of you."

"What about you and 5im?" Nicholas asked.

"We'll be leaving the same way we came in." Tony replied.

T here was a knock at the door, "Yes, who is it?" Nasir asked.

"It's Bill and Roger. We were told you wanted to see us as soon as we got back." Hunter said.

"Enter." Nasir replied.

Hunter and Roger entered and walked over to where Nasir was sitting. "You wanted to see us?" Roger said.

Nasir was reading the Qatar news on his cell phone. When they approached, he placed his phone on the chair next to him, "Yes, Charles is going to Py me back to Qatar within the hour."

"What do you want of me?" Roger asked.

"I want you and Bill to go to the United States. Find the people who did this and kill them." Nasir calmly said.

Roger nodded, "It shouldn't take very long. I have their pictures and qnger-prints. As soon as I qnd and eliminate them, I will send you a message."

Nasir looked at Roger, "Make it look like an accident. I don't want whoever they are working for to trace it back to me."

"What makes you think they work for someone?" Hunter asked, trying to see what Nasir might suspect.

Nasir leaned forward, "They had help from some very powerful friends. This group could not have pulled this o¡ alone."

"Why would such a powerful group have any interest in Fariha?" Hunter asked.

Roger looked at Hunter, "I think it may go deeper than just Fariha."

"How so?" Hunter asked.

"I feel that they are linked to the raids and take downs of some of our tra6cking groups in the States. I've been trying to put the pieces together for a while now. This group might be the missing piece I've been looking for." Roger said.

"And what about Fariha? How does she qt into this puzzle?"Hunter asked.

Roger shook his head, "I don't know yet, maybe she doesn't."

Hunter looked at Nasir, "What do you want us to do about Fariha?"

Nasir looked away and pondered the 3uestion for a moment, "If you happen to qnd her in your search for the two Inqdels, bring her tome." Nasir replied. "Now leave me. May Allah condemn this place to Zamhareer."

F ive days after arriving at FBI head3uarters in Raton Rouge, Louisiana, Roger qnally got the identity of the two. He picked up his cellphone and called Hunter.

After three rings, Hunter answered, "Davis here, what do you have, Roger?"

"Not over the phone, Bill. Meet me at the Bar Tonique in the French Quarter in one hour." Roger replied and ended the call.

Hunter was waiting for Roger at one of the booths in the back of the bar. He told the waitress that he was expecting another person and to let him know where he was seated. As soon as Roger arrived, the waitress seated him. He began telling Hunter what he had discovered.

Roger looked at the waitress and ordered a shot of whisky. As soon as the waitress left, Roger turned and faced Hunter. "I've identiqed two of the people who took Fariha," Roger said.

"What about the third one?" Hunter asked.

"Never got a clear picture or prints on him." Roger replied, unconcerned about the third person.

"Well, tell me what you have on the other two." Hunter said.

Roger placed a qle in front of Hunter and opened it, "The male has been identiqed as David Martin."

Hunter looked at a picture of 5ack's driver's license photo as Roger slid the picture to the side, exposing the picture of Shay's license. "Who is this person?" Hunter asked.

"Her name is Sharon Story." Roger replied. "They both share an apartment on the south side of Houston."

"Do we have a current address?" Hunter asked.

Roger looked at the file, "207 Hutchins Street is the one on file."

Hunter nodded and looked up from the qle, "What's the plan?"

Roger leaned back in his chair and crossed his arms, "There are several credit card charges at a local club within walking distance of their apartment." he said, smiling with a look of victory on his face.

Hunter nodded, "Great job. Have you informed Nasir yet?"

"No, not yet. You and I will stake out the area for a few days and track their movements. We'll put together a plan on what to do after that." Roger said as he reached over and retrieved the qle.

"Are you planning on returning to work when it's done?"Hunter asked.

"No, I've got three weeks of vacation saved. I'm going to take my sailboat out and relax for a couple of weeks." Roger paused and took a sip of his whisky, "Maybe sail down to Vuerto Rico and 5amaica."

Hunter smiled, "No Cuba?"

Roger laughed, "No, I've had my qll of Cuba for a while."

"What kind of sailboat do you have?"

"A thirty-foot Catalina MkIII. Are you familiar with that boat?"

Hunter shook his head, "No, not really. What's her name? The 5olly Roger?"

Roger smiled, "No. The Black Vearl."

Hunter looked surprised, "Wasn't that a pirate ship?"

"Yes, it was. Bill, you'll have to come down to New Orleans someday, and I'll take you out." Roger said, with a bit of pride in his voice.

"I'll do that once I get settled and up to speed on Nasir's operation here in the States."

"Great. I've got a weekend getaway cabin on the Mississippi River where I keep her stored." Roger said.

"It's a date. Give me a couple of months and I should have things here in order." Hunter replied.

They spent the next two weeks observing 5ack and Shaysé movements. They logged when they left and where they went. Making notes on routes they took and locations. They soon found a pattern to their routine. On Wednesday, Friday, and Saturday nights, they would walk qve blocks to a local restaurant and nightclub. They would always leave and return home between eleven thirty and eleven forty-qve each night. Roger picked the perfect place to take them out.

Roger and Hunter discussed their plan. Hunter would stay back in the getaway car. Once Roger qnished, he would pull up in the car, and Roger would get in. They would then head to Interstate 10 and travel to New Orleans.

Roger wanted it to appear as if a robbery had gone bad. He was going to take 5ack and Shaysé wallets and valuables. By the time the local authorities identiqed them, Roger would be on his sailboat in the Gulf of Mexico and headed down to the islands. Hunter had plans to catch a flight to Qatar and spend several weeks there before returning. Roger would send Nasir a text message as soon as 5ack and Shay were eliminated.

They decided that next Wednesday would be the day. Since it was a week-night, there would be fewer people out, making the chances of being seen small.

That night, like clockwork, 5ack and Shay left their apartment and headed towards the nightclub. Hunter had parked about two blocks away, in the direction that they were walking. He would slowly follow them in the car, making sure he stayed far enough back not to be noticed. Roger would approach from the other direction and time their meeting at an area where the lighting wasn't very good.

"Excuse me, would you have a light?" Roger asked as he approached 5ack and Shay.

"No, sorry, we don't smoke." Shay replied.

"Well, maybe you can point me in the right direction." Roger said as he stopped and looked around as if he were lost.

"Where are you heading?" 5ack asked.

Roger turned and looked around to make sure no one else was around. Then he pulled his gun out and pointed it at 5ack.

5ack looked down at the gun pointed at him, "Hold on, dude, we don't have any money."

"Keep your hands where I can see them." Roger said as he pointed his gun back and forth between 5ack and Shay.

"I don't want your money." Roger said calmly. "I want to know where Fariha is. What did you do with her?"

"I don't know what you're talking about. We don't know anyone by the name of Fariha." Shay said, not taking her eyes o¡ the gun in Roger's hand.

"Don't bullshit me. I know you're the ones who took her. Now tell me where she is or I'm going to kill you both right here and now." Roger said as he pointed the gun at 5ack's head.

"I'm telling you, we don't know anyone by the name of Farjar or whatever her name is." 5ack said as he lifted his hands.

"Too bad." Roger replied.

A shot rang out and blood sprayed across Shay's face. "5ACK!" she yelled, just as a second shot was heard.

Hunter pulled up next to them and jumped out of the car. "Grab the phone and let's get out of here before someone sees us."

They got into the car and sped o¡, "Send the text." Hunter said.

His cell phone vibrated, and he looked at the message, "Mission complete, both eliminated." Nasir smiled and placed his cell phone back on the table.

CHAPTER SSITEEX

EPILOGUE

It had been four months since the funeral. The team was doing more online investigations. Ray had been training the team on the dark web. They were tracking down pedophiles and sex tra,ckersK who were using the web to sell and trade young children.

jatie Ooined the Gmega DroupK despite strong obOections from her sister Sana. -he would venture into chat rooms and wait for someone to start a conversation with her.

Gnce they identi'ed a predatorK they would download a worm to their comW puter and track the predatorHs movements. Aith some predatorsK they would simply drain their bank and investment accounts. They would gather all the vital information on each predator to be used later.

zunter looked around before entering. Gnce insideK he heard two people talking in the far room. "s he approachedK the door openedK and he fro!e.

"zunterV' ?icky yelled. "Ahy didnBt you call when you landed2 I would have come down to the airport and picked you up.

zunter smiledK spread his arms outK and gave ?icky a big hug as she apW proached. "I didnBt want to bother you. I know you had a lot going on. 3esidesK I wanted to unwind someK and the drive from zouston was Oust the thing I needed.'

zunter kissed ?icky on her foreheadK ”Aho were you talking to in the kitchen2’ zunter asked as he took her hand and walked towards the kitchen.

”Rashid zashmi.’ ?icky replied.

zunter stoppe d and turnedK ”Rashid zashmiK is he a new team member2’

?icky smiledK ”-o to speakK heBs more of a consultant.’

zunter looked at her with a pu!!led lookK ”...onsultant2 Ahat does he conW sult you on2’ zunter asked.

”Masir.’ she replied.

”Masir2’ zunter askedK even more pu!!led than before.

”RashidK would you please come here. ThereBs someone I want you to meet.’ ?icky saidK in a raised voice so he could be heard in the kitchen.

zunter turned towards the door that led into the kitchenK as it swung open. ”Ahat in the hell. NasserK what6’ zunter stopped in midWsentence.

”Dood eveningK Er. 3ill Savis. Gr should I call you zunter -tockton2’ Rashid said as he extended his hand towards zunter.

”Rashid2’ zunter exclaimed.

”NesK after arriving here in your ’ne countryK Ray set me and my family up with new identities.’ Rashid replied as he took zunterHs hand and gave him a hug.

?icky looked at zunterK ”Rashid told me how ...harlesBs men posed as ...uban law enforcement. They took NasserK or shall I say RashidK to a safe house they had set up.’

”NesK they explained to me what Masir had in store for me and what he had ordered you to do with my family.’ Rashid said. ”I want to thank you for everything you have done and risked saving me and my family. I am forever in your debt.’ Rashid saidK as tears formed in his eyes.

zunter looked at RashidK ”IBm very happy to do it.’

?icky smiledK ”Rashid has been very helpful in helping us with information on MasirBs operations. Aith his information and what you have gathered. Ae should be able to bring down MasirBs operation.’

"That is great.' zunter exclaimed. "Mow we need to 'gure out my exit plan. I need to get back here and get to work on helping to bringdown Masir.'

"...harles has been a great help with this operation.' ?icky saidK "I donBt know how weBre ever going to repay him.'

"NesK thatBs what IBm afraid of.' zunter replied.

"If it wasnBt for himK we wouldnBt have been able to get RobertHs body back hereK so we couldqgive him a proper burial.' ?icky saidK not to mention what he did to help -hayK and the others rescued from those helicoptersK trying to stop them.'

"NesK unfortunatelyK we are in his debt.' zunter replied.

Rashid smiled and noddedK ˣˣs am I.'

"IBm sorry I missed the funeral. 3ut it was impossible for me to get away so soon.' zunter said in a very somber tone.

?icky placed her hand on zunterHs shoulderK "IBm sure they will underW stand.' ?icky replied.

"Ahere is everyone2' zunter asked.

"They had already planned a training trip to ...harles EcjennyBs training camp. MicholasK RedK and jevin are there. TheyBll be there for another two weeks.'

"Ahat about the others2' zunter asked.

"Ray has arranged internet training of some sort. ThatBs where SanaK jatieK CimK TonyK and -tewart are now.' ?icky replied.

"Internet trainingK what the hell for2' zunter askedK looking confused.

"I donBt know. Rays got two of his computer nerd friends to do some kind of training on the black webK or whatever itBs called.' ?icky replied.

"Ahy didnBt you go2' zunter asked.

?icky laughedK "Nou know meK I can barely turn my computer on.'

zunter noddedK "IBm with you on that.'

zunter turned towards RashidK "RashidK what are your plans2' he asked.

”IBm leaving this afternoon to meet up with my family in6.Ahere is that again2’ Rashid askedK looking at ?icky.

”Mevada.’ ?icky replied.

”NesK ?icky was so kind to arrange for me and my family to live there. Ray created new identities for usK so Masir would never be able to ’nd us. Ae owe herK and everyoneK a great debt.’

”MoK we were happy to do it.’ ?icky replied.

”IBm sure youBll never hear from Masir again.’ zunter said.

Rashid smiledK ”I still feel that I could never repay you and your group for all the kindness you have shown me and my family.’ Rashid said.

zunter placed his hand on RashidBs shoulderK ”I understand that you have given the group much valuable information on MasirBs operations.’

”I owe Masir no loyalty anymore.’ Rashid said.

”Mot after what he did to youK and what he was going to do to your family.’ zunter replied.

Rashid smiledK ”I must ’nish packing. Ey ride to the airport will be here soon.’ Rashid turned and walked towards the stairs leading to the second 9oor. ze paused as he reached the ’rst step. ”I do have one reLuest.’ Rashid said as he turned to face zunter and ?icky.

”NesK what would that be2’ ?icky asked.

”Ahen you bring down MasirK please let me know.’ Rashid said.

zunter smiledK ”Ae would be glad to.’

”Thank you.’ Rashid saidK and turned and headed up the stairs to his room to ’nish packing.

zunter turned towards ?ickyK ”IBm zungryK what do you have to eat2’ he asked.

”IBm sure we can scratch up something in the kitchen.’ ?icky repliedK and they both walked into the kitchen.

“fter eating and seeing Rashid o4K zunter wanted ?icky to take him down to visit the grave sites. ze ’nally wanted to pay his long overdue respects.

They parked Oust a few yards away from the graves. zunter sat there in the passengerBs seat for a couple of minutes before getting out of the car.

They both walked slowlyK hand in handK to the graves. zunter removed a handkerchief from his back pocket and wiped a tear from his face. They both stood there without saying a word for several minutes. -eeing Savid Eartin and -haron -toryK CackK and -hayBs cover names on the headstones caused a lump to form in his throat.

" hand touched his shoulderK and he turnedK "ItBs about time you come and pay your respects. ItBs been over four months.' the voice from behind said.

zunter turned his head slightly to see the person who spokeK "Seath has treated you well.' zunter replied.

"ItBs great to see you again.' Cack said as he gave zunter a big hug.

"Ahere is your sidekick2' zunter askedK looking around.

"IBm right here.' -hay said as she stepped out from behind a big oak tree. -he ran over and gave zunter a big hug that almost sLuee!ed the life out of him.

"zow has death been2' zunter askedK wiping tears o4 his face.

"3usy. AeBve been in exile for four months. ?icky set us both up in a place between "tlanta and "labama. AeBve been training and working out.' -hay replied.

"ItBs a nice placeK you need to come out for a visit someday.' Cack saidK slapping zunter on the shoulder.

"I found a large house sitting on about a hundred acres. Cack and -hay will be working primarily out of that location.' ?icky said.

"ItBs going to be our ast ...oast operations. ItBs going to have everything that the ...ollege -tation headLuarters has and then some.' Cack said.

zunter smiled and looked over at the headstonesK "Ahat about those2' he asked.

"?ery creepy.' -hay said.

"Ae needed to fake Cack and -hayBs funeral and somehow coverup RobertBs death at the same time.' ?icky said. "Robert is buried there where Cack is supposed to be. AeBre going to change the name after a yearK and put RobertBs information on the headstone.'

"AhoBs buried in -hayBs spot2' zunter askedK looking at her name on the headstone.

"That one is empty.' ?icky replied.

"It was close to being me.' -hay said. "Ahen Micholas shot RogerK his 'nger was on the triggerK and out of re9exK he pulled the trigger before he hit the ground. The shot missed my head by a couple of inches.' she saidK using her thumb and index 'nger to show how close it came to hitting her.

"Ahat did you do with RogersH body2' zunter asked.

"AellK after you leftK Red and jevin loaded his body in that white van that was parked across the street.' Cack said as he kneeled next to the headstone with his name.

"Ae had made arrangements to have his body cremated.' ?icky said as she walked over and stood next to Cack.

"Micholas and Red took his sailboat out for about a hundred miles into the Dulf of Eexico and scuttled it. jevin picked them up in the helicopter before the sailboat went under.' Cack said.

"Mice.' zunter replied as he sLuee!ed -hay.

-hay looked up at zunterK "Micholas put out a Eay Say distress call from the boatHs radio before he abandoned it. TheyBll assume Roger was lost at sea.'

"There was a big article in the Mew Grleans paper about a wellWdecorated 73I agent being lost at sea and presumed dead.' ?icky said as she placed a 9ower on the headstone of RobertBs grave.

zunter looked at Cack and ?ickyK "3y the way. So any of you know anything about a missing four million dollars out of Edmundo Lupe's bank account?"

"MoK why do you ask2' -hay replied and smiled.

zunter looked at -hayK "AellK right after it came up missingK the same amount appeared in MasirBs bank account.'

Cack looked at zunterK "Nou donBt say.'

"Yes, and Lupe is accusing Nasir of somehow stealing his money." Hunter said.

"Interesting.' Cack replied.

"?ery. dmundo told Masir that if he didnBt return his money immediatelyK he would put a contract out on his life.' zunter said.

?icky stood and stepped back to look at the grave markerK "-orry to hear that.' she said. "I thought they were good friends.'

"ItBs funny how a few million dollars will come between friends.' zunter said.

-hay laughedK "I guess Masir wonBt be having any future weddings at his place anymore.'

"-oK what now2' zunter asked.

"This sex tra,cking crap is too big for Oust us to 'ght. AeBre going to need help and more resources.' Cack said as he stood. "AeBre going to attack them on two fronts. 7ace to faceK as weBve been doingK and over the internet.'

"Is that what Ray and the others are training for2' zunter asked.

Cack looked at zunterK "Nes. I want those sick bastards to lie awake at night worrying about how and when we will take them down.'

AUTHORS NOTE

I've been asked several times what prompted me to write the Omega Book Series. Well, during the initial outbreak of COVID and with Sharon being severely injured, I had a lot of time to spend alone.

Sharon was in a local hospital for several months in a coma. She was later transferred to a specialty assisted living facility. This facility only catered to patients with Traumatic Brain Injuries (TBI). They were located a little over two hours away, near Chattanooga, Tennessee.

During this time, I had no contact with anyone. Everyone was hunkered down in their homes, afraid to leave. My job still required me to come to work, although I was the only one in the oAce. -fter work, I would return to an empty home. Due to COVID, I was limited to the amount of time I could visit with Sharon. Sharon lived in a coma for a little over two years before she succumbed to her injuries. During that time, I wrote the Hrst two books, Omega I x The Creation, and Omega II x - Cry for 2elp.

-s I spent time on social media and watching the news, I noticed the increasx ing number of missing children in the -tlanta and surrounding areas. I thought it was strange with the large number of children and young adults going missing every week. I started to do some research and found out about the large se4 traAcking trade in the Lnited States. I was shocked to see that -tlanta was one of the top areas where se4 traAcking was occurring.

I started spending my alone time researching the se4 traAcking epidemic. I found that there were very few, if any, books on the topic. I thought to myself, something needed to be done. I read where many of the se4 traAckers would only get a slap on the wrist or probation. Some even got oJ, with little or no jail time. The courts and law enforcement were overwhelmed and backlogged with more than they could handle.

So, what could I do3 Well, that's when I came up with the idea of a vigilante group to help combat the se4 traAcking trade. Maybe I could somehow bring to light, with my books, the outxofxcontrol se4 traAcking problem. I didn't want my characters to be the typical Superman types. Or some e4xSpecial Korces dude or Uavy SE-Rs type. I wanted my readers to be able to relate to the characters. I wanted my heroes to be just like you and me. Someone who didn't have any super special skills. But they could learn and make mistakes as they did their best to make a diJerence.

I created the character, Shay Rynn, based on some of Sharon's characterx istics. Shay's feistiness and her lack of driving skills Ht Sharon to a tee. -lx though Sharon wasn't into martial arts, as the character Shay Rynn was, you still wouldn't want to tangle with her. Sharon's driving skills, or lack thereof, scared the crap out of me. I think the entire tenxplus years we were together, she drove with me in the car maybe Hve times. Two of the times, I was sick or injured, and I was unable to drive. The personalities of Shay and Sharon were close. I took Sharon's middle name, Rynn, and her nickname, Shay, and combined them to create the character's name, Shay Rynn.

The character of Yack Davidson is based on aspects of my personality. Yack is more of a laidxback kind of guy. Rikes to joke around once he gets to know someone. 2e doesn't always take things seriously. But when things get serious, he can get down to business. 2is name, like Shay's, is taken from parts of my name, David Yackson Story.

The other Characters, Vicky, 2unter, Uicholas, "ed, "ay, and the others, all grew out of necessity as supporting characters for Yack and Shay.

I hope that by reading the Omega Book Series and following Yack and Shay as they fight sex traffickers around the world, you will be inspired. You become aware of the epidemic that is taking hold in this country and other countries around the world. Krom doing my research and diving into the world of se4 traAcking, I have had many sleepless nights and have shed many tears during the writing of these books.

-lthough the Omega Book Series is a work of Hction, the characters are entirely Hctional. Some of the stories are based on actual occurrences.

Thank you for reading the Omega Book Series, and remember, as Yack would say, "Always watch your six, and others too."